T0354730

BECAUSE
I'M
BLACK

BECAUSE I'M BLACK

THE STORY OF JESSE WASHINGTON

DW DUKE
WITH
TAIWO FAGBOHUNGBE

ARCHWAY PUBLISHING

Archway Publishing books may be ordered through booksellers or by contacting:

Archway Publishing
1663 Liberty Drive
Bloomington, IN 47403
www.archwaypublishing.com
844-669-3957

Editorial Consultants: Randy Ladenheim-Gil, Oluwadolapo Jegede, Bejide Oluwatobi, A.

Cover Design: Tyesha Law

ISBN: 978-1-6657-5957-1 (sc)
ISBN: 978-1-6657-5959-5 (hc)
ISBN: 978-1-6657-5958-8 (e)

Library of Congress Control Number: 2024909017

Print information available on the last page.

Archway Publishing rev. date: 07/31/2024

PREFACE
BY TAIWO FAGBOHUNGBE

In the late nineteenth through the mid-twentieth centuries, countless lynchings occurred in the southeastern United States, primarily in Georgia, Mississippi, and Texas. The victims were generally of African American descent. It is estimated that during those years, three thousand to five thousand African Americans were executed by lynching in the United States. In most instances, the lynchings resulted from allegations of indiscretion against a White person. Many of those cases were based on false allegations. Why did they occur? What possible motivation could trigger such brutal behavior? Perhaps lynching provided a sense of solidarity among White persons in a culture with changing socioeconomics and dynamic structures. While lynching was encouraged or at least tolerated by many in the southern culture, adversaries of the practice began to emerge, eventually forming an organization that became known as the National Association for the Advancement of Colored People (NAACP).

On May 8, 1916, near Robinson, Texas, Lucy Fryer was murdered by an unknown assailant while alone at the Fryer farm. She and her spouse, George Fryer, were English immigrants who had earned respect in their community. Information of her passing quickly reached McLennan County District Sheriff Samuel Fleming, who investigated the matter with the assistance of law enforcement officers, a forensic investigator, and several members of the community. The forensic investigator confirmed that

Fryer had been killed by an unpolished blunt object striking her head. The nearby townspeople presumed that Jesse Washington, a seventeen-year-old Black man, who had been living with his sharecropper family on the Fryer farm for five months, was the most likely suspect. One of them stated that he had seen Washington close to the Fryer house a short time before Lucy's body was found. That night, the sheriff's appointees ventured to the Fryer farm, finding Jesse in front of the house where they were living, discovering him wearing bloodstained overalls. Jesse ascribed the stains to a nosebleed from a few days prior. Jesse, his sibling, Billy, and their parents were transported to nearby Waco to be interrogated. Jesse's brother and parents were discharged shortly after being detained, but Jesse was held for further questioning. His examiners in Waco announced that he denied complicity in Fryer's passing but that he offered conflicting insights regarding his activities. Gossipy tidbits spread after his capture that he had been in an altercation with a White man a couple of days before the homicide.

On May 9, Fleming transported Washington to an area known as the Slope Region to forestall vigilante activity. The Slope Region sheriff addressed Washington with Fleming present; Washington revealed that he had murdered Fryer following a dispute about her mule. He also told them where to find the murder weapon. Washington was transported to Dallas, where Fleming announced that he had recovered a mallet at the location Washington had described, which he believed to be the murder weapon. In Dallas, Washington provided an explanation that depicted the assault and murder of Fryer; this admission was published the following day in Waco newspapers. The press sensationalized the homicide, depicting Fryer's endeavors to oppose Washington's assault, notwithstanding that the specialist who had analyzed her body concluded that she was killed before she could offer resistance. A lynch mob gathered in Waco in front of the prison that night, looking for Washington, unaware that he had been transferred to Dallas. A neighborhood newspaper commended their vigilante activities.

Also that night, a private memorial service and entombment were held for Lucy Fryer.

On May 11, a jury assembled in McLennan Province and quickly returned an indictment against Washington. The trial was scheduled for May 15. A local newspaper published notification on May 12 of the trial date. Fleming ventured to Robinson on May 13 to request that residents remain calm, and Washington was appointed a panel of six defense attorneys, at least one of whom was a member of the Ku Klux Klan. On the morning of May 15, 1916, Waco's town hall filled to capacity for the trial of Jesse Washington. Onlookers filled the walkways around the building as observers tried to gain admission. Participants were predominantly White, though some Black persons also attended. As Washington was driven to the court, a person in the crowd pointed a gun at him but was quickly subdued. As the trial began, the judge endeavored to maintain order despite the unruly crowd. He instructed the attendees to remain silent. Jury selection was brief. Washington was advised of the charges against him and asked if he was guilty. He murmured what sounded like yes, which was interpreted by the court as an admission. The court heard testimony from law enforcement officers and the investigator who had inspected Fryer's body. The prosecution rested, and Washington's lawyer asked him whether he had committed the offense. Washington replied, "That is the thing that I done" and discreetly apologized. Washington's attorneys offered no defense. Joseph Taylor, the lead defense attorney, announced that the trial had been led decently, inciting applause from the crowd. The jury retired to deliberate.

After only four minutes, the jury announced they had a verdict, and the jury foreman reported a blameworthy decision with a sentence of death. The trial lasted for a total of approximately sixty minutes. Court officials moved toward Washington to accompany him from the court but were pushed aside by a flood of onlookers, who held on to Washington and dragged him outside. Washington initially resisted, biting one man. He was beaten, a chain was put around his neck and he was dragged toward the city corridor by an amassing horde; in transit to the corridor, his clothes were stripped off, and he was cut with knives and was repeatedly beaten with obtuse articles. When they arrived at the city corridor, Washington saw that a mob had brought wood for a blaze close to a tree. Washington, lapsing in and out of consciousness due to the pain, shrouded in blood, was soaked with oil, and hoisted into a tree by a heavy chain. His fingers, toes, and genitals were cut off with a large butcher knife. A fire was lit beneath the tree and Washington, hanged upside down, was raised and lowered into the fire and slowly roasted alive over a period of two hours. He attempted to pull himself out of the flames by grabbing the chain; however, he couldn't because his fingers had been cut off by the mob. German historian Manfred Berg opines that the effort was to extend his life as long as possible to enhance his anguish.

After two hours of this hideous torture, Washington succumbed. The fire was smothered, permitting spectators to gather souvenirs from the site of the lynching, consisting of Washington's bones and pieces of the chain. One participant took a piece of Washington's genitalia, while children extracted the teeth from Washington's skull to sell as gifts. When the fire was stifled, portions of Washington's arms and legs had been burned off and his middle and head were roasted. His body was cut from the tree and dragged behind a pony throughout the town. Washington's remaining parts were transported to Robinson, where they were displayed until a constable acquired the body later in the day and covered it.

The lynching drew a massive crowd consisting of at least fifteen thousand spectators, including local government officials and the chief of police, notwithstanding that lynching was unlawful in Texas. Sheriff Fleming had advised his team not to stop the lynching. Despite the brutality of this event, which was denounced by the president of Baylor University, located in Waco, no person has ever been charged with any crime arising from this event. Author Patricia Bernstein in her book, *The First Waco Horror: The Lynching of Jesse Washington and the Rise of the NAACP*, Texas A&M University Press, 2005, suggests that this lynching and torture were intended as a demonstration of brutal management of wrongdoing that would help Fleming's application for reappointment that year. Mayor John Dollins may have additionally urged on the mob to act with impunity because a lynching would be politically advantageous to his career. Telephones helped spread news of the lynching, permitting observers to assemble more rapidly than was beforehand conceivable. Neighborhood media announced that "yells of enjoyment" were heard as Washington was roasted alive, and only a few participants objected. Waco residents, who likely had no association with the provincial Fryer family, comprised the greater part of the group. A few people from neighboring areas ventured out to the city before the preliminary to observe the occasions. As the lynching happened in late morning, youngsters from neighborhood schools strolled downtown to watch, some moving into the trees for a superior view. Numerous guardians affirmed their youngsters' participation, trusting that the lynching would fortify confidence in racial domination. A few Texans considered a lynching to be a positive, soul-changing experience for youngsters.

I met DW Duke several years ago as the result of a mutual interest in English literature. I was completing my Bachelor of Arts degree in English literature at Adekunle Ajasin University in Ondo State, Nigeria. I encountered one of his books in my studies and contacted him for discussion. A friendship ensued, and over the years we have enjoyed a number of conversations about literature, philosophy, art, and the law. On one occasion he mentioned that he was writing a book about Jesse Washington. He explained that the evidence on which Washington was convicted appeared weak and that, quite possibly, Washington was an innocent man. I reviewed an article he had written in the *Riverside Lawyer* magazine, along with as much material as I could discover about Jesse Washington, and soon reached the same conclusion as DW. We decided this case possesses historical significance that should be examined, and for that reason, we decided we would create a biographical novel based on everything we could discover.

Our objective in writing this book is to bring the story of Jesse Washington forward for the same reason stories of the Holocaust are retold. Only by studying historical events can we avoid the mistakes that caused such suffering. The Jim Crow-era was a tragic time in American history. It was a time when human interaction was at its lowest point. In this book, we hope to capture the flavor of that era. Our division of labor involves substantial research on my part and extensive writing by DW. Our goal is to tell this historical occasion in a fashion that will induce readership of this story.

CHAPTER
ONE

HATRED BESPEAKS THE loss of the innocent whose soul hangs in the balance, potentially destined to suffer the fate of the guilty, as a sacrifice to an ancient prejudice. This, we may see, was the dilemma of Jesse Washington, tried in Waco, Texas, on May 15, 1916, for the murder of Lucy Fryer, his employer. But was he guilty of the crime of which he was accused? Or was he a victim of unimaginable circumstances whose fate would be determined by his race, confined at a time and place in American history when Lady Justice tipped the scales in favor of the lighter-skinned race, as if skin color itself were the measure of worth?

For thousands of years, the area now known as Waco, Texas, had been inhabited by indigenous populations. By the 1820s those living around Waco had become known as the Wichita Indians. After numerous conflicts between the native people and the settlers, Texas Secretary of State Stephen F. Austin entered into a treaty with the Wichita people who were eventually driven northward to an area that would become an army outpost known as Fort Worth. In 1849 the first log cabin home was built in Waco. By 1866 a community had developed and a 475-foot bridge was constructed across the Brazos River, connecting the heart of Waco to the neighboring territories.

The town continued to grow and eventually became the home of Baylor University and several other colleges. Cotton was the primary crop for farmers, though there were cattle ranches as well. In its early years of existence, Waco was a rough town inhabited by cattle drovers, gunslingers, and those running from the law. It was a town where justice was harsh, and lynchings were not uncommon. In the early twentieth century, Texas was a segregated state. Black persons were not permitted to use White public facilities such as restrooms and drinking fountains. White students and Black students attended separate academic institutions under the doctrine of separate but equal, based on US Supreme Court case *Plessy v. Ferguson (1896) 163 U.S. 537.*

Our story begins in April of 1915, at a small Baptist church, where Becky Baines, a student at Baylor University, taught a teen Sunday school class. Her aspiration was to become a missionary in a "foreign field," as it was called in those days. It seemed that perhaps teaching at the "colored church" would better equip her for teaching Black students in Africa. Clearly a prejudicial assessment, albeit an innocent one given her limited understanding of race relations and her dutiful intentions.

"Jesse, do you know why it's good to be kind to others?"

Jesse stared intently at the page of the church bulletin. Perhaps the words would magically drift up from the page and enlighten him, though he could scarcely read and write. "No, ma'am."

Becky smiled. "Are you sure? What does the Bible say about being kind?"

Jesse looked up from the bulletin. A smile beamed across his face. "Do unto others before they do unto you."

The class roared with laughter.

Becky smiled. "Jesse, is that really what it says?"

"No, ma'am. I was funnin'."

"OK, what does it really say?"

"Do unto others as you would have them do unto you."

"That's right, Jesse. We call that the Golden Rule. Do you always try to be kind to others?"

"Yes, ma'am. I do."

Jesse was favorably regarded in the community, though occasionally known to exhibit a slight temper. Not particularly studious, some said Jesse was "mentally retarded." Others said that wasn't so. Jesse did not see the value in formal education, so he did not learn to read and write. He believed he would be a farmer and did not see a reason to learn to read. Undoubtedly stubborn, he was averse to learning in the classroom, but he wasn't slow. Everyone seemed to like him. He was popular among the Black teenagers, but he didn't know very many White teens. In those days Black children played with Black children and White children played with White children, and they kept those friendships into adulthood. That was how it had been as far back as anyone could remember and that was how everyone believed it should be.

One of Jesse's most amazing features, and the one that did not go unnoticed, was his impressive physique. He was tall, handsome, and very muscular. He had worked in the fields his entire life and earned his well-proportioned musculature with commensurate strength. His appearance often brought the attention of women in the community, most of whom found him uncommonly attractive. Even the Caucasian girls would talk about "the stud" in the absence of men. But Jesse's appearance did not cause him to display arrogance. In fact, he was quite humble, almost to a fault.

After class, the students shuffled from the classroom into the stairwell leading up to the sanctuary. The church was a Victorian house that had been donated by an unknown local businessman. The smell of oak trim and paneling created a woodsy atmosphere. This was one of the most subliminal emotions of Jesse's life at this young age and was endeared to him. On this day, however, Jesse stayed behind to talk to Becky, as he sometimes did. She had taken a special interest in him, encouraging him to learn to read and write. Perhaps she found him attractive. He was, after all, considered one of the most handsome and physically fit young men in McLennan County. But such thoughts were considered impure at this time because Jesse was of a different race from Becky.

"Have you been working on the alphabet, Jesse?"

"I tried, ma'am. I just can't do it. It's too hard. I can't learn to read. I'm just not smart 'nough."

Becky smiled. "That's OK, Jesse. I won't push you. I think you can do it if you really want to. If you decide you want to, let me know, and I will be happy to work with you some more."

"Yes, ma'am," replied Jesse as he stood to go to the sanctuary.

The sermon that morning was delivered by Reverend Robertson, a former missionary who had returned home to accept a role in the Southern Baptist Conference leadership. He was a kind fellow in his sixties, with a slightly overweight build, graying hair, and a beard. He generally wore a three-piece suit with a silver pocket watch attached to a chain inserted into a buttonhole on his vest—silver because a gold pocket watch would appear ostentatious for a minister of a legitimate denomination. He didn't shout and wave his arms, as many of the ministers often did, but the congregation listened to him nonetheless. He spoke in terms they understood. On this day, he talked about his experiences with Africans in the mission field. He told amusing stories about the "natives in Africa," as he called them, much to the fascination of the African American congregation.

Jesse looked around the sanctuary, which was a large living room with a vaulted ceiling. He saw Cassie Williams sitting with her sister, Jenny, and her parents, John and Cynthia, another sharecropper family on the McKinley farm, where Jesse's family lived and worked as sharecroppers. Jesse caught her gaze and smiled politely. Cassie and Jesse had only recently noticed each other. They had known each other for several years, and although they found each other attractive, neither had considered the other a potential suitor until the day they encountered each other in a horse stall, tending to the same mare. A conversation ensued that led to a developing friendship and more.

Like Jesse, Cassie was unusually attractive. She had light, mystifying green eyes. Jesse called them "naughty eyes." Sometimes he called them "voodoo eyes," which Cassie did not appreciate. Everything about her fascinated Jesse. Physically fit from engaging in running and jumping games as a child, Cassie was considered a rare form of African beauty. Some said that just by seeing Jesse and Cassie together, it was known they were meant for each other. "They complement and contrast each other in the most serenely beautiful way," said an elderly White woman who once saw them unloading a wagon of cotton in town.

After the service, Jesse went with his family to the McKinley farm. Jesse's parents were Henry and Martha and had come to Texas with their children after leaving their home in Mexico several years earlier. They came looking for opportunities and work. They had heard that Black persons had more opportunities in the less-populated part of the country, and Waco had developed a Black middle-class community, though heavily outnumbered by the White population.

The Washington family enjoyed a Sunday dinner of fried chicken, potatoes, and baked beans, always a favorite with Jesse. After this wonderful meal, Billy, Jesse's slightly younger brother, went with him to play by the Brazos River, as they often did on Sunday afternoons. There they encountered Cassie and Jenny, who also liked to play by the river. Cassie was the same age as Jesse and Jenny was closer in age to Billy. As usual Billy walked with Jenny.

"Wha' d' ya tink 'ill happen to us when we grow up?" asked Cassie.

Jesse smiled when he heard Cassie speak pidgin, an English-based blend of languages in Africa that facilitated communication between tribes. Many descendants of slaves spoke pidgin when they were alone, especially those from Central and South America. Jesse and Cassie both grew up speaking both pidgin and formal

English in their homes. As teenagers, they often spoke pidgin playfully among themselves.

Jesse skipped a stone across the river. "What do ya' mean?" Turning toward her, he could not help but admire her appearance, as he had so often in the past. She was the prettiest girl he had ever seen. Her gentle features and soft skin caused him to think of her as an ancient Yoruba princess. Just gazing upon her caused his heart to leap. She was kind, gentle, and sweet. And those amazing green eyes. They almost threw Jesse into a trance.

"What are we gonna do? You know . . . I mean where 'ill we live when we grow up? What 'ill you do for a job?"

Jesse skipped another stone across the river. "I'm gonna get me a farm. A cotton farm, and grow cotton."

Cassie walked toward the water and took off her shoes. Her casual actions slightly excited Jesse. She kicked the surface of the water with her bare foot. "How are you gonna pay for it? Farms cost lots and lots of money. Where ya gonna get that kind a money?"

"I'm gonna work real hard and save every penny."

Cassie sat on the bank of the river dangling her feet in the water. "Becky, our Sunday school teacher, told me she wants to teach you to read 'n write. But she said you won't try. Don't you want to learn? I would help you too."

"Why do I need to learn to read 'n write?"

"Because you would have more choices when you decide what to do. . . for a job, I mean. You could even go to college. There's Central Texas College. That's a school for coloreds. You could go there. Maybe you would even become a colored doctor like Dr. George Connor."

Jesse laughed. "I don't want to be no colored doctor. I already told you. I wanna have a cotton farm. Besides, my grandpa was an overseer. He oversaw over one hundred workers. If working a farm was good 'nough for him, it's good 'nough for me."

Cassie paused a moment. "Think about what you just said, Jesse. You said your grandfather was an overseer. But he was still a slave. Don't you want better? Besides, cotton farming is hard work."

"No, it ain't. Cotton is light. A whole bag only weighs a tiny bit."

"Yeah, but you have to bend over all day to pick it."

Jesse laughed. "I will hire a bunch of cotton pickers to work on the farm. Why do you want me to go to college anyway? Why would it matter to you?"

Cassie giggled nervously. "Well, I don't know. You said you like me. I thought maybe . . ." Her words drifted off into a whisper.

Jesse glanced at her. Suddenly he felt an inexplicable affection for her. "You think you are going to be my wife someday?"

Cassie laughed. "Well, I don't know. You would have to ask me, and you are kind of pigheaded."

Jesse chuckled. "What'd you call me?"

Cassie laughed, stood up, and turned toward him. He approached her and she shoved him backward.

Jesse smiled. "You know what happens to girls who say things like that, don't you?"

"No, what?"

Jesse ran forward. Placing his right arm around Cassie's shoulders, he bent down, swooping her up with his left arm behind her knees. "They take a bath."

"No!" screamed Cassie with a laugh as Jesse threw her in the river. She sank beneath the water, then stood up in the waist-deep river. Soaking wet, she said, "I can't believe you did that."

Jesse laughed. "You didn't think I would just let you call me pigheaded, did you?"

She leaned over and scooped a handful of water, then splashed it on Jesse. "Well, I don't think I would ever marry a pigheaded guy like you anyway."

Jesse ran forward into the river, tackling Cassie. They began wrestling in the water.

"What are you two doing?" asked Billy, who had just walked up with Jenny.

"Jesse decided I need a bath," replied Cassie as they stood up in the water.

"Well, most people take off their clothes when they take a bath," said Jenny.

Cassie laughed. "Well that ain't going to happen. Do we look like heathens?"

"Chicken," said Billy.

Cassie splashed water on Billy. "I ain't chicken. But I also ain't no actress."

"An actress? What's that?"

"That's what they call the hookers downtown, over on Washington and Third Street by the river," said Jesse.

"Why do they call them that?" asked Billy.

Jesse laughed. "Probably 'cause it sounds nicer than hooker."

The teens were startled to hear a man's voice. "You young folks shouldn't be talking like that. It's not appropriate . . . especially in mixed company." They looked up and saw Reverend Robertson in his three-piece suit walking with his wife who was attired in a flowing dress, holding a paper umbrella above her head. They walked arm in arm; Reverend Robertson was using a cane.

"Sorry, sir," replied Jesse. "We didn't mean any harm."

"That's all right," replied Reverend Robertson. "You didn't know any better. Just remember for the future that topics like that are shameful and not appropriate in public." Perhaps it was Reverend Robertson's knowledge of the pervasive influence of legalized prostitution in Waco that caused his reactionary trepidation about the conversation. Wives complained that the prostitutes perverted their husbands, and many marital disputes derived from these solicitous engagements.

"Yes, sir," replied Jesse.

Mrs. Robertson smiled. "Jesse, you are such a fine young man. And you are handsome too."

"Thank you, ma'am."

Reverend and Mrs. Robertson walked on. As they strolled

down the path, Cassie said, "I wonder what you would look like in a three-piece suit, Jesse. I bet you would be right handsome."

"Oh, I don't know. It seems a little stuffy and uncomfortable to me. I like to wear loose, comfortable clothes. His vest looks so tight, I don't know how he can even breathe."

The teens sat on the bank of the river and talked for several hours. By the time they were ready to go home, the warm afternoon air had dried the clothes Cassie and Jesse were wearing. As they stood up, they noticed a group of White men in their twenties walking toward them. Jesse quickly counted five of them.

"Hey, who said you N_____s could play here on the river?" asked one of them. Jesse recognized him as Steven Dixon. He often saw him at the cotton gin in Waco.

"No one," replied Jesse.

"Then, why you here?" asked Steven.

"No one told us we couldn't be," replied Jesse.

"Are you a smart-mouth?" asked another man.

"No, I'm not. It's just that no one ever said we couldn't come to the river. We do it all the time."

Steven became angry. "Well, I'm telling you that you can't come here. If I see you here again, I'm going to kick your ass, bad."

Embarrassed, Jesse didn't know what to do. If he said nothing, he would seem like a coward to Cassie. If he said anything, he would have to fight. He knew Billy was too young and would probably be afraid to fight, and he doubted he could beat five young men, even though he was very strong for his age. Angry and embarrassed, he decided not to respond.

"What do you say, N_____ boy? You ain't gonna say anything? You're gonna be a coward."

Jesse was startled to hear a voice behind him. "Shut up, Steve. There are five of you and two of them. You wouldn't be so brave if it was one-on-one." Jesse turned to see a White teenager he didn't recognize. He looked bigger than the other men. He was wearing a black western-style hat, tight-fitting denim jeans, and riding boots.

His ensemble was completed with a white western-style shirt. To Jesse, he appeared downright prosperous.

"Stay out of it," replied Steve. "This doesn't concern you, Elijah."

Elijah walked over to Steve and with a quick right jab to the left eye sent Steve stumbling backward toward the river, where he fell sprawled out on the bank. Jesse was astounded that a White teenager came to his aid. He had never heard of anything like that happening before.

Steve sat up holding his eye but said nothing. Elijah looked at the other men. "Any of you want the same? How about you, Hays? You're a tough guy. Wanna give it a go?"

"No," they all replied almost simultaneously.

"Then get out of here," said Elijah.

Steve stood and joined the other young men as they climbed into a truck parked beside the road.

After they had gone, Elijah looked at Jesse and Billy. "Who are you? I haven't seen you around here before."

"I'm Jesse and this is Billy, my brother. We live over on the McKinley farm. Our parents are sharecroppers."

Elijah reached his hand forward and said, "I'm Elijah."

Jesse shook his hand apprehensively. No White person had ever offered his hand in a greeting to him before, except for the White ministers who came to speak at the church. Elijah then extended his hand to Billy, who shook it cautiously.

The young man looked at Cassie and Jenny. Touching the brim of his black hat, he nodded with a smile and said, "Ladies," then turned and walked away.

After Elijah had gone, Jesse asked, "Who was that?"

Cassie said, "Elijah Morrison. He's on the boxing team at the White high school. He lives with his aunt and uncle. They own a big cattle ranch."

Jesse laughed. "Wow. I didn't even have a chance to say anything to those boys. He just stepped in and took over. I was gonna deck ol' Dixon."

Billy said, "Jesse, you know you can't fight White guys. They would hang you for that."

"They could try," replied Jesse.

The events of the day remained in Jesse's thoughts that night. *Who was Elijah, and why would he stand up for colored kids? No one ever does that. Elijah could be a good friend if I ever see him again.*

The following day Jesse worked in the field. June was not a harvesting month, nor was it a plowing month. It was time to weed the fields to ensure the crop survived. As Jesse collected weeds, he thought of his conversation with Cassie. *Would it be better if I got an education?* He didn't know very many people who had a high school diploma, and he knew even fewer with a college education. *What would be the advantage in obtaining a formal education?*

After working in the field all day, Jesse was tired, but he thought it would be fun to walk into town with Cassie. The McKinley farm was south of town, near the Baylor University campus. Jesse liked to take a bath and put on his nice clothes to walk to the campus. The faculty and students were always friendly and welcoming, even though Jesse was Black. Baylor was adjacent to the Brazos River, and Jesse felt that he could take Cassie to the river by the campus without risking an altercation with the teens who had wanted to fight the day before.

As Jesse and Cassie walked along by the river at half past six in the evening, they heard an approaching automobile. Jesse turned to see a 1915 Model T pickup truck painted green, instead of the traditional black stock color for Fords. The vehicle passed at a high rate of speed, then suddenly made a U-turn and came back directly toward them. Jesse noticed there was only one person in the vehicle. As it pulled out, he recognized Elijah, who had come to his aid the day before.

Elijah pulled the truck alongside Jesse and said, "Hey, Jesse. Last night I found out you know my cousin Becky from the colored church."

"Becky's your cousin?"

Elijah left the engine idling as he talked. "Yeah. Becky came over to our place for dinner last night with her parents. Anyhow, she was telling me about a colored boy she knows named Jesse with a brother named Billy. I knew right away she was talking about you."

Jesse nodded. "Miss Becky is really nice to all the students in her Sunday school class. They all like her."

Cassie nodded. "Everyone likes Becky."

Elijah replied, "Well, any friend of Becky is a friend of mine. She likes all the kids in her class. Hey, I am going uptown for a bite to eat. Do you want to join me?"

Jesse leaned against the door of the truck. "They won't let us in a White restaurant."

Elijah leaned over and opened the passenger door. "This place is OK. The owner doesn't care about the color of your skin as long as your money is green."

Jesse helped Cassie into the truck, then climbed onto the seat next to her. "I didn't know they had any places like that in Waco."

Elijah put the truck in gear and released the clutch, rolling the vehicle forward. "This place is a grub house for ranch hands. Most of them are Black folks, but White folks come in too, so it's really the White people who are breaking the segregation laws. But no one cares. And the food is better than any place in town."

The thought of eating in a restaurant with White people intrigued Jesse. Clearly a new experience, and one that seemed ominous at that. When they arrived at the eatery, Elijah parked the truck on the street in front and they disembarked. Upon entering the establishment, Jesse heard unfamiliar music. The stage supported a dozen musicians playing strange instruments that fascinated Jesse. "What kind of music is that?" he asked.

"Jazz," replied Elijah. "Do you like it?"

"I think so. What's that curved instrument he is blowing?" Jesse pointed at one of the musicians, who happened to be Black.

"That's called a saxophone. You've never heard one before?"

"No, I have never even seen one."

The three sat down for dinner. When the band took a break, Elijah motioned for the saxophone player to join them at their table. Elijah stood and extended his hand to the sax player. "Hey, Tony. It's good to see you. The band sounds great today. These are my friends, Jesse, and Cassie. Good people."

Tony shook Elijah's hand, then Jesse's. As was the custom, he did not extend his hand to Cassie, a female, but instead touched the brim of his ivy golf cap with his index finger. Cassie abruptly extended her hand to him and said, "You are really good on that instrument."

"Thanks. Are you two from around here?"

Elijah replied, "Join us if you like. Jesse and Cassie live on the McKinley farm."

Tony sat down at the table. "I only have a fifteen-minute break, but I'll have a Coke."

The waitress, in her western-style uniform, came over to the table and smiled at Cassie. "What can I get for you?" She placed a Coke in front of Tony, who glanced at her and smiled.

Before Cassie could respond, Tony said, "Order anything on the menu. It's on me." He looked at the waitress. "Shelly, get them anything they would like from the menu."

After Shelly had taken the orders, Tony said, "I've met Farmer McKinley. He seems like a nice old guy."

"He is," replied Jesse. "He helps us a lot. Just last week he barbecued the entire side of a cow for his hired workers. That was so good."

"Does he raise cattle or just cotton?"

"He raises some cattle, but mostly it's a cotton farm. He used to be a cattle drover, so he wants to raise cattle too. He has a huge spread. I think Pa said it's about a thousand acres."

Elijah nodded. "That's a good-size spread. Jesse, you know those guys who were giving you a hard time down by the river yesterday?"

"Yeah. I know who you're talking about."

"Do they know where you live?"

Jesse looked at Elijah inquisitively. "I'm pretty sure they do. It ain't no secret that we're living on the McKinley farm. Is that bad?"

"No, I would just recommend that you try to avoid those guys if you can. They're nothing but trouble."

Jesse nodded with a puzzled expression.

After a few minutes of conversation, Tony stood up. "I need to get back up onstage. We're playing at a club in Dallas next Saturday evening. If you folks aren't doing anything, we'd love for you to come and listen. It is going to be more of a concert than a supper club gig."

Elijah replied, "That sounds like fun."

Tony reached into his pocket and pulled out a flyer with the name and location of the club. He handed the flyer to Elijah and walked toward the stage. He turned back and shouted to Elijah, "Stop by if you can."

Elijah smiled at Jesse. "We'll be there."

CHAPTER
TWO

THE WEEK PASSED quickly for Jesse. Elijah invited him to travel to Dallas with another friend named Mike, who attended high school with him. They were planning to listen to Tony's band. The excitement overwhelmed Jesse. The music he'd heard at the club fascinated him. It was a style he had never heard before, but it had a familiar sound about it. It seemed to have similarities to sounds he'd heard as a child. He couldn't remember where he heard those sounds, but he knew he had heard them before.

The Model T pickup rolled down the highway with the sound of the wind blowing in the windows, which were open on both sides. Elijah drove and Jesse sat in the passenger seat. Mike was in the rear bed of the truck, lying on his back with his feet propped up on the tailgate. His head was resting on a bag of grain.

"How fast will this go?" asked Jesse loudly enough to be heard over the wind.

"I've had her up to fifty miles per hour. It will outrun a fast horse, and it can drive that speed for hours."

"Do you like it better than a horse?"

"It depends on what I am doing," replied Elijah. "If I'm going a long distance or into a busy town, I prefer the Model T. It can travel much farther and faster than a horse, and it is easier to control in town. But a Model T would be worthless on rough terrain or a mountainous region. And a horse can go through much deeper water than a Model T if you have to ford a river."

Jesse laughed. "This is a Ford. It should be able to ford a river."

Elijah chuckled and shook his head.

Jesse glanced out the rear window into the rear bed of the truck. Pointing his left thumb behind them, he said, "Mike's fast asleep. I don't know how he can sleep with all that wind."

"He worked late last night and wanted to sleep, so it worked out well with him back there. I sleep best when there is wind," said Elijah as he downshifted the truck to slow going into town. "This place is called Hillsboro."

As they drove through Hillsboro, Jesse noticed that several people waved at Elijah. "How do all those people know you?"

"Oh, I come through here all the time. I stop for lunch when I'm headed to Dallas. They have a nice restaurant just up the street there." Elijah nodded his head toward the street they were crossing. "They have the best fried chicken. They have some kind of spice that will burn your face if you aren't ready for it."

Jesse looked at the beautiful Victorian homes on each side of the highway as they drove slowly through the town. He contemplated building a Victorian house on the cotton farm he would someday own. "I like these houses."

Elijah nodded. "The detailed carpentry is exquisite."

"What is it? Exquisite? I never heard that word before."

"Oh. It means very detailed and precisely done. High quality."

Jesse had learned a new word. He rehearsed it in his mind so he could use it when speaking with Cassie. She would be impressed. As they reached the north end of town and headed out on the open highway, Elijah accelerated. The top speed of the Model T was approximately fifty miles per hour, but Elijah rarely exceeded forty.

"Elijah, can I ask you a question?"

Elijah nodded. "Sure, you can ask anything."

"Most White people won't hang around coloreds. Why are you different?"

Elijah nodded. "Because I know that the only difference between Black persons and White persons is the color of their skin."

"Really? That's what you believe?"

Elijah nodded again. "Yes, that's what I know."

"But why do other White people think Black people are bad and stupid?"

"Ignorance," replied Elijah.

"Ignorance? You mean people who think Black people are stupid are ignorant?"

"Yes, they are."

"How do you know that?"

"Because I have studied this issue for years."

Jesse appeared puzzled. "Then why are there separate water fountains and restrooms? If there is no difference, why don't everyone use the same one?"

Elijah shrugged and said again, "Ignorance."

They drove in silence for several minutes. Jesse looked at the fields on either side of the road. "Why they ignorant and you ain't?"

"I learned that as a child. My grandparents were abolitionists."

"What's that?"

"Abolitionists opposed slavery. They were Republicans living in Massachusetts before they moved to Texas. My aunt and uncle taught this to us since I was a small boy. My grandfather is a doctor. He says biologically, colored folks and White folks are basically the same except for skin color, and he says intellectually they are the same."

Unconvinced by Elijah's previous answer, Jesse asked again, "Then, why so many people say colored people are stupid and why we use separate bathrooms?"

"Because there are perceived benefits that come from that structure. Benefits for White people."

"Is it bad?"

"My grandpa operated a medical clinic for colored folks. And my grandmother ran a school for colored children. That is how they know this. They have been around colored people for years. They both told me that there are no differences between colored people and White people except the color of their skin."

"But lots of doctors say that Black people are stupid and evil. Are they ignorant too?"

Elijah paused for a moment, then shrugged. "I think a lot of people know better, but they say colored people are inferior because they are trying to maintain a social structure that is favorable to White people. Grandpa calls the system 'institutional discrimination.' That is what he calls the laws that require Whites and Blacks to use different facilities."

"Your grandpa sounds like a smart man."

"He is."

"Have you ever been to other countries, Eli?"

"Yes, I have traveled quite a bit. Mostly to Canada, but I have been to Europe and Africa too."

"Do other countries have slaves?"

Elijah shook his head. "Some countries have slaves, but the huge Atlantic Slave Trade was destroyed when Britain abolished slavery. Before that, Britain was the largest slave-trading nation in the world."

"You know a lot about this."

"Actually, I recently applied to Yale University. My essay to the admissions office was about the Atlantic Slave Trade."

"Where's Yale University?"

"Yale is in a town in Connecticut called New Haven. It's on the East Coast."

"Where's that?"

"Connecticut is a small state near Massachusetts and New York."

"Why don't you just go to Baylor? It is right here. Becky goes to Baylor. Is Yale better 'n Baylor."

"They are both great universities. My family has always gone to Yale, which is part of the reason I am going there. Also, Yale is Congregational, whereas Baylor is Baptist. Our family is Congregational."

"I've heard of Baptist, but what is Congregational?"

"Congregational is another religious denomination like Baptist."

"Oh. When will you learn if you are accepted at Yale?"

"I already got admitted. They sent the acceptance letter last week."

"When will you leave?"

"August."

"Wow. Congratulations."

Elijah smiled and glanced at Jesse. "Thanks, Jesse."

The young men drove in silence for several minutes. Jesse was happy for Elijah, but he would be sad to see him go. He had known him for only a week but already considered him a best friend. Jesse asked, "What was your essay about? I mean, I know it is about slaves, but what'd ya write?"

"I wrote about the abolition of slavery, but it was largely focused on the man I believe was most responsible for changing the way Britain thought about slavery. His name was William Murray, and his title was Lord Justice Mansfield. He was a judge in the king's court."

"What'd he do?"

Elijah laughed. "You're a million questions today."

"I never heard anyone talk about this before. I don't mean to be rude, but I would like to know what you wrote."

"I have a copy of the essay at the house if you want to read it."

"Didn't Becky tell you? I can't read. She's been tryin' to teach me, but I figure I won't need it to be a cotton farmer."

"No, she didn't say anything." Elijah laughed. "OK, I'll give you an essay report. But it might be boring."

"No, this is important to me. My grandparents were slaves."

"OK, the Atlantic Slave Trade began in the 1400s when Portugal began importing Africans to serve as slaves. In 1562 Britain joined the slave trade and began transporting slaves to Britain and other locations, mostly to plantation colonies. By the seventeenth century, Spain, North America, Holland, France, Sweden, and Denmark had joined the slave trade."

"Those are all countries, right?"

"Yes, they're countries in Europe and, of course, North America is today the United States, where we live. Although Portugal was the first nation to import slaves, Britain soon became the largest transporter of slaves."

"How'd dey transport 'em?"

"Mostly by ship. They would chain the slaves to boards laid out like beds in rows from one end of the ship to the other. They gave them almost no food and water so they wouldn't have to take them to use the toilet very often. Every week or so they would take them out and hose them down with cold ocean water from a pump."

"How long was dey on the ship?"

"It depends on where they were going. If they were going to the American colonies, it would take about three months."

"That's a long time."

"Yes, and many of them died on the way."

"So, what'd dat judge do to stop it?"

"He ruled on two cases that shocked Europe and struck a major blow to the slave trade. The first case was called *Somerset v. Stewart* and was heard in Britain in 1772. Somerset was a slave who was bought by Stewart in Boston and taken to Britain. He escaped but was captured by Stewart and put on a ship that was leaving for Jamaica. Some White friends of Somerset filed a petition for his release. Lord Mansfield searched the laws of England and Wales and found no legal authority for slavery. In the absence of either statutory or case authority for slavery, Lord Mansfield decided that Somerset could not be held as a slave.

"The second case heard by Lord Mansfield involved a slave ship called the *Zong*. To fit more slaves on the ship, the captain brought an inadequate supply of water. As a result, the slaves became ill, and to keep the illness from spreading to the crew, the captain ordered one hundred thirty-three male and female slaves to be thrown overboard, resulting in their drowning. The owners of the ship then filed an insurance claim seeking to be reimbursed for the one hundred thirty-three slaves who were thrown overboard."

"But he didn't bring enough water. Why should de insurance have to pay?"

Elijah replied, "That is exactly what Lord Mansfield said. Under British law, if the slaves were thrown overboard to save the lives of the crew, the insurance would have to pay. However, in this case, the slaves got sick because there was not enough water on the ship, and that was the captain's fault. In addition, during the course of the voyage the ship passed eight ports where the ship could have stopped and obtained water but failed to do so, even after the slaves became ill. Lord Mansfield ruled that because of these facts, the insurance company did not have to pay. He decided that the slaves were killed to collect the insurance and not to save the crew. That case was called *Gregson v. Gilbert* and was decided in 1783."

As they drove down the highway, Jesse pondered all that Elijah had told him. It made little sense that people would subject others to slavery simply because they looked different. And it made no sense to Jesse that people would be treated poorly today simply because of the color of their skin.

Elijah downshifted the Model T as they approached another town. "This place is called Milford. We deliver cotton here."

Slowing to thirty miles per hour as they entered Milford, Elijah continued, "We deliver cotton to that warehouse over there."

Jesse saw a cotton gin next to a large warehouse on the left side of the road. On the right side he saw a group of Black men working on the road. He thought it unusual they were doing road work. Usually, government jobs were reserved for White men because they paid well. Ordinarily, the only work for Black persons was sharecropping.

They drove in silence for a time. Finally, at approximately 7:00 p.m., the travelers arrived in Dallas. Elijah stayed on the main highway until he came to a cross street, then turned left and onto Jefferson Street. There they found the Phrygian Jazz Club on the left side of the street. Elijah parked the Model T, and they climbed out of the truck. The closing doors of the truck awakened Michael, who sat up with a start.

"We're here," said Elijah.

Michael slowly climbed out of the bed of the pickup. As he stepped down on the sidewalk, Elijah asked, "Did you have a nice nap?"

Michael nodded. "Yes, I was really sleepy. I didn't get much sleep last night. How did you like the ride, Jesse?"

"It was fine. Elijah and I got to talk a lot."

The three young men walked into the restaurant. They found a table near the right side of the stage. Jesse sat facing the stage so he would not miss anything. He saw the same musicians who were at the club in Waco. Tony nodded hello. They ordered dinner and listened to the jazz band. After about five songs the band took a break. Tony joined Jesse, Mike, and Elijah. "Hey, guys, how was your drive?"

"It was good," said Elijah. "It's really nice out tonight."

Tony leaned back in his chair. "Eli, do you want to play the next song?"

Elijah nodded. "I could do that."

Elijah's comment startled Jesse. "Do you play an instrument?"

Tony laughed. "Eli is only the best classical/jazz guitarist in all of Texas."

"Really?" Jesse looked startled. "I din't even know you could play."

Elijah laughed. "It's just something I picked up over the years."

After a brief introduction, Elijah joined Tony and the band onstage and played a four-song jazz set. His skill amazed Jesse, who had never seen this style of playing before. As he watched Elijah's fingers move swiftly up and down the neck of the guitar, he wondered how he found time to practice. He was on the boxing team, he was a scholar, he worked on his uncle's ranch. Jesse thought about his own life. What could he do if he chose to work like Elijah? Maybe he could be a farmer and learn to read and write.

The men enjoyed themselves for several hours. At a little after ten, Elijah said, "Hey, Jesse, have you ever been to Dallas before? I can show you downtown if you like."

"No, I never been here before."

Mike tapped Jesse's shoulder with the back of his hand. "Let us show you around. It's a big city. They have over a hundred thousand people living here. That is about three times the size of Waco."

Elijah stood up. "Let's go. I'll show you around. I'll be right back." He walked over to the side of the stage, where Tony was waiting to begin his sax solo. He said something to Tony, who smiled and nodded. They shook hands, and Elijah joined Jesse and Mike as they exited the club.

The men walked to the truck. Mike started to climb into the bed, but Jesse grabbed his arm. "I can ride back there now. You were back there all the way from Waco."

"I really don't mind," said Mike. "You and Eli probably have a lot to talk about. You know he's leaving for college in a few months. He won't be around after that."

"I know," said Jesse. "I'm gonna miss him."

Elijah, who overheard the conversation as he took hold of the crank to start the engine, laughed, then shouted, "Hey, I'm going away to college, I'm not dying."

Jesse laughed. "I know, but we're still gonna miss you."

As the teens climbed into the truck, Jesse looked up and down the streets. There were streetlights on all the streets. There weren't this many streetlights in Waco. When it got dark it was simply dark everywhere. But the streetlights illuminated much of the town in Dallas.

"Are those lights electric?" asked Jesse.

Elijah shifted the truck into gear and pulled away from the curb. "No, they're gas lamps. This area, where there are a lot of lights, is called the Gaslamp District."

"Are there electric streetlights?"

"I heard that they have some in Boston, but most streetlights are gas."

Jesse noticed that the streetlights were orange and yellow, but toward the base, they had a bluish glow. He observed the light they cast on the brick buildings. Jesse thought the images interesting and pleasant.

As they drove up and down the streets of Dallas, Elijah would occasionally comment on a building. "Over there is the Dallas courthouse. They call it the red courthouse because it is made of red sandstone and granite."

Although the street was dark, gas lamps illuminated the building. Jesse was amazed at the beauty of the structure. "I ain't never seen anything like that. What do they call that kind of building?"

"That is what you would call Romanesque architecture. It was popular in the eleventh century and was a blend of several different types of structure."

Jesse turned back to see the building as they passed. He thought of the beautiful Victorian houses he saw in Hillsboro. He wondered what the red courthouse looked like inside. He imagined oak-paneled walls and oak stairways similar to the old mansion that served as the church he attended. He imagined the enchanting aroma of the wood.

Just as they crossed the intersection past the courthouse, they heard someone pounding on the rear window. Mike was waving as Jesse looked back into the bed of the truck. Elijah pulled the truck over to the right side of the street and leaned his head out the window.

Mike leaned over the left side of the truck. "Hey, you guys want to get something to drink? Maybe lemonade or a milkshake?"

Elijah looked at Jesse, who smiled and nodded.

"That sounds good," shouted Elijah. "But who's open this time of night?"

Mike said, "There is an ice cream shop a couple of blocks up here on South Houston. On the right side."

Elijah nodded. "Oh, I remember that place. I think it's called Knolles or Noel's."

"Yeah, that's it. Only it's called Knolles, spelled K-n-o-l-l-e-s. They just pronounce it Noels in Texas."

Mike and Elijah laughed. Jesse smiled, though the humor eluded him.

"Are they open this late?" asked Elijah.

"Yeah, they're open until midnight. The ice cream shop is in a pharmacy. That's why they're open so late."

Elijah laughed. "Let's go get some ice cream."

He placed the truck in gear and pulled out onto the street. As they drove along the paved road, Jesse noticed that there were no gas lamps the farther from the courthouse they traveled. It was dark on both sides of the street, as if they were in the country. Up ahead he saw a building with the lights on inside.

Elijah pulled the truck over to the side of the road in front of the ice cream shop and turned off the engine. In the window was a sign that said, "Whites Only." The three teens stepped out of the truck. "I'll wait out here," said Jesse, knowing that black persons were not permitted to enter a White establishment.

Elijah put his hand on Jesse's shoulder. "We'll be quick. What kind of shake do you want?"

"Do they have chocolate?"

"I'm sure they do."

"That's what I'll have then, please."

"You got it. We'll be right back." Mike and Elijah entered Knolles. Seated at the soda bar, which spanned from one end of the building to the other, were about a dozen young men and women. The soda fountain operator was running back and forth, trying to quickly fill orders. At the end were two empty seats. Elijah and Mike sat there as they waited for the operator, whose job was commonly known as a soda jerk.

Elijah glanced out the front window at Jesse and the truck. Jesse saw him and smiled and waved. Elijah and Mike turned their attention to the task of buying milkshakes. Jesse stood outside the truck, enjoying the warm summer air. He noticed a group of young men walking toward him. He counted five of them. As they approached, they stopped speaking and stared at him. He chuckled slightly and whispered to himself, "Do rednecks always come in fives?"

The young men walked up to Jesse. One of them said, "What do we have here?"

Another said, "It's a N_____ leaning against a truck. You stealin' that truck, boy?"

Jesse knew that trying to communicate with these men was likely pointless. They were looking for someone to beat and Jesse was a Black man outside alone at night with no one to assist him. He stepped away from the truck and faced the approaching men. This time he didn't have to worry about Cassie or the others. He was prepared to fight, all five of them if necessary.

The first young man who spoke said, "Look at this. I think this fool is fixin' to fight us. Do you think you can whip us all, boy?"

As the young men approached Jesse in a threatening manner, Elijah and Mike returned from inside the pharmacy carrying three milkshakes. "What's going on here, Jesse?" asked Elijah.

One of the young men said, "You two friends of his? You friends with this N_____?"

Elijah took the two milkshakes over to the truck and placed them on the hood. He then took the one Mike was carrying and placed it on the hood with the others. He walked over and stood next to Jesse. Mike stood on the other side of Jesse, and the three faced down the five young men. Elijah sized up the men. "So, what's it going to be, fellows? Do you want to take us? We've got you outmanned. There are three of us and only five of you." Jesse and Mike laughed.

The young man who talked the most suddenly rushed forward toward Jesse with his right arm raised, holding a metal pipe in his hand. Elijah stepped forward with his right foot, then suddenly spun around with a backspin kick into the assailant's face with his left foot. He continued to spin in the same direction and resumed his previous position. As quickly as he planted his left foot on the ground behind him, he jumped forward between two other assailants and simultaneously planted the palms of his hands in the sternum of each man, knocking the wind out of them as they abruptly fell to the ground coughing and gasping for air.

By this time, a third man had rushed toward Jesse, who was not to be caught unaware. Jesse rushed forward and with his right hand grabbed the young man's belt, thrust him around 180 degrees so his back was to him, then with his left hand grabbed the collar of the man's shirt. Jesse hoisted the man above his head and held him there with both hands as the young man frantically kicked his legs and waved his arms, trying to get free. Jesse threw him on the fifth man, who was just standing as the events transpired. The weight of the thrown man was sufficient to cause the fifth man to lose his balance and fall on the ground with the thrown man on top of him. After a few moments, the five men got to their feet and limped away.

Mike stood motionless, amazed at what he had seen. "You guys are like the Barnum and Bailey three ring circus. I've never seen anything like that. What was that you did, Elijah? I have never seen anybody fight with his feet like that before. That was weird. And Jesse, you picked that guy up and threw him like a bag of potatoes."

Elijah laughed. "I learned that from an Asian man who worked on our ranch one summer. That is a fighting style from China." He walked around to the driver's door of the truck. "We better go before they come back with guns. I've got two loaded rifles under the seat. We'll be fine, but we shouldn't stick around and wait for them. Somebody might get killed."

The three retrieved their milkshakes, then the men climbed into the truck. This time Jesse got in the bed and sat down. He was amazed that Elijah could fight like that. He recalled seeing a man fight using his feet many years ago when he was a young boy and he knew that Elijah must have studied the same style of fighting.

As they pulled away from the curb, Jesse noticed that a truck about a block behind them had turned on its lights and began following them. He tapped on the window. Elijah rolled his window down and leaned out. Jesse shouted, "I think those guys are following us." Elijah looked back and saw the truck.

They drove through the streets of Dallas for a short time to see if the truck was following. After turning on several different streets, it became apparent that it was. Elijah turned a corner, turned off his lights, and made an abrupt U-turn, then parked along the side of the street. As the second truck came around the corner, Elijah suddenly turned on the truck lights, so they were shining directly on the second vehicle. They immediately recognized the five men they had fought a few minutes earlier. Elijah quickly grabbed one of the rifles and shoved the barrel out of the window so the men could see that they were armed.

As the truck drove past them, Jesse noticed that the lights were just lanterns hanging from hooks on each side of the truck. Jesse and Mike both stepped out of the truck with the rifles in their hands. The truck went up the street for two more blocks, stopped, and turned around, then parked at the side of the road. Elijah, Mike, and Jesse waited beside the truck to see if the men were going to come back up the street.

Elijah walked toward the back of the truck. "These guys

must be armed. They saw my gun sticking out the window. They wouldn't continue following us if they were unarmed."

Mike replied, "Yeah. What do you think we should do?"

"Let's just wait here to see what they do."

Jesse said, "Hey, Elijah, I noticed that they didn't have headlights like yours. They just had lanterns hanging on the side of the truck."

Elijah nodded. "That's true. That is a pre-1915 Model T. Mine is a 1915 model. That's the first year they had electric headlamps on the truck."

Eventually, the truck following drove toward them, then abruptly turned onto a side street and disappeared.

The three companions drove around Dallas a little longer, then decided to return to Waco around midnight. Jesse had much to think about. Elijah dropped him off at the McKinley farm around 2:00 a.m. He went inside and crawled into bed. This had been an action-filled week, one of the most interesting of his life. He had made a new friend, the kind of friend one keeps for a lifetime.

The following morning Jesse awakened early to feed the hogs. They got hungry in the morning and began making noise. Not wanting to disturb anyone's sleep, he put on his overalls and ran quickly to the barn, where he grabbed a bag of feed consisting of barley, wheat, and corn. He dumped it into the trough, and the pigs began competing for a place to feed. Jesse was amused. "You folks are noisy and messy."

"They sure are," said Cassie, who had walked up behind Jesse unannounced. They both laughed.

"How long you been standin' there?"

"Long enough to hear you telling the pigs 'bout being messy and noisy.

Jesse smiled. "You shouldn't walk up on a guy like that. You don't know what he might be doing."

"Doing, like what?"

"Well, he might be fixin' to use the toilet, or he might be talking to the animals. You would think he is crazy."

"Jesse, I already know you crazy." She laughed and punched Jesse lightly on the shoulder.

Jesse turned to walk back toward the barn. "I need to get another bag of feed. Those guys eat like pigs."

Cassie laughed. "That's mean."

"How can it be mean? They are pigs. Besides, they don't have any idea what I said."

Cassie replied, "I think animals are smarter than we give them credit for."

Jesse went to the barn and returned about five minutes later. He walked over to the trough and dumped in a second bag of feed. "Look at 'em. They fall all o'r each other tryin' to get to the food."

Cassie nodded. "Jesse, do you see that little white-and-black one over there? He's all by himself and he isn't coming over to feed."

"Yeah, I see him. He do that all the time. He waits 'til the others are finished before he comes over to eat. His mom abandoned him and he had to raise himself."

"I've never heard of a pig standing back and waiting to eat. I didn't know pigs could have that much self-control." Cassie stroked the back of her neck.

"Some do. This one's a real gentleman. I often save back a bowl of feed for him. Then when da others leave, I slip it under da fence for him."

Cassie kissed Jesse on the cheek. "You're a good man, Jesse."

Jesse and Cassie walked to the house together, holding hands.

CHAPTER
THREE

THE FOLLOWING MONDAY morning, Jesse was up before dawn for his morning run. It was his exercise routine. Every other morning, he would get up early and run five miles. On the alternate days he would exercise in the barn, using homemade weights consisting of buckets of sand on a steel bar. Jesse's exercise program was intense. He didn't know the origin of the program, but he had learned it from his father and grandfather.

As he ran across the cotton field toward the creek, he inhaled the aroma of wet sage from an early-morning rain. He had run this path every day for over a year. With each footstep he could feel a surge in energy, as if the energy came up from the ground itself. He approached the edge of the field and followed the path into the canyon that wound down to the creek at the base of the valley. He noticed that it was darker than usual as he entered the tall grass that lined the muddy bank of the creek. He had arrived earlier than on most days. Slightly concerned about possible unseen dangers in the darkness, he quickly dismissed the thought as he turned a corner in the grass leading straight into the water. Jesse saw something shoot quickly toward his left leg just below the knee;

then he experienced the most intense pain he had ever felt in his life. Collapsing onto the muddy ground, he knew immediately that he had been stricken by a rattler. He saw it slithering away up to a grassy knoll.

Jesse knew that he had to reduce his heart rate as quickly as possible by sitting motionless in the mud. He ripped off his shirt and, using the long sleeves, he tied off the leg just below the knee and right above the strike site. He then took his buck knife from his belt and cut his jeans so he could see the bite area. The area was already swollen and red; he could see the fang entry sites. He pushed on the swollen area, trying to force the wound to bleed. Using the knife, he lanced the wound between the entry sites, then took a small bottle of ammonia from his shirt pocket and slowly poured it onto the wound. It was common to carry a small bottle of ammonia in rattlesnake country to use in case of snake bites.

Jesse let out a short shout as he poured the ammonia onto the wound. The poison combined with the previous penetration into the bone by the fangs intensified the agony. He rolled back into the mud, wondering how long he would have to lie there before he could begin walking back to the house. Perhaps if he were missed someone would come looking for him. Deciding it was wise to get to dry land, he began pulling himself up the embankment. As he reached for a tree stump, he abruptly withdrew his hand upon hearing another rattler. Glancing to his right, he saw it coiled and prepared to strike. Less than three feet away, the rattler stared intently into his eyes. "What else can go wrong?" Jesse whispered to himself as he lapsed into unconsciousness. He fell back onto the bank with his upper body down the embankment. Turning his head to the right, he saw a rattler next to his face. He could feel the tongue flicking his cheek as the deadly serpent investigated him.

Staring into the face of the snake, Jesse had no concerns. He laughed and said, "You da one dat bit me ain't ya " The rattler was unalarmed with the speech and motion of his lips. It was almost as if the rattler had accepted Jesse as a natural element of the terrain.

Losing his senses, Jesse began talking to the snake. "You the one that gave Eve the apple. I better throw you away." Laughing and barely aware of his surroundings, Jesse reached over and grabbed the snake by the neck. He threw it backward over his head, not realizing he had fallen next to a large oak tree. The snake flew into the air and hit a low branch just above Jesse's head, causing the snake and several acorns and twigs to fall on his head. The snake slithered away, leaving Jesse wondering if the event had occurred or whether it was all in his imagination.

Jesse felt himself lapsing into unconsciousness. He awakened sometime later, seeing that the sun was high overhead. He surmised that it was approximately 10:00 a.m. With the sun beating down on him, he looked into the trees. He thought he saw dozens of snakes hanging from the branches. He blinked his eyes and realized they were just tree limbs.

He awakened again, several hours later, this time to the sound of voices. He looked up and saw Billy and Elijah leaning over him. Elijah waved his hand in front of Jesse's face. "Can you see us, Jesse?" Jesse did not respond. Although he could see and hear Elijah speaking, it seemed he was speaking to someone else, someone else inhabiting Jesse's body.

Jesse looked up to see Cassie next to Billy. She reached forward and took hold of Jesse's arm. "We're taking you to Baylor Medical College, Jesse. You're gonna be OK."

Jesse passed out again, and when he awakened, he was in a bed in the hospital. Cassie and Billy were there. Jesse looked at the clock, which said 7:06. "Is it night already?"

Cassie stood up and walked to the bed. "No, Jesse, it's Tuesday morning. You have been out all this time. You slept the whole day. The doctor said the reason you were out so long was probably that you were upside down on the hill. Your leg was higher than your heart and the poison went through your whole body. He said it could have killed you."

"Oh, my head is pounding." Jesse looked around the large

room, seeing dozens of other beds with Black men in many of them. "What are these guys in here for?"

A nurse walked up to the bed next to Jesse. "A wide variety of noncontagious injuries and illnesses. You don't have to worry about catching anything from them. You are fortunate, Jesse. We have an experimental method of dealing with rattlesnake bites. It is called antivenom, and it was first used in 1895 with cobra bites. Here we have been experimenting with diamondback rattlers. The doctors could tell from your bite that it was a diamondback. That's almost the only kind of poisonous snake we have around here. Did you get a look at the snake?"

Jesse laughed. "Yeah, I saw it trying to get away. It was a diamondback for sure. Another snake came up to my face after I was bit. I don't know if it was the same one or a different one."

The nurse rolled back Jesse's sleeve. "My name is Sarah, by the way. I'm going to give you another injection of antivenom. What do you mean, it came up to your face?"

"After I was bit I tried to get up to dry ground. I tried to stand up and reached for a tree stump to pull myself up. Then I saw another rattler coiled by the stump, or it may have been the same one. I pulled back my hand and fell backward down the hill. I landed on my back, and the snake came up to my face. It got so close, I could feel its tongue."

The nurse paused. "Whoa. That's scary. Then what happened?"

"By then I thought I was gonna die anyway, so I started talking to it. It just kept staring at me. Even when I started talkin', it didn't do anything. It just kept lickin' me. I thought it was acting like a dog and wanted to be my pet. Then I figured maybe it was waitin' for me to die so it could eat me. I got mad and grabbed the snake by the neck and threw it, but it hit a tree and fell back down on my head."

Billy and Cassie started laughing, then the nurse. Finally, Jesse began laughing as well. "Oh, my head." He put his hand up to his head.

The nurse leaned him back on the bed. "You better relax. Did the snake bite your head or neck? We didn't see any bite marks there."

"No, after it fell on my head it ran away."

Sarah rubbed alcohol on his arm with a piece of cotton. "Do snakes run, Jesse?"

Jesse laughed. "No, ma'am. They crawl."

Sarah smiled. "I just wanted to test your cognitive capacity."

"My what?"

Elijah, who had just entered the room, chuckled. "She wants to see if you can think and understand."

Sarah nodded. "That's right. This will probably make you a little sick. The earlier dose went into your stomach; this one is going in your arm. Try to sleep. Dr. Rosser will be by to check on you in a little while. He has to finish his rounds in the White section. Then he will come to see you. He's interested in your case because of the experimental antivenom."

Fortunately for Jesse, the antivenom worked, and he soon began feeling better. He was discharged from the hospital after four days. He found it painful to walk on the leg that had been bitten, so he used a cane Henry made from a branch of an oak tree. He walked with the cane for several weeks, then eventually was able to walk without it.

Once he was ambulatory, Jesse was back working in the field. Every day he would pull weeds. Cassie would walk with him. As they walked, they talked about many things. Occasionally they would see a rattler that slithered away without causing harm. "Jesse, what was it like when you got bit by that snake?"

"It felt like someone hit me in the leg with a club. I never felt anything hurt so bad."

"Were you scared?"

"I din't think 'bout being scared. It all happened so fast. Then I was just tryin' to stay alive, but after a while, that din't even matter."

"I'm so glad we found you. I couldn't bear it if something happened to you."

Jesse laughed. "It'll take more'n a rattlesnake to knock me down."

"Talking about rattlesnakes, do you ever think about Steve Dixon and those guys?"

"What about 'em?"

Cassie shrugged. "I donno know. Do you ever worry that Dixon and his gang will try to kill us?"

Jesse sighed deeply. "I thought about it. That's why I like to go to places where he won't be. But I get tired a' that. We shouldn't have to stay away from someone just 'cause he's a bully."

"He's more than a bully, Jesse. He's dangerous. I think if he found us alone and no one else was around, he would try to kill us."

"I know he would."

"Jesse, doesn't that scare you? What if he tries to hurt us? How will we fight back?"

"I'd fight back if you weren't there. But I don't want to do anythin' that might get you hurt. Ever' time I see him, you're there."

Cassie pulled a weed next to a cotton plant and tossed it into the bag Jesse was carrying. "It really worries me that we might run into him, and I am worried that you might see him when no one else is around."

"He ain't good. But we can't be scared all the time. We have to stand up to these bad people."

"It's too dangerous, Jesse. You can't change the way it's always been. Africans have always been under the White man's boot. You can't change that."

Jesse shook his head as he pushed the plow out of a rut. "If no one does anything to change it, then it'll always be the same."

"But you can't do it alone, Jesse. It isn't safe."

"I gotta do what I can."

Cassie stopped walking and took ahold of Jesse's arm. "Don't get killed, Jesse. Don't make them mad."

"I don't know how. I don't know how not to make 'em mad."

CHAPTER
FOUR

THE SPRING OF 1915 was a good time for Jesse. He was feeling an emotion he had never felt before. It was a warm feeling that made him happy inside whenever he thought of Cassie. His mother told him that it might be love, and that he should pay close attention to his emotions. His heart would guide him, she said.

Whenever possible, Jesse and Cassie would work in the field together. It was the plowing season. Jesse would guide the mules and the plow and Cassie would walk beside him to remove any rocks that might be in the way. At first, no one questioned the reason she walked next to the plow, and it seemed that they would get away with this method of being together. One day, Mr. McKinley, the owner of the property, saw Cassie walking along next to Jesse. "Why is Cassie always walking next to the plow? Doesn't she have anything to do?"

"She is moving rocks out of the way," replied Cassie's mother, Cynthia.

"Rocks? What rocks? There ain't no rocks in that field." Mr. McKinley took off his hat and rubbed his forehead. "If that in't the darnedest thing." He shook his head and walked away. Cynthia looked at Martha and smiled.

Later that evening, Jesse and Cassie were sitting together on a bale of hay in the barn. Cassie asked. "Did you hear that Becky is leaving for the mission field now?"

"Yeah, she told me. She said she's finished with the university in June and will be goin' to Sierra Leone. I wonder who'll teach her class at church when she's gone."

"I don't know. I know the kids really like her. It'll be hard to find someone they will like so much. We should git her a goin' away present."

"Like what?"

"I donno. Maybe a box of chocolates."

Jesse nodded. "That'd be nice. I'll be sad to see her go."

Cassie told the other students, and they were all glad to pitch in to buy a box of chocolates for Becky. When the time came for her to leave, they held a party in the Sunday school class. It was a sad moment, but everyone knew that Becky was needed elsewhere. Becky introduced her replacement, a junior from Oklahoma who was also studying to become a missionary.

"This is Andrew," Becky said. "He is going to take my place as the new Sunday school teacher."

"Kabo, bobos and titties," said Andrew. "That is Krio for hello, boys and girls." The students giggled.

Awkwardly, Becky quickly interjected, "Andrew is learning Krio, the dominant language in Sierra Leone. He plans to be a missionary there too." Smiling at Andrew, she said, "Andrew, we have been learning conversational Krio in this class, so they should be able to converse to help you practice. They helped me so much."

"That's wonderful," replied Andrew. He looked toward the class. "I look forward to learning with you."

"I explained to Andrew that you are studying the book of Matthew. I hope all of you will listen to Andrew and be the wonderful students you were with me. I'm asking you to work with him to help him develop his teaching skills. This is new to Andrew, just as it was to me four years ago. You all helped me so much and we all learned together."

Tearfully, Cassie said, "We'll miss you, Miss Becky. You have taught us so much." She stood and walked to the front of the class with the box of chocolates. "This isn't much, but it is all we could afford. We wanted to give you something to show how much we'll miss you." She gave the box of chocolates to Becky.

Becky reached for the box. "Thank you so much. I love chocolates. It's the best gift you could have given me."

The students stayed after class to visit Becky, and most of them did not go to the main sanctuary for the morning service. They talked about Becky's anticipated experiences on the mission field. The parents knew they were having a special party for Becky, so they were not troubled that the teens did not come up to the main service as they usually did. Eventually, everyone said goodbye to Becky, and the students went their separate ways.

After Sunday dinner Jesse and Cassie decided to go down to the river as they had often in the past. As they walked along the bank of the river, Jesse watched the road that ran along the river, somewhat apprehensive that the boys who started the fight with them before would show up again. As time passed, his concern dwindled until it was nothing more than a distant consideration.

As they stood by the bank of the river, Jesse heard something approaching on the road at a high rate of speed. In time he could see that it was a black Model T Ford sedan. When the vehicle drew nearer, Jesse could see who was in the car. It was the same five boys he had encountered before, and Steve Dixon was driving. As the car passed, Jesse noticed it was towing something. The boys in the car were shouting and cheering, as though they had just won an important sporting event. The car stopped in front of Jesse and Cassie, and the men got out. "Hey, Washington. Look at this," shouted Dixon.

Tied to the rear of the car was a naked Black man covered

with blood from having been dragged on the gravel road. He was moving slightly, which was the only way Jesse could see he was still alive. In the distance, a crowd was running toward the car. A man in the crowd was pushing a red wheelbarrow that had something in it causing smoke to rise from it. Jesse could smell the familiar smell of roofing tar. "They're gonna tar and feather him," said Jesse.

The wheelbarrow stopped next to the man lying in the street. The man pushing the wheelbarrow took a shovel and shoveled a scoop of the hot tar, then threw it on the naked man, who screamed in anguish. The crowd roared with laughter. Another man opened a bag of white chicken feathers and dumped them on the naked man. He then took a club and began beating the naked man mercilessly.

Instinctively, Jesse started to run toward the victim to assist him. Cassie grabbed him by the arm to prevent it. "You can't help him, Jesse. There are too many of them. There must be two hundred people up there."

Jesse knew Cassie was right, but it was hard to refrain from running up to help. He took Cassie's hand and began walking away down the river.

"Hey, Washington!" shouted Steve. "You're next. This is what happens when you N____s touch a White woman. Be smart and stay with that N_____ girl you got there. Maybe then you'll survive." He laughed loudly. "There's our next one, guys. That N_____ there. We're gonna tar and feather him one of these days. Or we'll hang him from a tree. Mark my words."

Jesse stopped momentarily and looked back at Steve, who turned directly toward him. "You got something to say?"

Cassie pulled his hand and said, "No, Jesse. Let's go."

Jesse turned and continued walking. The teens untied the rope that was hooked to the back of the vehicle, jumped in, and drove away. The crowd turned and walked back toward the city, leaving the burned, bleeding man lying in the gravel road.

After the crowd had dispersed, Jesse and Cassie walked over

to the injured man, who was lying, moaning, and writhing in the road.

"We have to get him somewhere safe before they come back," said Jesse.

"I don't think they're coming back, but we need to get him someplace where someone can help him."

Jesse leaned down over the man. "Can you hear me?" he asked.

In a struggling, whispering voice, the man said, "Yes."

"What's yer name?" asked Jesse.

"Richard."

"Can you git up?" asked Jesse.

The injured man attempted to stand up but fell back on the ground. Jesse looked around and saw a wooden plank lying in the dirt at the side of the road. He walked over to the plank and carried it back to the injured man. He noticed a hole in one end of the plank. He removed the rope from the injured man and tied it to the plank. "I'm gonna have to drag you outta here," he said. The man did not respond.

"How can I help?" asked Cassie.

"I can do it," replied Jesse. "Just help me roll him onto the plank."

Jesse laid the plank on the road next to the injured man. He and Cassie rolled him onto the plank. Jesse began dragging him down the road toward the McKinley farm. After walking for about ten minutes, they heard a vehicle approaching from behind. The Model T driven by Steve Dixon slowed to a crawl next to Jesse, who was dragging the injured man. Inside, the teens were laughing loudly and boisterously. "Look he is hauling out the trash," shouted one of the teens in the truck. The laughing grew louder.

"What are you trying to do?" shouted Dixon. "He is already dead, or at least he will be by the time you get him to wherever you are going. Where are you going anyway?"

Jesse did not reply.

"Hey, I asked you a question. Where are you taking him?"

"Just someplace where he can get some help," replied Jesse.

"You're wasting your time. But now you see what happens when a N_____ man messes with a White woman." Steve shifted into second gear and sped down the road, throwing dirt and stones on the injured man and Jesse.

When they eventually arrived at the Washington bungalow on the McKinley property, Jesse laid the board down and turned around to examine the man he had been dragging. The victim wasn't moving. Checking his wrist, then his neck for a pulse, Jesse shook his head, then got to his feet. "He's dead."

Cassie and Jesse stood looking at the burned dead man as Henry and Martha came out to investigate. "How'd this happen?" asked Henry.

"A mob near the city did this to him. They dragged him behind a Model T, then they poured hot tar all over him and covered him with white chicken feathers. I think he would have died from the dragging alone, but with the hot tar, he didn't have a chance. There was nothin' I could do to stop them. There must have been a hundred or more."

Jesse and his father dragged the man on the plank into the barn and put him in a horse stall. Then they walked into town and asked every Black person they saw if they knew a Black man named Richard and told them what had happened. No one knew who he was. They stopped by the undertaker's office and asked if he would take the body. He declined but didn't say why. Jesse and his father already knew why. Eventually, Jesse and Henry walked back home.

The following morning Jesse's father said, "It doesn't look like anyone is going to come for him. We can't leave him in the barn. The body will decay, and we'll get rats. We might as well go ahead and bury him."

Later that day Jesse and his father dug a shallow grave in the field near the Washington home. "I don't know who he is," said Jesse's father. "I don't believe I can do anything else for him."

Jesse and his father placed the man in the grave and covered him with dirt. Jesse's father took two pieces of wood he had brought from the barn and taking a hammer from his belt and a nail from his pocket, he fashioned a small cross that he forced into the ground at the head of the grave. He tapped it several times with the hammer to ensure that it was embedded sufficiently in the dirt to withstand the elements.

Jesse continued to stare at the cross on the grave for several minutes. "I don't believe I can either."

"What did you say?" asked Cassie, who had followed them to the field.

Jesse shook his head slowly. "Nothing." He said good night to Cassie, then went into his family's house. After sitting in the rocker by the fireplace for about a half hour, he went to bed hoping tomorrow would be a better day.

Throughout the summer Jesse remained active, helping to keep the farm productive. This meant walking through the fields looking for weeds and pulling them. Cassie always went along. She would carry a canteen of water and Jesse would pull the weeds, then throw them into a burlap bag. Occasionally Farmer McKinley would look at them from the house, then laugh and shake his head.

One day, as they walked through the rows of cotton shrubs, Jesse took Cassie's hand in his. "What would you say if I asked you to marry me?"

Cassie laughed. "It doesn't work like that, Jesse. You can't say, 'what if.' You have to ask me, then see what I say."

"But what if you say no? Then I would feel stupid."

She squeezed his hand. "Not as stupid as you will feel if you never ask, and I would have said yes."

They laughed as Jesse let go of her hand and got down on his right knee.

"Oh, you are going to kneel and ask me, right now?" Cassie laughed.

Jesse stood up with a weed in his hand. "No, I was just pulling this weed."

"Darn Jesse, you sure are evasive."

"Evasive. What do you mean?"

"You want to ask me to marry you, but you don't do it. Why?"

"I'm only sixteen," he replied. "And you are only fifteen. Someday, maybe."

"Jesse, why we beatin' about the bush? We both feel the same way, don't we? My grandma got married when she was only ten, and my mama was only fourteen."

"I feel something, Cassie. When I think about you it makes me happy. Mama said I should pay attention to these feelings, but I just don't know yet. And I want to be set up with my farm before I get married."

They walked along the row of shrubs in silence for a time. Cassie laughed, then shoved him. "Well, you know that a girl can't wait around forever . . . and besides, you may not be set up 'til you're fifty."

He laughed. "Thanks for believin' in me."

"No, I don't mean I think you can't do it. I just mean it might take a long time. We could work together on having a farm."

Jesse took her hand again. "I don't want to get married 'til I'm at least twenty. By then I'll have a plot of land and a little house. Then I'll get more land and more land. One day I'll be a big rancher, just like those White ranchers."

"You dream big. I never heard of a colored rancher."

"That's 'cause everyone stays on the plantation and works for the White man. I'm gonna be different. The White man's gonna work for me."

"I don't know, Jesse. That's big talk."

"It ain't big talk. It's real. You'll see."

"Why you asking me about gettin' married if you don't want to marry me now? I don't understand you, Jesse."

"Because I want to know you'll say yes before I ask you to marry me."

BECAUSE I'M BLACK | 45

"See, that's what I mean! It doesn't work that way. You have to ask, outright."

"But what if you said no? Then what?"

"Then you would feel stupid." Cassie laughed.

Jesse smiled. "That was downright low."

Cassie slowed her walk and looked at Jesse. "Why do you think I would say no?"

"Maybe because you want to be married to a colored doctor." Jesse barely finished his sentence before bursting into laughter. "You and your colored doctors."

Cassie shook her head and laughed. "Jesse, if you love someone, you love them the way they are. If you don't want to be a colored doctor, that's OK. You can be a cotton-pickin' rancher. A colored one. If I love you, I'll love you either way. I just want you to be the best at whatever you choose."

"You know, I was down at the army recruiter's office last week."

"What were you doing down there? You ain't joinin' the army, are you?"

Jesse's face exhibited a little excitement. "I thought about it. I heard that the war in Europe is gettin' big and that the United States might join in it."

"Where'd ya hear that?"

"I heard it from town folk. They said President Wilson's talkin' about joinin' the war."

Cassie frowned slightly. "I thought President Wilson didn't like the war."

Jesse shrugged. "He din't, but I guess he changed his mind . . . or maybe something 'bout the War changed. I don't know."

Cassie walked hand in hand with Jesse, her head looking toward the ground.

"You know, Jesse, I would really miss you if you joined the army."

"I would miss you too, Cassie."

Later in the afternoon, Cassie and Jesse walked to the house.

Jesse dumped the bags of weeds into the firepit, where they would be burned on Saturday. He and Cassie walked over to the pump that sat beside the well. The aroma of beef cooking above an open fire drew them around the house to the barbecue pit. Sitting at the picnic tables were Cassie's and Jesse's families. Mr. McKinley was brushing barbecue sauce onto the side of beef. Henry and John were turning the eight-foot iron skewer that pierced the side of beef. "It sure was nice of you to invite us to have a barbecue tonight," said Henry.

Mr. McKinley continued brushing on the barbecue sauce. "My pleasure. I thought you folks deserved a nice barbecue. You're doing a great job in the fields this year." Mr. McKinley laughed, then smiled at Jesse and Cassie. "And you two are doing a great job keeping the weeds out of the field. Just don't make any babies out there."

Cassie looked startled. "What? We wouldn't do that."

"Thank you, sir," Jesse replied.

Mr. McKinley continued. "It's good that Cassie walks with you to watch for rattlers. They're all over around here."

Jesse thought to himself, *I never told anyone she was looking for rattlers. I guess I will let him believe that.* He exchanged smiles with Cassie.

"How long you been cookin' this side o' beef?" asked Jesse.

"We started about noon," replied Mr. McKinley. "Slow cooking over a low fire is the best way to go. The beef will fall off the bone."

"This is gonna be good," said Henry.

John nodded and smiled. "Oh yeah."

"You better believe it," said Mr. McKinley. "We should put the beans on. This beef is almost done."

"Where'd you learn to cook like this?" asked Jesse.

Henry replied, "Don't you know, Jesse? Mr. McKinley used to drive cattle. He was a cowboy."

"Is that true?" asked Cassie.

Mr. McKinley stopped brushing the sauce on the cow and put

the brush in the bucket of barbecue sauce. "That's right young lady. I drove cattle from El Paso to cattle towns in the Midwest like Abilene and Dodge City for over twenty years. Later I drove them from El Paso to San Francisco. I enjoyed it, but one day I realized that sittin' on a horse eatin' dust for twelve hours a day and going a month without a bath just didn't suit me no more. So, I had a little money saved up and the missus and me decided to get our own little spread. First, we looked around El Paso and San Antonio, because I knew those areas better. We didn't find anything that we loved. Then we found this ranch. It was owned by a cotton farmer who was too old to farm, and his kids all went to Baylor and became doctors. So, we got it at a great price. I figure I'll raise a few hundred head of cattle that we'll drive to the Waco Yard and ship them out on the railroad."

Mr. McKinley's comments excited Jesse as he contemplated the possibility that he and Cassie might someday marry and have a farm. He found himself gazing at her and admiring her beautiful features, as he often did. He thought her the prettiest girl he had ever seen. He pondered, *Maybe I should ask her to marry me soon. If I wait too long, she might be gone. Someone else might snatch her up.*

Cassie giggled, then whispered, "Jesse, why are you staring at me?"

Before Jesse could respond, Mr. McKinley announced in a loud voice, "OK, folks. Gather round. We're ready to cut the beef. Who would like to say grace?" He looked around the yard, and then his gaze met Jesse's. He smiled. "How about you, young man? You're old enough to say grace."

Jesse smiled nervously. "I don't know if I can say the prayer right. Pa usually says it."

Henry replied, "It's OK, Jesse. You're man enough now."

Saying the prayer was a man's job, and it was an honor. A rite of passage. Jesse lowered his head. "Yes, sir. Let us pray. Dear Father in heaven, thank you for friends and family and our bounty. Thank you for Mr. McKinley, who prepared it. Thank you for this food, and we ask that you bless it for our bodies. Amen."

Several of those present repeated, "Amen."

"Let's eat!" shouted Mr. McKinley with a laugh. "Let's form a line on this side. Bring your plates and I'll cut each of you a slice of beef."

They enjoyed a great meal that evening with family and friends. The McKinleys stayed out with them until after nine. Afterward, Jesse and Cassie sat on a bale of hay next to the barn and talked until past midnight. They talked of love and trust and goals and dreams. It seemed they talked about every imaginable topic, and then another topic would come up.

Cassie talked fast in her excitement. "Jesse, what do you think happens after we die?"

Jesse shrugged. "Says in the Bible it gets hot or cold." He laughed.

"But I mean, what do you think we see and feel?"

"I think it depends. If a person is good, then I think it's good when he dies. But if he is coldhearted, he doesn't have that peace."

Cassie leaned back against the barn, "Jesse, you're so wise, but you don't like books. Why, Jesse, don't you like books?"

Jesse laughed. "Are you going to tell me to be a colored doctor again?" He paused and looked up at the moon. "I just like to know what I feel around me. Books are make-believe to me."

Cassie lifted her left foot up onto the bale as she hugged her knee with her arms. "I understand. Which one will you have, Jesse? When you die, I mean. Will you have peace?"

"Shahid."

"What?"

"Shahid."

"What's that?"

"I don't know. My grandmamma used to say it. She said she heard it when she was a kid. It means die serving God."

"Do you believe that, Jesse? That sounds scary."

Jesse stood up. He locked his hands behind his back as he had seen the older men at the church do, then he began to pace slowly back and forth in front of Cassie. Inwardly, she smiled. She admired his effort to appear gentlemanly, but his actions amused her.

"I don't know," he replied.

"Was that a foreign religion that said that, Jesse? Becky said we shouldn't listen to foreign religions. She said some of them don't believe like we do. Do you think that's true?"

Jesse lowered his head and said softly, "I suppose so." As a child, Jesse learned that when someone asks a question, you should always agree, if possible. He was taught that it was especially bad to disagree with one's boss. Jesse carried this perspective into his life with peers. He liked to please others by saying what they wanted to hear. "Grandmama said it was like a 'martyr' in our Bible."

Cassie and Jesse both grew silent. *Martyr* was a word they heard often as children. They heard of relatives or others in the culture of their parents in which Black persons had lost their lives or their freedom at the hand of some circumstance they did not understand. The word *martyr* had special significance for Jesse and Cassie. It was not just a person who was killed as a slave or in some other abusive fashion, it was a person who was righteous in God's eyes when he died.

Jesse and Cassie talked into the early morning. They took a clean horse blanket from the barn and covered up to keep warm. Suddenly they heard someone come up from behind them.

"Cassie," John said gruffly, "what do you think you're doing out here? It's two o'clock. You get up into the house, now."

Cassie stood up and whispered, "I'll see you in the morning, Jesse." She walked quickly toward her family's bungalow with her father. Jesse stood up and walked to his home.

The next morning, Jesse awakened, got out of bed, and walked over to the open window. He put his head through and looked out across the yard toward the Williamses' bungalow. He saw a white shirt blowing in the wind on the clothesline in the backyard. Cassie was nowhere to be seen.

As Jesse pulled his head back inside, he wondered how he could ease the situation with Cassie's father. *He must believe I'm a horrible person.* Jesse knew what he must do. He got dressed, walked into the kitchen, and made a quick breakfast of cornmeal mush. His mother had taught him how to prepare it. He mixed the cornmeal with milk, salt, and baking soda, then fried it into a patty like a pancake. When it was prepared, he put it in a bowl and poured milk on it. He ate slowly, occasionally looking out the window toward Cassie's house.

Nervously, Jesse stood up from the table and walked out the door, then over to Cassie's bungalow. He knocked on the door. John opened it.

Jesse cleared his throat. "Sir, I want to apologize for keeping Cassie out so late last night. We got to talking and had no idea how late it was."

John smiled. "It's OK. I shouldn't have got so mad. I looked in her room and she wasn't there, so I thought something happened to her."

Jesse felt a sense of relief. "Thank you, sir. We'll be more careful next time."

"It's OK, Jesse. I know you are a good young man. Sometimes when you are havin' fun time slips by."

"Thank you, sir."

"Have a nice day, Jesse."

As Jesse turned to walk back to his bungalow, Cassie's father went back inside the house. Jesse overheard him say, "I don't believe that. Jesse came over and said he was sorry for keeping Cassie out so late last night. He's a good boy."

CHAPTER
FIVE

DURING THE SUMMER of 1915, Elijah taught Jesse to drive his truck and was soon paying Jesse to deliver supplies to farms around Waco. Jesse loved the truck. Each week he would drive to a small ranch about an hour northwest of Waco to deliver produce from Elijah's aunt and uncle's ranch. On many of these occasions, Jesse noticed a small mountain range that he learned was called Kay Mountain. He also noticed a large clump of trees that seemed misplaced in this mountain-desert region. One day Jesse had a very light load consisting of two horse saddles and a blanket. Elijah had given Jesse permission to take passengers on his routes if he so chose. Jesse invited Billy, Jenny, and Cassie to ride along so they could explore Kay Mountain on the way back home after the delivery. They decided on an early start and left at 4:00 a.m. Jesse had instructions to leave the saddles in the barn if no one was up when he arrived. After completing the delivery, they drove back south toward Kay Mountain.

When they arrived at Kay Mountain Jesse parked the green Model T truck by the road near the base of the mountain, behind a long row of pampas grass that completely concealed the vehicle. It was now becoming light. Jesse, Cassie, Billy, and Jenny climbed from the truck and walked along the road toward the mountain. The beautiful reddish morning sun appeared on the edge of the horizon in the eastern sky. About a half mile off the road to the west was a huge clump of pine trees surrounded by a massive amount of vegetation encompassing about one hundred acres. These trees lined the base of Kay Mountain for a substantial distance. The area of the forest was hilly, with numerous ravines. Jesse had seen these trees on many occasions while traveling to and from Waco and was always curious to see them up close.

Jenny pointed at the small forest. "What is that large clump of trees over there at the foot of the mountain?"

Billy replied, "The river branches off into a creek in that direction and the trees line the water."

Cassie said, "Let's explore. Jesse, can we explore? Let's see what's in those trees and hills."

Jesse held his hand beside his face to block the rising sun as he looked toward the trees. "I don't know who owns this land, but I don't see any signs. I guess we can look around a little bit."

Leading the way, Jesse walked into the wooded area, pushing limbs and bushes out of the way. Cassie walked immediately behind, followed by Billy and Jenny. Jesse led them along a creek that wound through the hilly area away from the river. The smell of wooded vegetation generated a pleasant aroma of pine. "I love that smell," said Jesse. "Watch out for rattlers."

Cassie stepped over a fallen tree that was blocking the path. "This is interesting. I wonder if anyone ever comes in here."

Jesse nodded. "I know that people hunt in here 'cause I heard 'em talk about it."

The party continued until they came to a waterfall that drained into a beautiful blue basin filled with water so clear you could see fifteen feet down.

Jenny walked up to the edge of a large rock that hung out over the pond. Her companions approached behind her. As they stood looking into the water, Cassie slowly slipped off her sandals, then suddenly jumped off the rock into the water. When she came to the surface, Jenny said, "That caught me off guard. I wasn't expecting it."

Cassie motioned for them to join her. "Come on in."

Jesse removed his shoes, then dove in. Billy and Jenny followed close behind.

All four of them were excellent swimmers, and they splashed about for a half hour. Eventually, Jenny, Cassie, and Billy came out of the water onto the shore. They climbed back on the rock and lay down, letting the warm summer air dry their clothing. Jesse stayed in the water and began following along the edge of the pond, examining the shoreline. Looking for evidence of animal life, he pulled his face up to a rock wall that formed the edge of the pond. Moving along the bank with his face fifteen inches from the rock, he barely noticed that he was moving under the waterfall until the water began dumping on his head. Having been taught since a child never to stand under a waterfall, because there may be falling rocks and debris, he quickly pulled himself behind it. He found himself in a large, recessed area behind the fall. There he found a rock ledge.

On the shore, Cassie sat up and looked toward the water, "Where did Jesse go? He was floating along by the edge of the pond toward the fall, but I don't see him now."

Jenny sat up and put her hand above her brow to block the rising sun. She pointed toward the waterfall. "I think that's him over there behind the water."

Billy sat up and looked at Jesse behind the waterfall. "How did he get under there?"

The water impaired the view, but they could discern Jesse's image behind the falling water. The three continued to watch him move about behind the fall. As he looked at the wall of the bluff, which recessed several feet into the side of the hill, Jesse noticed a rock that appeared to cover something dark. He climbed out of the water and up onto the rock ledge. As his eyes adjusted to the lack of sunlight, he looked closer at the dark area behind the rock. He noticed that it appeared to be a hole in the rock face of the hill. Getting as close as he could, he looked inside but could only see darkness. He reached his hand into the opening but could not feel a wall. Concluding that reaching into a dark cave might not be particularly wise, Jesse stood up. Stepping back, away from the hole in the side of the hill, he looked again toward the opening but still could not see it well. Turning and looking toward the east, Jesse realized that within a few minutes the sun would rise over the tops of the trees and cast some light into the opening. He decided he would go tell the others what he found and come back in a few minutes when the sun was directly on the face of the fall.

Jesse dove through the waterfall and into the pond. He swam to the bank where Billy, Jenny, and Cassie were waiting for him.

Cassie asked, "What were you doing, Jesse?"

Jesse climbed up onto the rock and sat next to Cassie. "I found what might be a cave under the waterfall. I couldn't tell for sure 'cause it was too dark, but in about a half hour the sun will come up over the top of the trees and will shine on the waterfall. Enough light will come through so we can see if it is really a cave or just a hole in the rock face."

"Wow," said Billy. "I wish we had a lantern."

"I do too," replied Jesse.

Cassie leaned forward to see Jesse's face. "Do you think anyone knows about this place?"

Jesse shrugged. "I think people have been to the pond, but I don't know if anyone has seen the cave, if it is a cave."

Jenny pointed toward the east. "Look, the sun is coming over the trees now."

Jesse looked toward the waterfall. The sun was shining brightly on the falling water. Jesse could see the rock formation behind the fall. "Let's go." He jumped from the rock and into the pond, then swam toward the waterfall. The others followed.

They reached the other side of the pond, climbed up onto the ledge under the waterfall, and walked over to the dark area behind the rock. Much to their astonishment, not only could they see into the cavern, but they could see at least twenty feet into the cave. They had to stoop to get into the cave, but once they were inside, they could see a fair distance. A shiny glistening on the floor and the walls caused the sunlight to reflect, creating illumination. The reflections allowed them to see that the tunnel went deep underground.

"Why is everything so shiny?" asked Cassie.

Jesse scraped the wall with his fingers, and they became shiny. "It's some kind of dust."

Billy touched the wall with his fingers. "Think it's gold?"

Jesse reached down, picked up a rock, and threw it far into the cave. "I don't know. I wonder if anyone has ever been in here." The rock crashed into the wall a long distance into the tunnel.

"That went a long way," said Jenny.

"It did," replied Jesse. "Let's get lanterns and come back tomorrow. I want to see how far this goes."

"Will we get in trouble?" asked Cassie.

Jesse turned to walk out of the cave. "No one ever comes around here. I been over here a lot and ain't never seen a person around anywhere. I don't know if hunters ever found this cave."

The group left the cave, swam back across the pond, and climbed onto the bank. With soaking-wet clothes, they walked out of the woods and onto the dirt path headed toward the truck. They talked excitedly about their amazing find. Unsure of how their parents would react, they decided not to tell them of their discovery. Generally, in early August there wasn't as much work on the farm. They would get up before dawn to milk the cows, then relax until about 10:00 a.m. Then they would do chores before lunch. They enjoyed the leisure time. They often explored the terrain around Waco. The pond was nearly sixty miles from the McKinley farm, so it would take about an hour to get each way.

When they reached the McKinley farm, they agreed to get up at 4:00 a.m. to milk the cows and be on their way to the pond, with a lantern and supplies, by five thirty. Throughout the day Jesse thought of the excitement of finding the cave. He could only imagine what they would find in the morning. That evening he and Billy prepared the equipment needed to explore the cave. One lantern, a box of matches and two hundred feet of binder twine. As they discussed the task of crossing the pond and going behind the waterfall, Jesse realized it would be difficult to keep the matches dry. He retrieved a Ball canning jar that would be used to carry the matches. He found four leather saddle bags to keep their change of clothes while they swam under the waterfall. Jesse knew from walking into the entrance of the cave that it was cold inside. He had heard that caves usually were only about fifty-five degrees. They would need a change of clothes to put on once they came out of the water to go into the cave. They would be too cold wearing wet clothes.

The following morning, after milking the cows, the quartet set out for the pond. They were overcome with excitement, even more so than when they were leaving the cave the day before. Jesse drove and Cassie sat in front, next to him. Billy and Jenny were in the bed of the truck. The window of the truck between the cab and the bed was open, so they all could hear one another. As they drove down the road toward Kay Mountain, they sang songs from church: "Battle of Jericho," "Swing Low, Sweet Chariot," and "Amazing Grace." Their harmonies were exquisite, as always. During "Hold On," Cassie broke into an amazing solo that surprised everyone as they sang the harmony parts.

As they approached the path that led into the forest and to the pond, Jesse stopped the truck, and everyone jumped out. Jenny started to run toward the pond. By the time they caught up with her, she was already in the water, making her way to the waterfall. She bobbed up and down as she bounced along in the neck-deep water by the rock embankment. Billy laughed. "Baby, you look like a bobber." Everyone joined in the laughter.

Jenny laughed. "I hope a fish doesn't bite my butt."

Jesse was next into the water, followed by Cassie, then Billy. "Billy, you got those matches in the jar with the lid tight?"

Billy replied, "Yep. They'll be dry."

Jesse was careful to hold the kerosene lantern upright and as far above the water as possible as he went behind the waterfall. He had to keep the wick dry. Jenny was the first to climb on the ledge behind the wall. Her wet skirt stuck to her legs. Cassie laughed. "Jenny, you can see right through that white skirt. You look naked. That's why I wore jeans." Billy and Jesse pretended not to hear.

When they were all up on the rock ledge behind the waterfall, Jesse flipped the glass globe open to light the lantern. Billy struck a match and ignited the wick. Before Jesse had closed it, Jenny and Cassie were already in the cave. "Be careful, there could be rattlers," said Billy. "They like caves and water."

Cassie replied, "It's OK. It's like daylight with all the sparkling lights. Don't come in. We are going to change into dry clothes."

After the girls put on their dry clothes, Jesse crouched and walked into the cave. "Wow, these sparkles are gold. I think this might really be gold dust."

Billy followed Jesse. "Ya really think so?"

"Yeah, it looks like it . . . unless it's that pyrite stuff. Cassie, you and Jenny should slow down. Ya don't know what's in front of ya. Sometimes the floors of caves are really thin, and people fall through. Stay there and look away while Billy and I change. Don't walk farther than the light on the floor."

Cassie and Jenny stopped to wait for Jesse and Billy, who finished changing and left their wet clothes on the floor of the cave next to Cassie and Jenny's. Jesse walked past them and took the lead. They continued walking through the tunnel with glistening walls. Jesse walked slowly to test the floor with each step. The farther they walked, the larger the tunnel became. Soon the ceiling of the cave was over fifteen feet above their heads and sloped downward ten feet on either side. Jesse stopped walking for a moment. "Do you hear that? It sounds like water running."

Everyone stopped walking and listened. Billy cupped his hand behind his ear to hear better. "That is water. It sounds like it is miles away. This place goes on forever."

They continued to walk in the tunnel, eventually arriving at a fork with one branch of the tunnel leading to the left and one leading to the right.

Cassie stopped and put her hands on her hips, looking in every direction. "This reminds me of that riddle Becky told us."

"I remember that. How did it go?" asked Jesse.

Cassie looked at the ground for a moment. "I'm trying to remember. You come to a fork in the road. There are two twin brothers at the fork. One path goes to heaven and the other path goes to hell. The only thing you know is that one of the brothers always tells the truth and one of the brothers always lies, but you don't know which is which. You can only ask one question. What question should you ask?"

As she talked, Jesse wondered if the answer might tell them which tunnel to take into the cave. "I can't remember what Becky told us."

Cassie looked at Billy and Jenny, neither of whom responded. "You ask one of the brothers, 'If I asked the other brother which path leads to heaven, what would he say?' The brother who always tells the truth would point to the path that leads to hell because he knows that his brother would lie about which road leads to heaven. The brother who always lies would also point to the path that leads to hell because he knows his brother would always tell the truth and point to the road that leads to heaven so he would point to the path that leads to hell. So, you take the other path."

Jesse laughed. "Every time I hear that, I can't believe how smart someone was to come up with it."

Cassie said, "I think we should pray."

Jesse laughed again. "Pray for what?"

"That we don't get hurt in here." Cassie reached out her hand to Billy, who was next to her right side, and Jesse, who was on her left. They took one another's hands, and they formed a circle.

Cassie prayed. "Dear Father in heaven. Thank you for showing us this place. Please keep us safe here. Amen."

Jenny replied, "Amen."

Jesse glanced at Billy with a smile. "Alrighty then; now we'll be safe."

Cassie laughed. "Are you making fun of us, Jesse?"

He shook his head and laughed. "No."

Cassie punched him gently in the shoulder and laughed too.

Jesse walked forward and shone the lantern into the tunnel to the left. He looked in as far as he could see. Then he walked over to the tunnel that led to the right. He looked in and listened, turning his head slightly to hear better. "Let's go this way."

Cassie walked over to the tunnel on the right. "Why?"

Jesse went into the tunnel. "Because this is where the sound of water is coming from."

"That sounds scary. What if we fall into the water?"

"Then we would be stupid," said Jesse. "Wait a minute." Taking the leather bag from his shoulder, he opened it and pulled out the roll of binder twine. He walked back to the fork of the tunnel and looked around. He saw a large rock that he tried to move. "Billy, help me with this."

Billy walked over to the rock and helped Jesse lift one side of it. Then they let it back down. Jesse asked, "Cassie, can you put the end of the twine under the rock when we lift it up?"

Cassie went over to the rock. Jesse and Billy lifted one side of it again, and Cassie quickly slipped the end of the binder twine under the rock, then they let it back down.

Jesse picked up the binder twine and gave it a tug to ensure it was secure. "Now we won't get lost if we come to any more forks."

He led the way into the tunnel, carrying the lantern with one hand and letting the binder twine unroll behind him with the other. Finally, he handed the twine to Billy. "You do that. I can't do it with one hand."

They walked in silence for a time. The farther they walked, the closer the water sounded. Eventually, the sound of water turned into a mild roar.

"That ain't a trickle," said Jesse. "That's a waterfall."

Jenny said, "This is scary. Maybe we should go back."

"It's OK," replied Jesse. "Just be careful where you step."

Finally, they came to the end of the binder twine. Billy gave it a slight tug. "That's the end of the rope."

Jesse glanced at the twine, then kept walking. "It's OK. As long as we are in this tunnel we just go straight. We'll come straight back out."

The team continued to walk for what seemed like an eternity. Suddenly, they felt a draft of warm air. They found themselves walking up to a large opening into complete darkness until Jesse held up the lantern. The youth were amazed as they saw they were looking into a cavern the size of a gymnasium. The walls and ceiling glistened and sparkled from the reflection of the light of the lantern. On the far side of the cavern, they could see what appeared to be water pouring from the side of the mountain into some kind of pool.

"Wow," said Billy. "This is amazing."

Jesse lowered the lantern to their feet. "Stop, we are on a ledge." He shone the light into the cavern and stepped forward. The floor of the ledge turned up sharply nearly three feet at the edge of the pit. This allowed the teens to brace themselves as they leaned forward and looked into the hole. Jesse picked up a rock and tossed it into the hole. Several seconds later he heard it hitting the wall of the pit. The rock continued making sounds as it hit against the wall, until it had traveled so far that the sound could no longer be heard. "That's really deep."

"Is that where the warm air is coming from?" asked Cassie.

Jesse nodded, "I think so. I think we took the path that leads to hell." Everyone laughed at his comment. "Look, this ledge is at least ten feet wide, and it looks like it goes all the way around." Their eyes began to adjust as they peered into the dark hole. "Is that a light down there?"

Cassie leaned forward. "I don't see anything. Why does the ground curve up right at the edge? It is like it was made to keep people from falling in."

"I think it is because the water rushes from over there when that pool overflows and goes around the pit like a swirling above a drain. So, this ledge is like a riverbed we are standing in that was built thousands of years ago from rushing water." Jesse held the lantern upward. High overhead, he could see a faint glistening of the sparkling dust on the walls of the cave. "We should get some of that dust to see what it is." Jesse stopped speaking. "There it is again. Do you see that light down there? It looks like it's miles away, down in that hole."

Billy leaned forward to the edge of the pit. "I saw it. How could there be light down there?"

Jesse replied, "I don't know."

"I saw it too," said Cassie.

Jenny reached for Billy's hand. "Me too. How's that possible? Are there people down there?"

Jesse replied, "I don't know. The lights were moving. I'm going to turn off the lantern. Don't panic. I want to kill all the light up here so we can see better what's down there. Don't get too close to the edge and lay down on your belly so you don't lose your balance. Brace yourself on the ledge."

Jesse blew out the flame of the lantern and the four friends lay prostrate on the edge of the ledge, looking into the pit. A short time later a faint light appeared far below. Jesse shouted, "Hey, down there."

Looking into the pit, they saw a second light next to the first one, then both lights disappeared.

"Wow, did you see that?" exclaimed Billy, leaning farther into the pit.

Jesse got to his feet and lit the kerosene lantern. "We better go back." Turning, he started back through the long tunnel that led to the waterfall and the pond. The group followed in silence until they reached the fork near the entrance of the cave. As they walked into the small chamber that formed the junction, Jesse tugged on the binder twine slightly but found no resistance. He walked over to the rock under which they had placed the end of the twine. He saw the twine lying on the ground away from the rock. He lifted it off the ground. "How did that happen? It was under the rock when we went down."

Cassie looked around the cavern, then blurted out abruptly, "Hey, which tunnel did we just come out of?"

Jesse pointed. "That one."

Cassie replied, "Yes, the tunnel on the left. But which tunnel did we go down?"

Simultaneously the four friends expressed amazement that they had exited from a different tunnel than the one they had entered.

"How did that happen?" asked Jenny.

Jesse shook his head. "I don't know. We must have crossed over from one tunnel to another down there and didn't even know it. So that's why they say to bring a rope. But how did that rope get out from under that rock?"

Jenny turned to walk toward the distant light of the entrance of the cave under the waterfall. "I don't understand this. Now this really is getting scary. Let's get out of here."

They walked to the entrance of the cave, changed back into their wet clothes, jumped in the water, and swam to the other side, changed into dry clothes, then walked back to the truck. On the way they talked about what they had found and of the strange events of the day. They climbed in the truck and headed back to Waco.

After dropping off his companions, Jesse took the truck back to the ranch where he was to meet Elijah. Although the teenagers had decided not to tell their parents about the cave, Jesse didn't see any harm in telling Elijah.

"How was your trip?" asked Elijah as he gave Jesse a glass of iced tea.

"It was great. I took Billy, Cassie, and Jenny with me. We had a good time, especially when we found a cave."

"You found a cave?"

"Yeah, at Kay Mountain. I've driven past there a lot, but this time we decided to stop and explore. We parked the truck by the side of the road and walked to a wooded area near the mountain. When we got there, we found a pond with a waterfall. Behind the waterfall was a cave."

"Really?"

"Yeah, it was great. We went back today with a lantern. We had to swim to get behind the waterfall."

"Where is this place?"

"It is at the foot of Kay Mountain. It isn't far from the farm where I delivered the saddles."

Elijah leaned against the truck and looked toward the ground introspectively. "I think I would like to see this place."

"I can take you there if you like."

"I would like that. How about today?"

"Sure, I can take you there now. Should I bring Billy, Cassie, and Jenny?"

"If they want to come, that would be great. I am working today, but I should be done about three o'clock. Why don't you take the truck to your place, do whatever you need to do, then come back with your friends and we will all go."

"OK, I will see you around three."

Jesse went back to the McKinley farm and told Billy, Jenny, and Cassie about the plan. He asked Billy to bring an extra lantern and to refill both with kerosene. Jenny and Cassie were excited about going back to the cave. They wanted to explore even deeper.

At three o'clock Billy and Jenny climbed into the back of the truck while Jesse and Cassie climbed into the cab. Jesse drove to the Morrison ranch to pick up Elijah. When they arrived, he was standing out front with a bag of clothes and a flashlight. Cassie opened the door and jumped out. "Here, Elijah, you can ride up here with Jesse so you guys can talk. What's that in your hand?"

Elijah replied, "I don't mind riding in back with Billy and Jenny if you want to ride with Jesse. It's a flashlight."

Cassie climbed into the back of the truck. "No, that's OK. You can ride up front. I have never heard of a flashlight. What does it do?"

"I can't show you now because it has to be dark, but I will show you in the cave. It's like a lantern, but it focuses the light in a specific direction." Elijah climbed into the passenger seat of the truck. Jesse put the truck in gear and pulled out on the road, heading northwest on Meridian Highway.

Jesse and Elijah laughed and joked as they drove. Elijah asked many questions about the cave and surrounding area. "Did you see any farmhouses nearby?" asked Elijah.

"No, we didn't see any buildings or farms. There was something strange, though. When we were exploring the cave, we came to a big open cavern. It was a giant room inside the mountain that was about as big as the gymnasium at the university. But there was no floor. There was a giant hole that went straight down. The strange thing was, when we looked down in the hole, we saw lights moving around down there."

"Lights?"

"Yeah. First there was one, then there was a second one. I yelled into the hole, but we didn't hear anything except an echo. Then the lights disappeared."

"Were the lights moving?"

"Yes."

"Then it seems it almost had to have been people."

"That's what I was thinking. But there was something else weird. When we went into the cave, we found two tunnels, one going to the left and one going to the right. We took the one on the right, but when we came out, we were coming from the one on the left. None of us know how that happened."

Elijah looked at Jesse inquisitively. "You must have circled back without knowing it. How else could it have happened?"

"That is what we thought, but there is something else. Before we went into the tunnel on the right at the fork, we took a two-hundred-foot piece of binder twine and put one end under a heavy rock, so we could follow it just in case we got lost. When we came out of the tunnel the binder twine was lying next to the rock."

"Maybe you didn't put it under the rock as well as you thought."

Jesse shook his head. "No. I tugged on it after we put it under the rock. It was solid."

Elijah shook his head and shrugged. "That sounds like the stories the kids tell in the youth group at the church." He laughed. "Hmm. I am anxious to see this place."

After driving for a little more than an hour, they arrived at the field near Kay Mountain. Jesse pulled the truck off the side of the road and turned off the engine. They climbed out of the truck. Elijah pointed toward the wooded area. "Is that where the cave is?"

Jesse nodded. "Yeah, that's it."

After walking for a few minutes, they reached the wooded area and walked to the pond. They removed their shoes and, holding their dry clothes and lanterns above their heads, they entered the water, made their way to the waterfall, and went behind it. They climbed upon the ledge, changed out of the wet clothes and into dry ones, lit the lanterns, then went into the cave.

Jesse led the way, holding the lantern in front of himself. When they came to the rock that had been sitting on the binder twine, they saw that it was still there, next to the rock. "That's the binder twine I was telling you about," said Jesse. "We had it under the rock, but when we came back out of the cave it wasn't under the rock."

"Do you think you pulled it out by accident when you tugged on it?" asked Elijah.

Jesse replied, "I don't think so. I didn't tug that hard. Maybe an animal pulled it out."

Elijah nodded. "If you didn't pull it out when you tugged on it and an animal didn't pull it out, it seems that the only possibility is that someone else was in this cave when you were. That would tell me that someone else knows about the cave. Plus, you said you saw lights moving in the bottom of the giant hole. Only people could have created moving light, so there are people at least in the other part of the cavern."

As they walked deeper into the cave and past the distal end of the two-hundred-foot binder twine line, Elijah said, "Look to your left. There is a tunnel going off in that direction. I bet this is what happened before. When you were coming back up you accidentally took that tunnel and you probably never saw this tunnel that you had entered. You walked right past it. That is why you came out of the tunnel on the left."

"I think so too," said Cassie. "We walked right past the tunnel we came down and didn't even see it because it was dark, and the lantern didn't shine light on it. If there was a bear or a cougar in that tunnel, we never would have seen it. We could have gotten lost in here."

When they reached the giant cavern Jesse held up the lantern so they could see the massive underground rock formation. Elijah turned on the flashlight and pointed it toward the ceiling of the cavern. "This is bigger than a gymnasium. It is more like a stadium. This is beautiful. Do you see how shiny the walls are? This might be gold."

Jesse looked with amazement out over the cavern. "Wow, that

flashlight is amazing. We can see all kinds of things we couldn't with the lantern."

Elijah replied, "That's because the lantern doesn't focus the light. The flashlight creates a beam that focuses on the area you want to see. You just point the flashlight at what you want to see."

Elijah walked to the edge of the hole and shone his flashlight downward. "This looks like it is about a thousand feet deep." While the beam wasn't completely focused at that distance, it allowed the explorers to see the floor of the pit below. Elijah handed Cassie the flashlight. "Don't drop it." He reached into his pouch and pulled out a telescope. "Cassie, can you shine the flashlight straight down into the hole?" She did as requested.

Elijah looked down into the pit with the telescope. "Whoever had the lights you saw down there, they were human. If you look around down there, you can see a firepit, some logs arranged in a circle around it, and something that looks like tables." He gave the telescope to Jesse.

Jesse looked at the bottom of the pit. "You're right. People did this." He gave the telescope to Cassie and took the flashlight from her, then shone it into the pit.

Cassie looked around for a moment, then gave the telescope to Billy. He looked at the area at the bottom of the pit and asked, "So what's this? What are they using this area for?"

Elijah took the telescope from Billy and asked Cassie to turn off the flashlight. "That is what I thought. With this telescope, you can see down there without the flashlight. There is light coming in from a large opening. That means there is an entrance to the cave down there."

Jenny took the telescope from Elijah. "Let me see." She focused the telescope on the floor one thousand feet below. "Elijah is right. There's an opening down there where the sun is shining in."

Elijah pondered for a moment, then said, "We can go outside of the cave and find our way down there. It's still light outside, so it shouldn't be too dangerous. Maybe we can find out who these people are."

Cassie said, "I don't know. What if they're bad people? It might be dangerous."

Jesse replied, "We can be careful. If there's trees down there like there is up here, we can hide in them and get a good look. Maybe you and Jenny should stay up here. You can wait in the truck."

Cassie shook her head, "What if someone comes by and sees us sittin' in the truck?"

Elijah replied, "That might not be good. Maybe it would be better if you came down with us."

The explorers made their way back to the entrance of the cave, changed clothes, then jumped in the pond, swam their way to shore, and climbed up on the other bank by the rock where they came in. After changing back into dry clothes, they made their way back to the truck. Elijah decided it would be better to drive the truck off the road and hide it behind the trees that surrounded the forest area. They laid their wet clothes out in the bed of the truck and walked back toward the forest area.

Elijah said, "If we go over the hill above the pond, we should find a way down to the lower part of the cave."

Cassie pointed toward an area of the mountain just before the trees. "That looks like the lowest place. We have to go through the trees, but it looks like it will take us to the other side."

Billy nodded, "I think so too."

Elijah began walking in the direction Cassie pointed. "Let's try it."

The team of five set out toward the peak of the mountain. It was a constant climb. They made their way through the forest, climbing higher each step. After about fifteen minutes they reached the summit and began their descent down the opposite side.

"Who do you think the people are?" asked Jenny.

BECAUSE I'M BLACK | 69

Elijah replied, "I am thinking they may be Indians. There were a lot of Wichita Indians here before the White people drove them out. Maybe this is a group that didn't leave."

Jesse asked, "How long ago did they drive them out?"

"About fifty or sixty years ago. Some could have stayed hidden here, I suppose. I don't know."

As they walked, they noticed that the sun was growing closer to the horizon. "How will we find our way back in the dark?" asked Billy.

Jesse replied, "It'll be OK. We have the lanterns and the flashlight."

By the time they reached the bottom of the back of the mountain, another hour had passed. It was now nearly eight o'clock. They came out of the forest at the foot of the mountain. In the distance, they could see a large campfire and hear people saying something in unison. They turned off the flashlight and lanterns. Not knowing who the people were or even whose property on which they were trespassing, they decided it was wise to hide within the shelter of the trees. They quietly made their way toward the crowd of people. Finally, they were within three hundred feet of them and hiding in the trees; they stopped to listen.

Jenny started laughing as she looked at them. "They are wearing white robes and dunce caps. Who are these people?" No one else laughed.

Jesse looked at Jenny. "You really don't know?"

"Know what?"

"You don't know who these people are?"

"No, they just look silly to me. They must have been the ones who flunked out of school."

"Jenny, these people are the KKK," said Elijah.

Jenny sat upright with a start. "KKK? I have heard of them, but I didn't know they were around here."

Elijah replied, "I think they're everywhere."

The explorers watched them for about a half hour. They made

Jesse feel ill. "I don't understand how they can have so much hate for people they don't even know."

"I know," replied Elijah. "That seems foolish. Maybe that is why they wear dunce caps."

Everyone laughed quietly. Suddenly they heard a twig crack behind them. They turned and saw a group of about a dozen men approaching about forty feet behind them. Still hidden in the trees, Elijah said, "Shh. Be quiet. These people are dangerous."

They remained motionless in the bushes as the men in white robes and pointed caps walked next to them, within five feet of their location. Eventually, the men passed, and everyone breathed more calmly. They continued to watch as several hundred people in white robes and pointed hats gathered at the opening of the cave.

The sun began to set behind the mountain and the robed men erected a large wooden cross, then built a large bonfire around it. As the teens sat quietly in the bushes, they heard a rustling sound behind them. They saw another man wearing a white robe and coned hat who happened to glance into the bushes, seeing Jesse, then Elijah. Jesse recognized him as an attorney named Westwood Bowden Hays. He started to shout when Elijah jumped forward, striking him hard in the jaw with his fist, knocking him to the ground. Elijah turned and motioned for everyone to run back in the direction from which they had come. Hays began to get back on his feet. Everyone jumped to their feet and began running. Hays started to shout a second time, but Jesse shouted "dunce" then shoved the man back to the ground, laughed, and ran into the woods.

The group ran through the woods, following the path they had used coming down the mountain. As they ran, they heard the man who was struck, shouting for his companions to assist him. While there remained sufficient light to navigate through the woods, they were able to move quickly. Then they heard the roar of a pickup truck and men shouting. They knew they were being chased by members of the Ku Klux Klan.

As they ran through the woods, they heard a barking dog getting closer. "It sounds like just one," shouted Jesse.

Elijah pushed a large branch from the path and held it back so the others could pass. "I think so too." He grabbed a heavy stick from the ground and followed the others up the hill. The sound of the barking dog was quickly getting closer and soon was upon them. It lunged at Elijah, who was standing between the youths and the dog. He swung the stick like swinging an ax to cut down a tree. The stick struck the dog in the shoulder, causing it to fall to the ground, then run back toward the other men, whimpering.

By this time, the kids had a half-mile lead on the men chasing them. As they descended the other side of the mountain, they needed the flashlight to see where they were going. This gave them an advantage given that their pursuers did not have flashlights, only lanterns; hence, the teenagers were able to travel much faster than their pursuers because they could focus the light farther ahead. Descending required much less exertion than ascending, thus allowing them to move quickly. In a short time, they found themselves running along the stream that led to the waterfall. Soon, they were running down the hill from above and beside the pond. Finally, they ran across the field toward the road where the pickup truck was hidden behind a large clump of trees.

The five friends jumped into the pickup, Elijah and Jesse in the front with Cassie, Jenny and Billy in the back. Elijah pulled onto the road and headed back toward Waco, maintaining a speed of forty miles per hour as they traveled down the gravel road. A mile behind them were the headlights of several other vehicles. "Do you think they're chasing us?" asked Billy.

"Pretty sure," replied Elijah. "Don't worry, they can't catch this Model T."

Jesse felt an uneasiness as they sped down the road. *What if the truck broke down? What would these men do if they caught them? What would they do to Jenny and Cassie?*

Elijah glanced at Jesse as if he heard his thoughts. "Don't worry, Jesse, they'll never catch us. Besides, we have those rifles under the seat."

In time the lights behind disappeared. Jesse pointed to the rear of the truck. "They must have given up."

Elijah nodded. "It looks like it."

After driving for an hour and a half they arrived at the McKinley property. Elijah pulled the truck up to the front door of the Washington bungalow. Billy, Cassie, and Jenny slowly climbed from the truck bed. Billy and Jenny went to their respective bungalows. Cassie followed Elijah and Jesse to the front of the truck. Elijah leaned against the front left fender facing forward. "That was a bluenose."

Jesse smiled. "A what?" Cassie and Jesse laughed.

"A bluenose—a strange event. I mean those KKK guys."

Cassie laughed again. "I felt sorry for that one you guys knocked down. First Eli hit him in the face and knocked him down, then Jesse called him a dunce and pushed him down a second time."

Elijah and Jesse joined Cassie in the laughter.

"What did you think when you saw the Klan guys?" asked Elijah.

Cassie took Jesse's arm and leaned with him on the right front fender facing forward, like Elijah. "It scared me. I remember when I was little, the KKK came to a farm where we were living. They took one of the young men out of his shanty, tied him to a tree, and whipped him. It was because he argued with a store owner about the weight of some strawberries. Even the farm owner couldn't get them to stop until he chased them away with a shotgun."

Jesse frowned, "The weight of some strawberries? That's strange. Why would someone get that mad about some strawberries?"

Elijah adjusted his footing, still leaning against the truck. "It wasn't really about the strawberries. That was a pretext."

"A what?" asked Cassie.

"A pretext. That's where they have one thing and they try to make it look like something else. So, they pretended the fight was about strawberries, but it was really because they thought that the man was disrespectful to the White store owner."

"Why do they treat us like that? What did we ever do to them?" asked Cassie.

"We were born different," replied Jesse. "It's because we're Black."

After seeing the KKK rally the young people did not return to the cave. Jesse wanted to go back. but the others said it was too dangerous. Although Jesse thought the KKK members were evil, he also found them fascinating. *How can they gather so many men who hate Black folks? Where did they come from?* Jesse believed he knew where some of them came from. He had heard rumors that the local barber, the mayor, and the sheriff were all members of the KKK. Jesse didn't know if it was true, but the double lives these men lived—kind, pleasant, and moral during the day, hateful, angry, and ruthless at night—was perplexing. They reminded Jesse of a character in the novel by Robert Louis Stevenson, *The Strange Case of Dr. Jekyll and Mr. Hyde.* Becky had read this book to the students in the Sunday school class one summer when she was teaching them about "evil inclination" and the nature of sin.

For the rest of the summer Jesse pondered evil inclination and what caused some people to be evil. He wondered if the KKK considered themselves evil, or if they thought they were good. Elijah loaned Cassie and Jesse a book about the KKK so they would understand the danger of being near these people. Cassie read the book to Jesse. In it was a large drawing of a man wearing the KKK robe and the pointed hat. Jesse noticed that on the front of the robe was a large red cross. It was a design he had seen years before, while looking at a book Becky showed them about the Crusaders who invaded the Holy Land to fight the Muslims. He remembered seeing the same cross on the robes of some of the men at the cave.

One day Jesse was talking with Elijah about the KKK. "I noticed that some of the KKK wear a big red cross on the front or back of their robe. It is like a picture I once saw of the Crusaders. Becky said they were knights who invaded the Holy Land. Are the KKK the same people as those knights?"

Elijah shook his head. "No, the Crusaders lived a thousand years ago. The KKK just copied them. They probably think it gives them some kind of authority."

This puzzled Jesse. *Why would the KKK copy someone who lived a thousand years ago? Who were the KKK really trying to be?* Jesse did not find an answer to this question. But it puzzled him and would have puzzled him even more if he had known that someday his path would intersect with the Klan in an unimaginable way.

CHAPTER
SIX

THE VOLLEYBALL TEAM lined up on the court at Baylor University. All local churches were welcome in the league, including the churches attended by Black persons. They were known as colored churches, and this was one occasion where the races were permitted to engage in sports and socialize together. Even so, Jesse's church was the only Black church that participated, likely because the church was supported by the university. They called their team the Tigers. Most of the participants were college age, though some were still in high school. Billy, Jesse, Cassie, and Jenny were all on the team. They were the youngest members of the team, which had six good players and three alternates. Jesse was the most agile and usually scored the most points. The Tigers would handily beat the other teams 80 percent of the time.

Jesse saw one of the Baylor students bend his knees as he prepared to spike the ball for an easy score. Jesse was in the outside hitter position in the back row of the court. As the student leaped into the air, Jesse took two steps in a rapid run and jumped into the air nearly a foot above the head of his opponent and spiked the ball back across the net before the Baylor student's feet even returned to the ground.

The spectators jumped to their feet and cheered Jesse. His skill on the court exceeded even the best college-age students. "Go, Jesse," shouted a student from Baylor. He turned to the student next to him and asked, "How does he do that? It's like he flies. He must be five feet off the ground when he does that. And it's like he just sits in the air. It's like he floats."

Volleyball debuted in the United States in the winter of 1895 in Holyoke, Massachusetts. Developed by a YMCA physical education director named William Morgan, the game was originally called mintonette and drew from numerous popular games such as badminton, tennis, and handball. The game became so popular that within a few years it was played on church teams and in high schools across the country. Initially outpacing basketball in popularity, volleyball was well on its way to becoming the leading recreational game among young people. The games lasted well into the evening and even after dark. Spectators pulled their cars up to the edge of the court and turned on their lights to illuminate the playing area.

That day, as the clock approached 9:00 p.m., the final game came to an end. The exhausted players made their way to the showers. The team from the Black church stood in front of gender-identified lockers. Absent was the "No Coloreds" designation, as was generally found on public facilities throughout Waco. The United States was still a segregated nation. Not only was it unlawful for African Americans to use facilities used by Whites, but it was also unlawful for White persons to encourage such use.

As the Tigers stood by the entrances to the lockers, a group of athletic directors from several religious colleges approached. One of them stopped and looked at Jesse, "Congratulations, young man. I wish we had you in our athletic program at Baylor. You have a natural talent for sports."

Jesse smiled and looked shyly toward the ground. "Thank you, sir." Jesse knew it wasn't possible for him to attend Baylor, but the comment meant a lot to him.

"I'm Joe. You folks better get showered so you can join us for the weenie and marshmallow roast. You are coming to the weenie roast, aren't you?"

Jesse looked up at the coach, "We can't, sir. There aren't any colored showers, and we have to walk home."

The coach looked into the men's locker room, then came back out. "I tell you what, there is no one in there. Go ahead and use these."

He looked to his companions, who nodded. "It's OK. Jane, why don't you take the girls into the ladies' locker room, and we can all meet back out here in ten minutes. Then we will go to the weenie roast."

Jane, one of the Baylor administrators, smiled, and said "Ladies, come with me."

Jesse protested. "But sir, we'll get in trouble. The colored laws."

Joe smiled. "It's OK. We won't let anyone in until you're done. Then I'll drive you kids home in the wagon after the weenie roast. What time are you kids expected home?"

"They know we'll walk home so they know it could be as late as midnight," said Billy.

"OK, that will give you at least two hours to sit with us by the bonfire. You all live on the McKinley farm, don't you?"

"Yes, sir," replied Jesse as the boys walked into the men's locker room and the girls went with Jane into the women's locker room.

Several minutes later the team exited the locker rooms and they all walked toward the large bonfire down by the river. As they approached the teens sitting around the fire, one of them said loudly, "Hey, Jesse. I'm glad you guys could join us. Man, can you play!"

The crowd cheered and whistled. Jesse felt proud of his ability and was thankful it was appreciated.

One of the other teenagers stood up and walked toward the

fire. He picked up a handful of sticks and gave one to each of the members of the Black team. A young woman stood up and said, "Make yourselves at home. Over here are the hot dogs." She pointed toward the end of the table. "Down there are the buns, the condiments, and the marshmallows. There's chocolate by the marshmallows if you want it. There are logs by the fire you can sit on while you roast your weenies."

As the Black team took their food from the table and sat on the log by the fire, the teams began to sing hymns and campfire songs. After preparing their food, the Black team walked to the side of the campfire closest to the river. Many players were sitting by the water, and some were dangling their feet. Eventually, they began to sing "Swing Low, Sweet Chariot." As Jesse, Billy, Cassie, and Jenny began to sing their harmony parts, the rest of the crowd stopped singing so they could listen. After they finished the song, someone in the crowd said, "Wow! That was beautiful. Can you sing another one for us?"

Cassie whispered to Jesse, "What about 'Amazing Grace'? Everyone loves that."

Jesse began singing "Amazing grace, how sweet the sound." Billy, Jenny, and Cassie joined in. The crowd listened to every word as they sang. When they finished, everyone applauded.

As the crowd continued singing, Jesse noticed that many of the people had paired off as couples. Several of the men had their arms around the girl next to them. He looked at Cassie, who was sitting to his left. She looked so lovely. Her dark skin and braided hair were mesmerizing to Jesse. Eventually, he reached his arm around her. She looked at him and smiled, then leaned against him in a cuddling fashion.

As they continued to sing, Jesse thought of the kindness they were being shown by these White people. *Why are they so kind?* he wondered. He felt very welcome among these young people. He kissed Cassie on the top of her head. "Do you like these people, Cassie?"

Cassie nodded. "Yes, they are really nice."

"They are like Becky at Sunday school. I wonder why some White people are so nice and others so mean."

Cassie rested her head on Jesse's chest. "I don't know. Some people are just nice, I guess. I feel safe with these people. They really like you, Jesse."

He laughed softly. "I think they like the way I play volleyball."

Cassie nodded. "Yes, they have a lot of respect for you."

After the group sang for about an hour, Joe, the athletic director, stood and spoke for a time. He talked about the importance of inclusiveness in everything they did. He said that all people were God's children, and everyone should be treated like they were just as important as everyone else. He didn't mention race, but Jesse could not help but believe that was what he meant.

Jesse turned toward Cassie. "Have you seen Elijah tonight? He was going to try to be here for the games."

Cassie shook her head. "No, I haven't seen him. Maybe something happened and he couldn't make it."

Jesse nodded.

In a short time, Joe finished his message. "I know you didn't come to hear me talk all night, so let's sing a few more songs, then pack it in. Y'all have church tomorrow. Don't forget to go to church."

The crowd laughed. Jesse saw two men approaching the campfire from the distance. "Isn't that Elijah?" asked Jesse.

Cassie strained to see the approaching men more clearly. "Yes, and that's Samuel Palmer Brooks, the president of Baylor University walking with him. He came to the church a couple of times."

Jesse and Cassie watched as Elijah and Dr. Brooks walked around and greeted everyone.

Eventually, Elijah saw Jesse and Cassie. "Dr. Brooks, I would like to introduce you to a young couple here. This is Jesse Washington, and the lovely young lady is Cassie."

Dr. Brooks shook hands with Jesse and tipped his hat to Cassie. "Are you two in high school? You look a little young for college."

Jesse nodded toward Cassie. "She's in high school. I just work on the McKinley farm."

"What do you want to do when you graduate, Cassie?"

"I think I want to be a teacher or a nurse."

"That sounds fine. How about you, Jesse? Do you have any plans for your future?"

Jesse nodded. "Yes, sir, I would like to have a cotton farm."

"That sounds ambitious. I hope that works out for you. We have quite a few farmers around here."

Elijah said, "It was good seeing you," to Jesse and Cassie. "Dr. Brooks and I need to discuss some matters involving Yale University where I am going to attend. Dr. Brooks attended there too. Enjoy yourselves."

Dr. Brooks tipped the brim of his hat again. "It was nice meeting the two of you."

Dr. Brooks and Elijah continued greeting the other team members.

Cassie said, "I wish I could go to a university like this. Dr. Brooks said someday that may be possible."

Jesse shrugged. "Why? Aren't the Black colleges just as good as the White ones?"

"I think they are. I just don't think they should be separate."

"That's the way it is."

Cassie nodded. "I know, but do you think that is really good?"

"No, but there ain't much we can do to change it. Do you remember what Becky told us St. Francis a sissy said?"

Cassie laughed. "No Jesse. It isn't St. Francis a sissy. He was St. Francis of Assisi. It's a place in Italy."

Cassie looked into the fire for a few moments. She leaned back inquisitively. "Jesse, what do you think everyone thought when the president of the university came over and talked to us? He talked to colored folks. Do you think it bothered them?"

"Not really. In fact, I think they might have been bothered if he didn't come and talk to us."

Cassie looked deeply into Jesse's eyes to understand his meaning. "Really?"

Jesse smiled. "Yeah, I think so."

Cassie and Jesse sat together until it was time to leave. They talked about many things. They talked of goals and dreams, desires, and simple things like how to roast a chile pepper. For Jesse, these moments embodied all he could desire. The girl of his dreams on his arm, admiring him, showing affection; for Cassie, it was a time of comfort, trust, and love. These were moments that Jesse and Cassie shared together every night on the McKinley farm. These moments provided a time to relax and converse with depth as they contemplated various topics. The talk was simple, to be sure, but the depth of thought was profound. Perhaps it was their connection, or whatever caused them to feel such a bond, but they knew they were meant for each other. Often Cassie would say she could not go on if she ever lost Jesse. Those words caused an unpleasantness for Jesse, as if there was some unfortunate destiny that awaited them. He often wondered if others felt the same sensation. It was difficult for Jesse to think of how things might be in the distant future. He could not imagine his future the way other people seemed to imagine theirs. One evening he decided to share his thoughts with Cassie. They were sitting on the bale of hay where they often sat next to the barn. Jesse put his arm around Cassie and held her close. "Do you ever wonder what is going to happen in the future? I mean, do you ever wonder where we'll be ten years from now?"

Cassie cuddled closer to Jesse. "Sometimes I think about it. I think about what I am hoping for."

"That's weird," Jesse replied. "When I try to think of what it will be like in the future, it is like there is nothing there. It's blank, like a blank chalkboard . . . nothing written at all. I can't imagine it. It's almost like something is telling me not to think about it."

"That's scary, Jesse. Do you think it means anything?"

"I don't know. I feel sometimes like something bad's gonna happen and I am not supposed to think about it."

"You mean you think God doesn't want you to think about it?'

"I don't know, but it kind of seems like it."

"Why would God not want you to think about your future?"

"I don't know. I wish I could explain it better."

Cassie nodded. "It's OK, Jesse. You don't need to think about it. Think about things that make you happy."

"You always got good advice, Cassie. I don't often think of the future, but when I do it just seems empty."

"But you have talked about having a cotton farm. What happened to that idea?"

Jesse shook his head, then shuffled his feet nervously. "That is still what I would like to do, but when I try to picture it, there's nothing there."

The young couple sat quietly for a time. Finally, Jesse broke the eerie silence. "Eli will be going away to Yale in a few weeks."

"I know. I will miss him. He has been such a good friend. I heard Yale is a good school."

"Yeah, that is what Eli said. He said Baylor is good too, but his family has gone to Yale for over a hundred years. Plus, it is part of his church; that's why he's going there. I wonder what he was talking about with Dr. Brook that night at the volleyball games. They seemed to be working on something."

Cassie said slowly, "Elijah said that President Brooks also went to Yale, where he is going. He said they were working on something that has to do with that university. I wonder what it was."

"I don't know but I'm gonna miss Elijah. He has been a good friend. He doesn't know for sure he'll come back after he graduates. He's been thinking about becoming a big city doctor like his grandfather. He said he will probably be interning in the hospital in the summers."

"What hospital?"

He said, "Yale Medical School.'" Jesse continued, "Do you re-member when you told me I should go to college and become a doctor?"

"Yes, I remember saying you should think about it. Why?"

Jesse nervously cleared his throat. "I was thinking what that would be like."

"Are you really thinking about it?"

"Well, it would take a lot of work. I don't even know how to read yet."

"If you really want to, you could do it. I could help you."

Jesse coughed nervously. "I'll think about it."

Cassie laughed and pushed Jesse's shoulder. "Don't think too long or you will be an old man."

Jesse laughed.

In August, Elijah prepared to leave for Yale University. He asked Jesse to meet him on a Friday afternoon at the McKinley farm. Jesse was in the field when he saw the green Model T truck pull into the driveway in front of the bungalow. Following behind Elijah was a second truck, also a Model T, in the standard black paint. Leaving the plow and the donkey where they were, Jesse walked toward the truck. Elijah extended his hand; they greeted each other. "It's good to see you, Jesse. I'm leaving for Yale in a few days, and I just wanted to stop by to say goodbye. You have been a good friend and we have had good times together."

Jesse nodded. "Yeah, it has been fun."

Elijah glanced at the pickup truck. "I was wondering if you would do something for me while I'm gone. I have to be at Yale for registration on August 25."

"Sure, what is it?" replied Jesse.

"My uncle says it would mean a lot if you would continue mak-ing the deliveries. I said I would ask. You would need a vehicle. I thought I could give you the truck as advance payment. Uncle will pay you the same amount I have paid, and the truck is yours. So, the truck will be like an advance bonus."

Jesse frowned. "But you love that truck. I couldn't take it."

"Actually, you would be doing me a favor. Every year that truck decreases in value. It is called depreciation. I will be at the university for four years. I will only be here during the summers. That isn't enough time for me to need a truck, so it will be just sitting here the rest of the year. By the time I get back after four years, the truck won't be worth much. You can use it to make the deliveries for my uncle and you will also have transportation when you need to go somewhere."

Jesse shook his head. "That's too much, Eli. I can't take that."

"No, it's what I want. You would be taking a great burden off me if I knew you were still handling deliveries for my uncle."

"OK, if that is what you want me to do, I will."

Elijah reached in his pocket and took out the keys to the truck. He handed them to Jesse. "It is what I want you to do." He placed his hand on Jesse's shoulder and smiled. "Take care of Cassie." Jesse laughed and nodded. They embraced for a moment. Then Elijah walked to the second truck and got into the passenger seat. As the truck made a U-turn in the driveway, Elijah waved goodbye to Jesse.

CHAPTER
SEVEN

HARVEST SEASON WAS a good time for Jesse. Because of the fresh supply of food, they always ate heartily. Jesse was cleaning the barn one September afternoon in 1915 when Mr. McKinley came in and leaned against a wooden pillar. "How is everything goin', Jesse? Are you folks gettin' everything you need?"

Jesse nodded. "Yes, sir. We're gettin' on. We hold back enough crop to last the winter. We trade some of it, but most we sell."

Mr. McKinley nodded. "OK. By the way, I bought some long-horns. Have you worked with them before?"

Jesse raked hay into one of the stalls. "I seen them on the ranch in Mexico, but I ain't never work 'em."

"They're some of the best beef you'll find. Always keep your eye on 'em. Those horns are long and dangerous. It don't happen very often, but once in a while a rancher will get gored by a longhorn. I think it's usually an accident, but it does happen. It's best to be careful."

"OK, I will. How many did you buy?"

Mr. McKinley shifted his weight to his opposite leg. "Three steer and eight heifers. I am going to look for a longhorn bull at the fair in December. The herd should grow pretty quick. I figured this would be a good chance for you to learn about cattle since you would like to get your own ranch someday."

"That would be good," said Jesse as he came out and closed the gate to the stall. "I like working with cattle."

Mr. McKinley smiled. "I worked with cattle for a long time. Most of my life. I drove them all over the country."

"Did you like doin' that?"

"I did. I also liked sleeping under the stars, but sometimes it would get cold. That wasn't as much fun."

Jesse and Mr. McKinley left the barn to go to the house. As they walked across the barnyard, Mr. McKinley slowed and looked somewhat dazed. Jesse took ahold of Mr. McKinley's arm to help steady him. "Are you OK, Mr. McKinley?"

"Just give me a minute."

"What's happening?" asked Jesse.

"I get this ache in my chest every so often."

"What's it from?"

Mr. McKinley shook his head. "I don't know. First, I get this ache, then I feel light-headed."

"I wonder why it's doin' that. Did you talk to a doctor?"

Mr. McKinley took two pills from his pocket and swallowed them. "Yeah. He said it's my heart. He gave me some nitroglycerin pills to take when it starts aching."

Jesse looked startled. "Nitroglycerin? Ain't that what they use to blow things up on the railroad and in the mines?"

"Yeah, but it's watered down. It won't explode. The doctor told me to take it easy and lose some weight. I'm eating less now. If anything happens to me, Jesse, I want you to promise you won't give up on having your own ranch someday."

Jesse nodded, "I promise. But why do you think somethin' might happen to you?"

"Oh, nothin'. I mean just in case. I also ordered two heifers for your family, and the same for the Williams family. Because I bought a small herd, I got a really good price for 'em. We will need to brand 'em so we don't get confused who each one belongs to."

"I don't think my parents can afford two heifers, Mr. McKinley."

"It's OK. I already talked with John and Henry about them. They can pay me back over time. I won't charge interest. Mostly, I want to help your folks get established."

"That's a fine thing you are doin'. Pa didn't mention it to me."

Mr. McKinley nodded. "That's because I just told them a few minutes ago, before I came out to talk to you."

As Jesse and Mr. McKinley approached the bungalows, Martha came out. "Jesse, did Mr. McKinley tell you what he done? He gave us two heifers. He gave the same thing to the Williams family."

Jesse laughed. "Yeah, he just told me. Thanks, Mr. McKinley. That was really good of you."

Mr. McKinley smiled and waved at Martha as he turned to walk toward his house. "I'm glad I could help you folks. They'll be delivered in two weeks."

On a Tuesday afternoon, September 21, 1915, late in the day, Cassie and Jesse were sitting on the front porch swing of the Williamses' bungalow. The harvest season was a busy time, so they enjoyed every moment of rest. Usually, they worked until dark, but this day, they decided to quit early so they could watch the cattle come in.

Jesse picked up two branding irons that were leaning against a rail on the porch. "This is how we're gonna brand 'em." He turned the handle away from them so they could see the brand, which was a *W* with a line under it. "This is your family's brand."

Turning the handle of the other branding iron away from them, Jesse showed Cassie a *W* with a line on top of it. "Your family's brand has a line under the *W*. My family's brand has a line above the *W.*"

Cassie looked inquisitively at the iron. "Who made these?"

"Mr. McKinley hired a blacksmith in Waco. He din't charge much."

"But why are there only two? What is Mr. McKinley gonna use for his brand?"

Jesse shook his head. "Maybe he already has one."

Hearing cattle lowing in the distance, Jesse stood and looked up the road. He pointed. "Look, they're comin'."

Cassie stood and looked in the direction Jesse was pointing. She walked over to the front door, opened it, and leaned inside. "Papa, Mama, the cattle are comin'."

The Williams family came out to see the cattle. Jesse walked down off the porch. Hearing the commotion outside, Jesse's family came out as well.

Soon Mr. McKinley came out of the house and joined them as they all walked toward the road at the end of the lane. "Let's go get some steaks," he said with a laugh.

As if at a family gathering, the Williamses, the Washingtons, and Mr. McKinley all walked down the lane to greet the cattle. The cattle turned into the lane that led to the McKinley house and the bungalows. Two cowboys on horses were driving the cattle, one on each side. As the cattle came up the lane, the family members stood at the side of the lane so they could pass.

Cassie glanced at Jesse. "They act like they know where they are goin'."

Jesse laughed. "They probably heard how nice Mr. McKinley is." Overhearing his name spoken, Mr. McKinley glanced over at Jesse and smiled.

As the cattle walked past them, everyone turned and followed the cattle up to the corral adjacent to the barn. The drovers stopped in front of the barn and looked at Mr. McKinley. One of them asked, "Do you want them in that corral with the gate opened?"

Mr. McKinley nodded. "Yeah, right in there."

The cowboys drove the cattle into the corral and Mr. McKinley shut the gate.

The lead drover gave Mr. McKinley a bill of sale and Mr. McKinley gave him a check. "Thanks for bringin' 'em out here."

"Thank you, sir," replied the drover as they rode back down the lane toward the road.

Everyone gathered around the corral and leaned on the fence, looking in at the cattle. Mr. McKinley took a small pail of blue paint and said, "OK, you folks choose the ones you want. One family chooses first, then the other. Who wants to go first?"

John said, "Go ahead, Henry."

Henry laughed. "No, you go."

Mr. McKinley took a quarter out of his blue jeans pocket and flipped it in the air. "Call it, Henry."

"Tails."

The coin landed in the dirt inside the corral. Mr. McKinley looked down. "Tails it is. Which is your first pick, Henry?"

Henry pointed at a cow standing next to Mr. McKinley. "That one there would be fine."

Mr. McKinley took the bucket of paint and drew a W with a line above it on the cow's hide.

He looked at John and smiled. "John?"

John pointed at a cow standing by the fence. "How about that one over there?"

"Good choice." Mr. McKinley walked over to the cow and painted a W with a line under it. "The W with a line above it is the Washington brand and the W with a line under it is the Williams brand. OK, Henry. It's your turn."

Henry protested. "No, sir. It's your turn."

John nodded his head. "Yeah, it's your turn."

"OK." Mr. McKinley looked at the cows. He walked over to one of them and painted an M with a line under it. "Does everybody see that? A line above a W is Washington, a line under a W is Williams, and an M with a line under it is McKinley."

John and Henry laughed simultaneously. "So, that's the reason you only wanted two irons. You just turn one upside down and we have three brands."

Mr. McKinley laughed. "That's right. Because I bought two, I got the second one half-price, and it is like getting three because we can use one of them twice." The others joined in the laughter.

The men continued this process as Mr. McKinley painted the cows. After all the cows had been painted, Mr. McKinley said, "OK, men, tomorrow we'll brand 'em all. The steers are for butcherin' next year. When I buy a bull at the fair in December it'll have time with each of the cows, and you can grow your herd too. One bull can handle up to thirty cows. We'll only have sixteen cows, counting the heifers. We'll rotate his time with them."

Jesse leaned over and whispered to Cassie, "Lucky bull."

Cassie giggled. "Jesse, that's bad." Martha, who was standing behind Jesse, tapped him lightly on the back of his head with her knuckles.

Cassie touched her head against Jesse's head. "Is that what you want, Jesse? A string of girls? Well, you ain't gonna get it." She laughed and tapped him on the back of his head where Martha had tapped him.

Jesse put his hands above his head, "Everyone's ganging up on me."

"You deserve it," said Martha.

Cynthia laughed. "Men will be men. They're all the same."

Henry and John walked over from the other side of the corral. "Who deserves what?" asked Henry.

Cassie laughed and pointed at Jesse. "This guy wants a string of girls like the bull. He wants to rotate them around every week."

"No, I don't. I just said, 'lucky bull' as a joke, and these women started in on me."

John stopped and looked up toward the sky with an ornery smile on his face. "Hmm . . . actually, that don't sound half bad."

Cynthia bolted toward him and began chasing him and hitting him with a towel. Jesse noticed her beauty as she ran in a flowing, light-blue dress. He looked at Cassie and noticed how similar they appeared. Cynthia looked much like her daughter, only more mature. The flowing blue dress gave elegance to each stride as she ran. Jesse thought of Cassie and Cynthia as a princess and a queen. Finally, John stopped running and said quickly, "I was joking. I was joking." He laughed and held his arms over his head. John and Cynthia embraced, causing everyone to laugh.

Mr. McKinley came out of the corral and closed the gate behind him. "OK, now I have some more good news. Do you smell that cooking from the house? The missus made chicken and dumplings. You're all invited over to our place for a bowl. Let me tell you, it is the best chicken and dumplings you ever had. Those dumplings are so good, they'll make you cry."

Everyone laughed as they turned and walked to the McKinley house. They entered, and Mr. McKinley showed them into the dining room. "Take a place around the table."

Jesse stopped and looked. "Hey, did this table grow? It is about twice the size it used to be."

Mrs. McKinley entered the room with a large pot of chicken and dumplings. She laughed. "No, Jesse. That's what you call table leaves."

"Wow, is that a new invention?"

Everyone laughed. Cassie said, "No, only to you, Jesse. I think a guy who wants a string of ladies better know what a table leaf is. He's gonna need a place for all those girls to eat."

Billy said, "I never heard of table leaves either."

Martha shrugged, "That's because you boys always work outside. Cynthia and Cassie used to work in a house. They saw table leaves there. I saw them in houses when I grew up." She looked over at John and Henry, who were listening. Cynthia pointed her thumb at them. "These two are still worried about how they are going to feed all those women." Everyone laughed again.

This time it was Henry's turn to step out of line. "How'd you know we were still thinking about that?"

The room filled with laughter as Cynthia said loudly, "Because men will be men."

Mrs. McKinley smiled. "I don't know what all I missed, but I do agree with that."

The three families laughed and joked until almost 10:00 p.m. Jesse had an opportunity to learn about each of his neighbors. He felt a closeness not only with Cassie but with everyone at the table. He studied everyone and enjoyed their laughter and happiness. He reflected on the joy he felt. *I hope this lasts forever.* He looked at Cassie. *It can't get better than this.*

CHAPTER
EIGHT

BRANDING CATTLE WAS considered a man's job. Most ranchers believed it unfit for women to participate, or even know about the process. Mr. McKinley, Jesse, Billy, Henry, and John stood in the corral, where a fire heated the branding irons to five hundred degrees Fahrenheit. They had moved all the livestock into the barn so they would not be spooked by the activities outside.

Branding was a painful process for the cattle. The hot iron was pressed against the hide just behind the hip, where it caused third-degree burns. It was an acquired skill that required burning carefully through the first two layers of skin but not through the third. A burn too deep could result in serious infection. If the burn was not deep enough, the hair would grow back and the brand would fade as the wound healed. Mr. McKinley had branded thousands of cattle in his years as a ranch hand and as a drover; he was an expert.

Each cow was brought into the corral one at a time. A slipknot was placed over the hind legs just above the hooves, and then the front legs were bound. On the count of three, the slipknots were pulled tight while Mr. McKinley pushed the animal, causing it to fall over on its side. The legs were quickly tied to a stake to keep the cow from kicking as the iron was placed against the skin. Most of the cows made a bellowing sound as they cried out in pain, but a few of them made no sound at all. Some did not even kick. Branding cattle was dangerous work. A wild kick could injure or even kill a man, which was the reason the legs were tied to a stake and the animal was held down by four men.

Jesse and Billy removed the ropes from one of the cows, allowing it to jump up and run around the corral. "Why do you think some of them don't resist at all and don't even cry out?"

Mr. McKinley placed the end of the branding iron in the fire to heat it for the next cow. "I noticed that years ago. The same is true when a cow is slaughtered. Some kick and fuss, while others don't do anything at all. Some are submissive, while others are very feisty. I figure that some don't fight or cry out 'cause they trust people and don't believe we would do anything that would harm them. They are almost like a child or a pet."

"Do you think maybe some of them can't feel it?"

Mr. McKinley walked over to the edge of the corral, reached through the fence, and took a glass of the lemonade Mrs. McKinley had placed on a table. "That might be true. I've always wondered if there isn't a better way to mark the animal than branding. People have been branding cows for thousands of years. In places where people share grazing land, it is the only way to identify cattle. They also do it to make it easier to catch rustlers."

The rest of the men walked over to the fence to retrieve a glass of lemonade. Henry took a glass from the table. "I was branding cattle as a young boy in Mexico. We usually did it a long way from the farmhouse. I remember they would bring in a hundred head all at once. Sometimes it would take weeks for us to finish branding them. I used to wonder if there wasn't a better way that didn't hurt the cattle. I never could think of one."

Mr. McKinley nodded. "I used to try to think of a better way too. I think all boys do, when they first start branding. But what else could you do? You can't paint them; the paint would just wear off. In some places, where they don't have to worry about rustlers, they tag the ear with a metal clip. But that won't protect against rustlers. They would just take off the tag. The mark has to be permanent. That is why branding is the only thing we can do."

Each time the iron was used it had to be reheated because the cow's hide would cool the iron. John leaned against the fence as the men waited for the fire to heat the iron again. "My pa told me that some slave owners used to brand their slaves. They would brand them just like we're branding these animals."

Mr. McKinley nodded. "I heard that too. I never seen it done, but I remember seeing lots of slaves with brands on 'em. I'm at least twenty years older than all of you. I remember when there were slaves. When I was a boy, they still had slaves. We didn't have any because we were too poor, plus my parents said slavery was evil. But I remember when I was real little seeing slaves with brands on their skin. Sometimes it was on the side of the face."

For a few moments, no one said anything. They just stood in silence as they reflected on Mr. McKinley's comments.

It took the entire morning and much of the afternoon to brand all the cattle. When they were finished Jesse took a bath and cleaned up to go visit Cassie and her family. He enjoyed his visits to Cassie's house. Billy and Jenny often visited with them, but on this day, they decided to visit Henry and Martha while Jesse and Cassie visited with John and Cynthia.

As they sat in chairs in the living room of the Williamses' bungalow, Jesse could not stop thinking about the story he had heard about slave owners branding the slaves with a branding iron. Then he remembered seeing a mark on the left shoulder of his grandfather. He never asked what made the mark, and his grandfather never talked about it. Jesse suddenly realized that his grandfather had been branded. This brought back the question Jesse asked himself often: *How can people be so mean to other people?*

Cassie reached over and took ahold of Jesse's hand. "What are you thinking about, Jesse? You're really quiet today."

Jesse glanced over at John. "I was thinking about a conversation we had today while we were branding the cattle. Mr. McKinley mentioned that some slave owners used to brand their slaves the way a rancher brands his cattle."

Cassie turned to face Jesse. "You mean, brand them the way cowboys brand cattle? I was watching from the window today. How could anyone be so mean?"

John shook his head. "Some people just are."

"But why did they brand them?"

John glanced at Jesse, then Cassie. "That's how they would identify them if they ran. The slave owners used to register their slave brand the same way cattle ranchers register their brand. The slaves were treated like animals. Then, after slavery ended, some farmers would brand sharecroppers so they wouldn't try to leave."

Jesse stared at the flower vase in the middle of the table. "I saw a brand on my grandpa's shoulder. I never knew what it was until today. I suddenly realized what it was."

"What did it look like?" asked John.

"It was like a circle with a cross inside. Grandpa never talked about it, and I never asked, but I knew it bothered him that it was there. I knew there was some deep, dark history he didn't want to talk about. Now I understand what it was."

Realizing that slave owners once branded their slaves and that his grandfather had been branded, Jesse could only think of the horrible life his own grandfather must have suffered. To Jesse, it was an evil so intense that there must be some resolution. There must be some way of causing people to understand the pain they caused others. He felt as if his desire to expose the horrors of slavery and the abuse of Black persons was met with an insurmountable resistance by society. The entire world seemed to be against his people. He felt helpless. It was difficult to think of going back to work the next day. Then he considered the kindness shown by some people like Becky, Elijah, Mr. McKinley, and Mrs. McKinley. Remembering the goodness in some people, Jesse was able to find the strength to carry on. It wouldn't be easy, but he couldn't give up. He had to keep fighting, and that was what he decided to do.

After the harvest season, the sharecroppers sold their cotton to a buyer to whom Mr. McKinley had sold for several years. He paid a fair price, and because the McKinleys always had such a bountiful harvest, the buyer sent wagons to the farm to pick up the cotton in raw form which he took to his gin, where he separated the cotton fiber from the seeds and dirt and made them into bales. Most sharecroppers sold their crops to the farmer who owned the farm they worked, but Mr. McKinley made arrangements for them to sell their cotton along with his directly to the buyer. "There is no reason to pay me to be a middleman. We'll just sell your cotton directly to my buyer, and that way you keep all the profit."

The fall season was a wonderful time for the Williams and the Washington families. They had plenty of money, having sold all their crops except what they held back for personal consumption. And because the crops were in, there wasn't a great deal of work to be done. Halloween was a popular holiday in Waco, but not one that the sharecroppers on the McKinley farm celebrated. Martha called it the voodoo holiday and told the boys it wasn't a real holiday. Far more interesting to the sharecroppers was the Texas Cotton Palace Exposition, which took place during the first two weeks of November. Cassie, Jesse, Billy, and Jenny loved the exposition and would spend at least two or three days enjoying the amusements. There were festivities, rides, games, and many activities that kept them occupied nearly every day during the event. Because of the harvest, they had a little extra money to spend. They used this opportunity to buy presents for Christmas and to have a good time.

Shortly after the exposition the families began planning for Thanksgiving. As in every other year, the McKinleys invited the sharecroppers into their home for a Thanksgiving Day dinner. The day before, the men would select a large turkey, slaughter and clean it, then give it to the women so they could prepare the meal. Jenny, Cassie, Martha, and Cynthia all worked with Mrs. McKinley to cook the food. They started late in the afternoon on Wednesday and worked for several hours. This was essentially a time for the women to work together and enjoy one another's company. After they finished the day's responsibilities the women would socialize until approximately 8:00 p.m. Cassie often told Jesse that the day preparing was almost as fun as Thanksgiving Day itself. Everything was prepared except for cooking on Wednesday, and then on Thursday morning the turkey was placed in the oven, and it would be ready to eat by noon.

On Thursday morning the women went to the McKinley house to finish the preparation of the meal. They put the turkey in the oven, made coleslaw, corn, mashed potatoes, gravy, fresh baked bread, and several other dishes to complement the meal. Jesse and Billy handled the morning chores because the girls were helping Mrs. McKinley prepare the food. In Texas, as in many rural areas in the United States, the noon meal was called dinner and the evening meal was called supper. Thus, the noon meal on Thanksgiving was called Thanksgiving dinner.

As they finished cleaning the barn stalls, Jesse could smell the wonderful aroma coming from the kitchen. Jesse leaned a pitchfork against the interior wall of the barn. "Wow, that turkey smells good."

Billy lifted his head to sniff the aroma. "Oh yeah. That will be great food."

The boys walked to the bungalow to get cleaned up and change clothes for the meal. Henry and John were sitting on the couch discussing the farm. They were talking about developing another eighty acres for growing additional cotton on the farm. Mr. McKinley had mentioned that for every new acre they developed, each family—the Williamses and the Washingtons—would be given one acre until each family had reached one hundred acres. John and Henry stood up as the boys came into the living room. Henry opened the front door. "Are you gentlemen ready for some food?"

"Yes, sir," replied both Jesse and Billy, almost simultaneously.

The men exited the house and walked across the yard to the McKinley home. As they walked up onto the front porch, Mr. McKinley motioned them into the house. The aroma of the food overwhelmed them. They were ushered to seats around the table. Mrs. McKinley came into the dining room with a large bowl of mashed potatoes. Behind her was Martha, carrying the turkey, and following Martha was Cynthia, with a plate of sliced beef. A few minutes later Cassie came in with a bowl of corn and Jenny had a plate of biscuits.

After all the food was placed on the table Mr. McKinley said grace. The conversation drifted from discussions about the new cattle to developing the new section of the farm. Mr. McKinley put a slice of beef on his plate. "The area I was thinking of planting is over on the north side of the farm. So far, we have used only four hundred acres of the land for crops. The other six hundred acres have been for grazing, but the small herd we have doesn't need but a fraction of that much land. Over on the north corner is some of the best farming land around. I spent hours walking it and looking around. There are hardly any rocks, and the dirt is soft. Last summer when the price of cotton dropped way down to six cents per bale, the price of seeds also dropped. I bought enough seed for three hundred acres. That is why I decided that if you fellows could plant an additional hundred for me next spring, I will give each of you one hundred acres. You should be able to make a pretty good income with that much land. That will still leave three hundred acres for grazing. That's more than enough for our small herd. That's enough grazing land for up to fifty cows on land as good as ours. We'll stop at twenty, though, to play it safe. So, we'll have crops as our main product and beef as a secondary one."

Henry nodded. "That is good of you to give us the land to get started and the cattle you gave us earlier."

Mr. McKinley took a piece of bread. "I'm thinking this will mostly be a breeding farm. We'll slaughter enough steer for our own consumption, and we will sell the offspring to neighboring farmers if you men are in agreement."

John replied, "I think that's a great idea, sir."

"I do too," said Henry.

After a wonderful meal, the men retired to the living room, where they made themselves comfortable on the chairs and sofa. The warm climate around Waco in November provided adequate warmth throughout most of the day. Toward late afternoon the weather began to chill. Mr. McKinley started a fire in the fireplace. After the kitchen was cleaned the women joined the men in the living room. Mrs. McKinley got out some checkerboards and checkers. The three families joked and laughed until well into the evening. Several times the Williamses and the Washingtons prepared to leave and the McKinleys persuaded them to stay longer.

Finally, at nearly ten, the families decided to retire to their own homes. Jesse and Cassie walked out to the barn where they often sat on the bale of hay and talked until midnight. This time together caused them to grow closer every day.

After Thanksgiving there wasn't much to do. Some sharecroppers would try to find construction work. Some would find jobs moving cattle to the large cities. Jesse enjoyed the free time, spending most of it with Cassie. Billy spent the time with Jenny. The affection between both couples grew stronger.

CHAPTER
NINE

IT WAS WEDNESDAY, December 15, 1915. The streets of Waco were blocked off for the very first McLennan County Fair. The exhibits included clowns, exotic animals, trapeze artists, livestock contests, a funhouse, horse races, and many other fascinating features. Mr. and Mrs. McKinley invited the sharecropper families to accompany them to the fair. This was one of the few events in Waco that Black and White families both attended. Anticipating the event all week, Jesse could scarcely conceal his excitement as he bathed and put on his best leisure clothes. The Williamses and the Washingtons rode together in a large hay wagon. Henry drove and Mr. McKinley sat next to him on the wagon seat. In the back of the wagon, Jesse, Billy, Cassie, and Jenny tossed a pigskin football from one person to the next. The football had been purchased by Mr. McKinley for the enjoyment of the sharecroppers, along with several other toys and games. One of the games, croquet, was especially popular with the sharecroppers.

Martha, Cynthia, and John talked about the crops. April 9, 1915, had been the latest freeze on record for Southern Texas. The sharecroppers had put out many of their crops in early April not anticipating a late freeze. Many of the local farmers lost much of their crop. Although Henry and John were concerned about the potential damage to their crops, they were pleased with the bountiful harvest.

John swatted at a fly that was buzzing about his head. "I'm glad we survived the freeze. A lot of people lost their entire crop. It was a good year for us, but I think we might want to plant a little later this spring."

Cynthia nodded. "I think you're right. I don't think the cold went that far down this year, but we don't want to risk it again. The folks who put their crops out earlier are gonna lose some."

Cassie tossed the ball to Jenny, who missed the catch, and the ball bounced out of the wagon onto the gravel road. Jesse quickly stood up and jumped off the wagon, watching it as it traveled. He chased the ball, running with a limp from the snake bite, retrieved it, tossed it in the wagon, then jumped back into the wagon—all in less than a minute.

Cassie began laughing. "Did you see that?"

Cynthia put her hand on her head and laughed too. "How could I miss it?"

John said, "That's a powerful boy. I notice he still has a little limp from that rattlesnake bite."

Henry nodded. "Yeah, he does. He's a strong kid. I seen him wrestle two and three other boys at the same time and beat 'em all. The doc said the reason his leg still hurts is that the snake bit into the bone. If it just goes into the flesh, it will heal in about three weeks, but if it hits the bone it can take up to a year, according to Dr. Lee."

The football bounced over to John. "Is he gonna wrestle in the matches tonight?" He tossed the football back to Billy.

Henry glanced back over his shoulder toward Jesse. "Hey, Jesse, you gonna wrestle tonight?"

"I might. I was thinkin' 'bout it. I wish I could wrestle in the White matches."

Everyone chuckled at the thought of this. Jesse tossed the ball to Billy.

Cassie spoke up. "You can't wrestle the White guys, Jesse."

"I know, but I wish I could. I could beat most of those guys."

Billy chuckled. "You could beat 'em all."

The wagon of fun seekers arrived at the fair, and Henry hitched the horses to a post designated for Black visitors. The teenagers climbed over the side of the wagon while the adults opened the tailgate and climbed down with caution. Mr. McKinley said, "Let's all plan to meet back here at six o'clock. That's two hours from now. We can eat supper, then we can stay for a few more hours."

"What time we gonna leave?" asked Jesse.

Mr. McKinley replied, "There's shows and activities 'til midnight. That's when they close everything down. We can stay 'til midnight if you folks want to."

The teenagers strolled toward the games and entertainment section, while the adults walked to the livestock shows. As the teenagers wandered along Sixth Street looking for games to play, they noticed that there were few Black persons at the fair. Cassie said, "There ain't many colored folks here tonight."

Jesse looked up and down the streets. "I only see us. I know they'll be here in a little bit for the wrestlin' matches. Maybe they all went somewhere to do somethin'."

Cassie asked, "What time are the wrestling matches, Jesse?"

"They start at seven."

They came to a booth with a basketball hoop and several basketballs sitting on stands on the table. Participants would get three shots for a nickel. If a participant could make three out of three shots, they could choose from one of several toys. Jesse walked over to the line and stood behind a participant. Billy and Jenny followed him. Cassie stood next to Jesse. "Do you think you would be good at basketball, Jesse?"

"I think I could play. I've been practicing at the hoop by the barn. Dribbling the ball is hard to learn, but I have practiced that too. If I win, I'll give you a prize."

Suddenly, Cassie said, "Jesse, that's Steve Dixon over there. He is coming this way. He's with those guys who tried to start a fight with us at the river. Let's go so we don't have no trouble."

"I ain't afraid of those asses," replied Jesse. "I ain't gonna run ever' time I see a cracker."

Billy stepped forward and said softly, "Cassie's right, Jesse. They'll try to start a fight. You can't fight a White man, Jesse. They'll lynch you for it."

Cassie took Jesse's arm. "Please, Jesse, let's go. I don't want no trouble."

Jesse stepped out of the basketball line and the four walked over to Jackson Street. They turned right past the church and began walking toward the river. As they walked around the corner of the church, Jesse glanced back at Dixon and noticed that he and Hays seemed to be looking in his direction.

Cassie asked, "Do you think they saw us?"

Jesse frowned. "I don't care if they did. I ain't gonna hide from them all night."

As they strolled down Jackson Street toward the river, they noticed their parents with the McKinleys looking at a young but large bull that was being shown. Mr. McKinley asked, "What do you think? Should I buy this one? I think he'd be a great breeding bull."

Henry nodded. "He looks like a goodin' fo' sure. The farmer says he produced some nice heifers last year."

As the teenagers approached, Mr. McKinley glanced over at them. "What do ya think, Jesse? I'm thinkin' about buying this here bull."

"He looks like a fine one, sir."

The teenagers watched as the auction began. When the bidding on the bull approached $90 the bidders began to drop out. Finally, Mr. McKinley was the highest bidder at $103. They led the bull to a side stall. Mr. McKinley, Henry, and John turned to walk to the stall. Jesse turned to walk with them just as he saw Dixon and Hays standing behind him. Dixon and Jesse looked at each other momentarily but neither said anything. Jesse turned toward the other teens. "Let's go pay for the bull."

The teens walked with the men to the stall where the bull was penned. Billy said quietly, "Did you see Dixon standing right behind us?"

Jesse glanced at Cassie. "Yeah, I did. He didn't say nothin'."

Cassie took ahold of Jesse's arm. "I think that was 'cause Mr. McKinley was with us."

As they walked away, Steve Dixon and his friends approached the fence where Jesse and his friends had been standing. "Good evening, ladies," said Dixon. "Are you buying stock today?"

Jesse, who overheard the conversation, thought it peculiar Dixon would be friendly to the women. He even heard his mother engaging Dixon in conversation.

Cassie said, "Steve Dixon is on his best behavior today. Prolly 'cause the McKinleys are here."

Jesse replied, "Yeah, that must be the reason. It ain't 'cause he is a nice guy. That I know."

Mr. McKinley paid for the bull and the auctioneer agreed to keep the bull in the pen until the McKinleys were ready to leave.

As they walked back over to the women, Jesse noticed that Steve Dixon and his friends had left. "Who were you talkin' to, Mom?"

Martha smiled. "I don't know them. They just started talking to me. They were nice boys."

"Be careful of them, Mom. They ain't good people."

Martha's face appeared perplexed. "They were nice boys."

"No, Mom. Remember the man who tried to start a fight with me when Cassie and I were at the river and who dragged that man behind his car and killed him?"

"Yeah, I remember."

"That guy you were talkin' to . . . that's the guy."

"What?"

Jesse nodded.

"Then why was he talkin' to me if he hates coloreds?"

"He was warnin' me."

"Warnin' you what?"

"He was warnin' me that if I don't kiss their boots, they can get to you."

Martha looked at Cynthia, who was standing on the other side of Jesse, listening to the conversation. Cynthia returned her gaze and nodded. "I think he's right, Martha."

Martha looked to see if Henry had noticed anything untoward. He was walking back with Mr. McKinley and John. Mr. McKinley looked up and saw Cynthia, Martha, and the teenagers. He smiled, unaware of the conversation with Steve Dixon. "We were gonna meet at six, but since we're all here now, why don't we go ahead and have supper?"

"That's a good idea," said John. "I'm hungry now anyway." The others nodded affirmatively.

Mr. McKinley said, "There's a nice barbecue restaurant around the corner. I come in here sometimes when I'm in town on business."

They followed Mr. McKinley to a restaurant with a sign that said, "Barbecue Ribs." To the amazement of the sharecropper families, under the sign was a smaller sign that said "Coloreds." Jesse suddenly realized that Mr. McKinley was taking them to a colored restaurant. He thought it interesting, then realized the reason. The sharecroppers couldn't go with the McKinleys to a Whites-only restaurant. They would be arrested. So, the only way the McKinleys could eat with the Black sharecroppers would be if they went to a restaurant for Black persons. Once inside, Jesse looked around the large dining room. He noticed quite a few White persons eating there, though most of the customers were Black.

Mr. McKinley took out a pipe and lit it with a match. He smiled at Jesse as he puffed. "Jesse, before we leave, I should introduce you to Moses. He is the man who owns this restaurant. He's a colored man. He also owns a ranch. The steaks we eat here are from his ranch. I know you would like to have your own spread someday. I thought you would like his arrangement."

Jesse replied, "Thank you, sir. I would like to meet him."

The group enjoyed a delightful meal of barbecue beef ribs, corn, mashed potatoes, beef gravy, and biscuits. "I think I died and went to heaven," said John. "That was the best meal ever."

Everyone laughed. Billy said, "That was really good barbecue sauce."

Mr. McKinley nodded. "Yeah, it's the molasses he uses in the sauce. He gets the perfect mix. Jesse, you didn't eat much. Are you feeling OK?"

Jesse nodded. "I'm gonna wrestle at seven o'clock. I don't wanna eat too much."

Henry smiled. "So you're gonna do it?"

"Yes, sir. I enjoy the matches."

Mr. McKinley stood up abruptly. "Moses, can you come here for a second? I want to introduce you to someone." He motioned for a middle-aged Black man to come over to their table. "Moses, these are the Williams and the Washington families. They work on our farm. This is Cynthia, and her husband, John." He motioned toward Henry. "This here's Henry and his wife, Martha. These two young ladies are Cassie and Jenny Williams. And these boys are Jesse and Billy Washington. They haven't been here before, but I wanted to introduce them. Jesse here wants to own a farm someday, like you."

Moses smiled. "It is nice to meet all of you. Thanks for coming in. If you need anything, just ask." He looked at Jesse. "So, you want to have a farm? Do you want to raise cattle or crops?"

Jesse stood up and shook Moses's hand. "I was thinkin' I would grow cotton, but I might raise cattle too. But first I have to raise money to buy a farm."

Moses nodded. "It takes a long time to earn enough money to

buy a farm, but you might be able to get a loan. That's what I did. That way you don't have to wait for years and years."

Jesse looked at Moses inquisitively. "A loan?"

"Yeah, that is how I got started. A local rancher gave me a loan to help me get started. I couldn't have done it without that loan. That was six years ago. I made my last payment in March. Now I own the farm and the restaurant free and clear. I'll tell you what, Jesse, how old are you now?"

"Sixteen."

"When you turn eighteen, you can legally own property in Texas. Come and see me then. I'll introduce you to some local businessmen who ain't afraid to loan money to coloreds."

Jesse smiled. "That would be a good thing, sir. Thank you. I would be obliged if you did that."

"OK, well, come and see me when you're eighteen and we'll see what we can do."

"Yes, sir."

After a wonderful meal, Mr. McKinley paid the check, and everyone stood up to leave.

John said, "Are we all going to watch Jesse wrestle?"

Mr. McKinley smiled. "I would sure like to see it."

Cassie joined in. "Me too."

They left the restaurant and walked over to Sixth Street, where the wrestling matches were held. Jesse walked up to the booth with a sign that said, "colored Wrestlers." He placed his hands on the table and leaned forward. "I want to sign up to wrestle."

The attendant looked up and smiled. "Ah, yes, Jesse Washington. I remember you from the Cotton Palace last year. You're a lot bigger now, and you were good even then." He pushed a piece of paper to Jesse. "Sign here." He pointed at the paper. Jesse made an X on the line. Cassie stepped forward and wrote Jesse's name for him.

Jesse walked over to the roped-off wrestling ring. He saw

several bookies taking bets on wrestlers. One of them walked over to Jesse. "You Jesse Washington?"

"Yeah."

"You wanna earn a quick hundred?"

Jesse appeared puzzled. "A hundred what?"

"A hundred dollars."

"What do I have to do?"

"See that big fella over there? His name's Moose."

Jesse nodded. "I see him."

"Let him win when you wrestle him. He is gonna beat you anyway. You might as well make some money at it."

"You mean throw the match? If you think I'm gonna lose anyway, why do you want me to throw the match?"

"Thinkin' you're gonna lose ain't the same as knowin' you're gonna lose. If I am gonna set the odds ag'in ya, I gotta know you gonna lose."

Jesse shook his head. "But I ain't gonna lose."

"We'll see, Jesse, but if ya wanna make a hundred bucks, just tell me you ain't gonna win."

"I could use a hundred bucks, but I ain't gonna throw a match."

The bookie shrugged. "That's your choice."

He walked over to Moose. "When you get in the ring with Jesse Washington, that guy over there on the bench, beat the tar out of him. There's gonna be a lot a money ridin' on you."

Moose looked at Jesse and nodded.

The bookie slapped Moose on the back. "Go get 'em."

A few moments later the matches began. Two young men faced off. One quickly overpowered the other, not the result of strength so much as skill. The second match lasted longer than the first due to a more equal pairing of competitors. Jesse was scheduled for the third match. He grabbed the top rope and pulled himself up and over the ropes into the ring in a single fluid motion. His muscles glistened with the grease placed to prevent his opponent from securing a grip. Such tricks were legal in a world where there were few rules of the game. The only rules were no striking, hitting, or kicking. This was purely a grappling competition. Jesse had learned many tricks of the art of wrestling, passed down through the family from an ancient tribe in Africa.

Jesse took a low, crouching position as he swung his arms loosely, waiting for the moment to assault. His opponent abruptly moved to grab Jesse's biceps, but his hands slipped off from the grease. Jesse quickly stepped forward with his left foot, planting it between his opponent's feet. He reached his left arm under the crotch of his opponent and threw him backward over his shoulder. His opponent landed on the plywood floor with a thud. Jesse turned around and jumped on his opponent, pinning him in less than a minute. The crowd of spectators roared with excitement. Jesse could hear people saying his name, "Jesse! Jesse! Jesse!" which gave him a sense of pride.

Jesse was declared the victor and he stepped out of the ring. He had stirred the crowd, and now the excitement level was high. In a short time, the small crowd of spectators had turned into a large crowd consisting not only of Black persons but White persons as well. After a few more matches the disqualifications began. Any competitor who lost more than one fight had to drop out.

Finally, Jesse was up again. The crowd cheered as he climbed into the ring. Some were chanting his name. He gazed at his opponent, a young man in his twenties. It would seem a teenager Jesse's age would be no contest for a man more than five years older. They faced off in the ring. The opponent moved in a circular fashion around Jesse. Both were crouching slightly. The opponent thrust himself forward several times to give the appearance he was attacking. Jesse was undeterred. Finally, the third time his opponent lunged forward Jesse suddenly jumped underneath him, landing on his own buttocks, then fell backward on his back, underneath his standing opponent. He threw his left leg around his opponent's hip, catching him unaware and slamming him to the plywood floor. Jesse pinned him almost as quickly as in his last match.

Jesse was announced the winner and he began to leave the platform when the referee shouted, "Hold up there, Jesse. We are going to change the rules. We have a champion. Jesse will stay in the ring until someone beats him." The referee took a twenty-dollar bill from his pocket. "I'll give twenty dollars to the first man who can beat Jesse Washington in a match." He waved the twenty-dollar bill in the air. "And Jesse gets twenty dollars just for bein' a champion. Here we go."

A large young man climbed into the ring. He was the person the bookie called Moose. Jesse knew from his appearance he would be more formidable than the others. Like Jesse, his arms were strong and muscular. Even more puzzling to Jesse, as they began to wrestle, was that he knew all the moves Jesse knew, and he countered each of them appropriately. The audience watched in fascination the agility of these two young fighters. Although they grappled with intensity and strength neither man was able to put the other on the mat. Finally, during the third round, Jesse's opponent got the upper hand, and Jesse was thrown against the ropes. His opponent pushed him backward against the ropes with all his strength as he held Jesse entrapped.

Using the flexion of the ropes, Jesse threw himself forward into his opponent, knocking him to the mat. Jesse dove on top of him as he attempted to affect a pin. Moose rolled over into a prone position and held himself from the floor to prevent Jesse from pinning him. In this deadlocked position they remained until the third round ended.

As they sat in their respective corners, the young men established eye contact. For a brief moment, they both smiled. Jesse nodded his head, and Moose nodded back. They both knew they had met their match. Jesse felt that the next round could go either way. They nodded to show respect for each other.

Soon the referee tapped the bell with a drumstick, signaling the beginning of the fourth round. The crowd was on its feet, knowing it was watching a match of great strength between two powerful young men. Both were skilled in fighting, and both were very strong. In the fourth round, they both decided the audience deserved a good show. They were much more fluid and undertook much greater risks. The result was a fascinating match between two powerful men who could toss each other about like rag dolls. Although each repeatedly threw the other to the mat, neither could pin the other.

This high-energy wrestling continued until the ninth round. Finally, Jesse felt he had a solid hold on his opponent that would result in a pin. Just as he pushed the opponent's shoulder to the mat, Moose suddenly twisted and freed himself from the hold. They were both in another deadlock position from which neither could move.

It was the end of the ninth round. The referee sounded the bell. The men stood to their feet and the referee shouted, "I'm calling this one a draw. Each competitor gets twenty dollars." The crowd roared with excitement.

As they stood in the center of the ring, the opponent extended his hand. Jesse shook it. "I'm Jesse Washington."

"Luke Lincoln. They call me Moose."

"You from 'round here'?" asked Jesse.

"No, I'm from Austin. I came down to stay with my aunt and uncle for the fair. I'll be showin' cattle tomorrow. The farmer where my aunt and uncle live has some nice cattle. Some of the best in Texas."

"You live in the city?" asked Jesse. "I mean in Austin, the city."

"Yeah, I live on the south side of Austin. We have small farms where I live. Most of them are less than five acres. We just grow enough food for ourselves, and we work the big farmer's land.

"You don't live on the farmer's land, like sharecroppers?"

"No, but his farm isn't far away. We ride over in a wagon every day."

"You own your own farm?"

Moose nodded. "Yeah. It's a small farm, but it's ours."

"So, you aren't really sharecroppers?" Jesse wore a puzzled expression.

Moose laughed. "No, we just have jobs on the farm. Sharecropping is dying out up by the big city. Now everyone just has a job."

The thought of having a job and not working as a sharecropper intrigued Jesse. It seemed to be one step closer to freedom, and one step closer to living like a White man.

Jesse liked Luke Lincoln. He seemed to be a nice fellow and a good fighter. Luke was one of the few men Jesse ever met whom he deemed worthy of a true friendship. In his thoughts, Jesse pictured Luke Lincoln, Elijah Morrison, and himself, spending time together. *We would be great friends,* he thought. Although he never saw Luke Lincoln again, Jesse was pleased to have met him.

The families stayed at the fair until half past eleven, then climbed into the wagon and headed back to the McKinley farm. Large lanterns mounted on the front of the wagon near the seat cast enough light on the dirt road ahead for Henry to see where he was driving the horses, provided he traveled slowly enough. Tied to the back of the wagon was the bull that Mr. McKinley had purchased at the fair. Jesse had enjoyed a wonderful day with his family and his best friends. *These are good people,* thought Jesse as he looked at his own family members, then at Cassie's. And the McKinleys were such fine folks to invite the sharecroppers to the fair.

CHAPTER
TEN

IT WAS THURSDAY, December 16, 1915, when the tragedy occurred. Jesse awakened to the sound of people talking loudly and
running about the farm. He climbed out of bed, put on his clothes,
and walked into the kitchen. The house was empty. He opened the
outside kitchen door and went out into the yard. He saw a crowd
of approximately twenty people, including Cassie's family and
his own, standing by the front porch of the McKinley house. The
McKinley house was about five hundred feet from the sharecropper bungalows. Jesse walked up to his father. "What's going on?"

Henry turned to Jesse. "Mr. McKinley died last night or early
this morning. Mrs. McKinley tried to wake him, but she couldn't.
I went into town to fetch the doctor. He looked at Mr. McKinley
and said it was a heart attack. He wasn't that old. Mrs. McKinley
is taking it real hard. Some neighbor women are in there with her."

Jesse reflected on the kindness Mr. McKinley had shown his
family over the past few years. In some ways he reminded Jesse of
Elijah. Skin color meant nothing to either of them. It was as though
all people were the same. That was the reason Jesse admired both
of them. They were uniquely honest in their views of the world.

The family had a quiet funeral for Mr. McKinley. The body was displayed in the McKinley home for three days, then the funeral was held in the yard. Jesse and Cassie attended the funeral together. Jesse was saddened by his passing. He had hoped that he could learn about managing a farm from Mr. McKinley. He had offered to teach Jesse farm management because he knew Jesse would like to have his own farm someday. He didn't really know if it was possible because of the restrictions on Black persons, but he was determined to try.

Jesse and Cassie sat next to each other on chairs in the yard. Cassie had been crying. "It's hard to believe what happened to Mr. McKinley. He was such a nice man. I remember he let us come here when he didn't really need any help. He had just bought the farm and it was harvesting season, but nothing had been planted that spring because the former owner had died. He bought this place from the bank. He got a great deal. Even though there was no work that year he let us live here anyway and gave us food."

Jesse nodded. "He really was a good man. One time he told me not to let anyone tell me I can't have a farm. He said I could do anything I set my mind to if I'm willing to work hard enough. He never said anything about colored people not being able to own a farm like White folks do."

"I think someday you'll have a farm, Jesse. I know it's what you really want. What do you think will happen to us now? Mrs. McKinley can't run a farm."

"I don't know. Maybe she'll sell it."

"Where will we go if she does?"

Jesse put his hand on his neck as he reflected. "I don't know."

"What if we get separated, Jesse? I couldn't live without seeing you every day."

Jesse nodded, then looked at Cassie. "Yeah, that would be bad."

Cassie's eyes drifted thoughtfully toward the ground, "Let's make sure everyone knows we want to stay together. We will have to go where we can find work, but even if we get separated, let's just agree that we will always stay close."

"I agree with that. We will always need to know where each other is. Then, when we can, we'll get back together."

Cassie reached toward Jesse and took his hand in hers. "Whatever happens, Jesse, I want you to know that I love you."

Jesse smiled and looked into Cassie's eyes. "I love you too Cassie."

Nothing seemed the same after Mr. McKinley died. His widow mentioned often that she did not know what to do. She did not know how to do the bookkeeping or any of the chores on the farm. She did not understand what had happened. She seemed lethargic and in a daze. Jesse noticed that she did not talk as much after Mr. McKinley's death.

Every day Jesse worked unusually fast and hard because he desired to see Cassie after his chores were done. Cassie would often ride along with him when he made his deliveries. Fortunately, they were able to make most of the deliveries on weekends, so it did not cut into Jesse's other chores on the farm. Each time they drove past Kay Mountain they were reminded of their harrowing experience with the KKK. One day, as they were driving past the mountain, Jesse asked, "Do you want to stop to swim in the pond?"

Cassie appeared startled. "Jesse, that's too dangerous. That's where the dunces gather. Besides, we don't have any swimming clothes or clothes to change into. And the water would be freezing. This is December."

Jesse laughed. "We don't need clothes. How long have we been together?"

"Jesse, you are the devil himself. Do you mean you want to swim with me without clothes?" Cassie began laughing fiercely and shaking her head. "You are the worst boy I have ever known."

"Well, I thought I would try. Besides, we have never seen the KKK people up on this side of the mountain."

"Yeah, but remember, somebody moved that rope from under the rock the first time we went deep in the cave."

Jesse shrugged, "Yeah, I guess that's true." He glanced at a book Cassie had on the seat next to her. "Why do you always bring that book? You never read it."

"I just keep it with me in case we break down."

"What's the book about? Maybe you could read some to me."

Cassie laughed. "I don't think you would like me to read it to you. It is a book about algebra."

"What's algebra?"

"It is a type of mathematics. It was invented by a Muslim man."

Jesse whispered the word *Muslim*, then said, "I remember Grandma using that word. Didn't you say it was a foreign religion? Becky said we should stay away from foreign religions."

"I don't think math is part of the religion. Plus, they teach it in the high school, so I guess it's OK."

Jesse remembered his grandmother. At least that was who they said she was. She often spoke of a desert region called the Sahara where she lived before she was sold and transported to America. She served a powerful sultan who treated her as his favorite until one day he simply told her she had been sold. Two days later she was in chains on a ship bound for America. She never saw her sultan again. She never understood why he gave her up on such short notice. She believed he did it abruptly to avoid causing them both pain with a long-drawn-out goodbye. She also believed that his wife had forced his hand. She used to tell Jesse that she was like Hagar in the Quran: the handmaiden of Abraham who bore him Ishmael, the ancestor of the Muslim people.

Upon arriving in Central America, she found herself working as a housemaid on a large plantation in Mexico, where it was her responsibility to prepare Middle Eastern dishes two nights each week. Jesse didn't know her very well. She became ill and died while he was very young. Shortly thereafter the family moved to Texas, where they found work as sharecroppers. The family had worked on several farms until they found the McKinley place. Of all the farms where they had worked, Jesse liked the McKinley farm the best.

After the death of Mr. McKinley there seemed a cloud over the farm. Mrs. McKinley almost never came outside like she did before she was alone. Cassie and Cynthia tried to draw her out and engage her in conversation but to no avail. Mrs. McKinley simply did not respond. A few weeks earlier she was always happy and smiling. She would often come over to the bungalows of the share-croppers just for conversation. Sometimes she would bring freshly baked oatmeal cookies for the children. All of that stopped when Mr. McKinley died. Whereas they were accustomed to seeing her nearly every day, now they saw her only a few times during the rest of the month of December. The farmhouse had been updated with indoor plumbing, so it was necessary for her to leave the house only to obtain groceries. However, young women from the church would stop by the house every Saturday morning to see what groceries she might need, and they would go to the store for her.

In years past, on Christmas Day, the McKinley family would always prepare a feast of turkey, mashed potatoes, gravy, corn, cranberries, and biscuits. It was served with cold iced tea. The McKinleys would invite the sharecroppers into their home to share their meal around the dining room table. Jesse loved those days, but now he knew they were gone forever. This year there would be no Christmas dinner at the McKinley home.

On December 22, 1915, a stranger driving a black Cadillac arrived carrying a male passenger. They parked directly in front of the McKinley farmhouse. The men climbed out of the car wearing suits and black Borsalino fedoras. One was carrying a brief-case. They walked up the three steps to the front porch of the McKinley farmhouse and knocked on the door. Jesse watched from the kitchen window of the Washington family bungalow. The men stayed inside for less than a half hour; then they came out, tossed the briefcase in the back seat, got back into the car, and drove away. Jesse didn't know for sure what they were doing but he was concerned that Mrs. McKinley had sold the farm.

A few days later, Jesse heard the news he dreaded but antici-pated: "Mrs. McKinley sold the farm." The family that bought it was bringing their own sharecropper family with them, which meant one of the families currently on the farm would have to leave. The buyer had talked to a family who had a farm ten miles south of Waco. They were George and Lucy Fryer, who had im-migrated to the United States from England about eight years before. They were well respected in McLennan County. The Fryer family agreed to allow the Washington family to move onto their property as sharecroppers. There was a bungalow on the property where they would live.

On a cool winter afternoon, Jesse and Cassie stood beside the barn where they often spent the evenings alone, conversing about their plans for the future. Jesse put his arm around Cassie, and they walked to the bale of hay they often used as a bench. Sitting there together, Cassie rested her head on Jesse's shoulder. "What are we gonna do, Jesse? Robinson is a long way away from here."

Jesse shrugged. "It isn't so far when you have a truck. It's only about a fifteen-minute drive."

"Fifteen minutes seems like an eternity when we're apart. This is going to be hard."

"I know, but maybe it won't be so bad. We can get together sometimes after work and every weekend."

Cassie nodded. "I suppose so. It just seems like we will be so distant. All the time we lived here, we were together every day, of-ten all day long. Now I will be lucky to see you once a week. Jesse, you know I love you, don't you?"

"Yes, I know, and I love you too. Were you surprised when Mrs. McKinley sold the farm?"

"I was a little at first, but we had said that might happen, so I don't think I was too surprised. I was surprised at how fast she did it."

Jesse shrugged. "Well, I guess I knew it was going to happen. I just didn't really believe it. Maybe I didn't want to believe it."

"How will we stay in touch during the week, Jesse? I heard that some farms have these talking wires, or . . . I forget what they call them."

"Oh, you mean telephones?"

"Yeah, telephones. I heard that some houses have them, but they don't have them out on most of the farms yet. If they did, we could talk every day. So how will I know if you are coming to see me?"

Jesse noticed the brightness of the sun. It seemed unusually bright for December. "I will pick you up at the same time every Saturday. That way you will always know when I am coming. Then, when I am coming to see you during the week, I will either just come over or we will plan it on the weekend."

Cassie nodded. "That would work." Cassie began to cry softly. Then she began to cry uncontrollably. "I will miss you so much."

Cassie and Jesse held each other closely. Jesse didn't cry aloud, but he felt a terrible emptiness in his chest and his throat was dry and scratchy. "I love you, Cassie. This will just be temporary; then, when the time is right, we will be together on our own cotton farm."

Cassie wiped the tears from her eyes, then chuckled. "Jesse, always the dreamer."

CHAPTER
ELEVEN

MRS. MCKINLEY MOVED out abruptly. One day the black
Cadillac showed up again, with the same two men who had visited the house previously. They knocked on the door, and Mrs.
McKinley came out wearing a winter coat and a hat. One of the
men opened the back door of the car for her. The other man carried two large suitcases from the house and put them in the back
seat. Mrs. McKinley started to climb into the car, then looked
over and saw the Williams and the Washington families standing in front of their bungalows. While the men carried several
more suitcases out to the car, Mrs. McKinley walked toward the
sharecroppers. They all began walking toward her, and they met
in the yard.

Mrs. McKinley said, "I'm leaving now. I sold the farm to a
family, as you know. I sold all the furniture, the cattle, the supplies,
everything. I told them that four of the heifers were yours, and that
they have the W brands on them."

Henry put his hand on his neck. "Thank you, ma'am."

Mrs. McKinley nodded. "I know it probably seems really fast
for me to sell and leave. The truth is this family put in an offer over

a year ago. Mr. McKinley always said he didn't want to sell. But after he died, I knew I couldn't stay here. Too many memories that are too painful. Last week I decided I needed to get out of here as fast as I could. I was having nightmares. I called my brother, who is a real estate agent in Dallas. That's him driving the car. I told him I wanted to be out right away. It is too hard to stay here."

Martha asked, "Where are you going now?"

"The family that bought the farm has a two-hundred-acre farm near Waco. They wanted a bigger place and they liked this, so they traded their farm as part of the purchase. I am moving there. I asked my brother to arrange everything as fast as he could. I'm leaving all the furniture, and the house I bought is furnished, so it will all work out."

Cynthia stepped forward and took Mrs. McKinley's hand. "We're gonna miss you, ma'am."

"I will miss all of you too," replied Mrs. McKinley. She reached out and took Martha's hand. Tears were in the eyes of nearly everyone present. Mrs. McKinley turned and walked over to the black Cadillac and climbed into the back seat. The driver closed the door and walked to the other side of the car as the other man got in on the passenger side. The car started up and drove away. Neither the Williamses nor the Washingtons ever saw Mrs. McKinley again.

The following morning, a Model T automobile pulled up in front of the house. A young man and woman exited the vehicle and a young girl, about the age of seven, climbed out of the back seat. The little girl ran excitedly to the front door of the house and opened it, then ran inside. She let out a shrill scream of excitement. She came back out the front door and said, "It's a big house."

The man and woman walked up the porch steps. The little girl pointed at the sharecropper families. "Who are those people?"

The man looked over at Jesse and Cassie, who were standing on the front porch of the Williamses' bungalow and waved. "Those are the sharecropper families that live here."

The family went into the house, where they remained for

approximately a half hour. Then the man came out and walked over to Jesse and Cassie. "Do you live here?"

Jesse nodded. "Yes, I'm Jesse Washington and this is Cassie Williams."

"Oh yes. Your family is moving to Robinson." He looked at Cassie. "And yours is staying here. I'm Sam, the new owner of the farm."

Cassie nodded. "It's nice to meet you, sir."

Henry, Martha, and Billy came out of the bungalow and walked up to Sam. Henry said, "I'm Henry, this is my wife, Martha, this is our son Billy and this is our son, Jesse."

"I understand you went over and met the Fryer family."

Henry nodded. "Jesse and I went over and met them."

"You know that you have to move out?"

Henry replied, "Yes, we understand."

"The new sharecropper family will be here on the fifteenth of January. The Fryers are good people. I've known them for years. You will like it there. I'm sorry you have to go, but we have a family that has been with us for five years. I had to bring them, and we don't have a need for three sharecropper families."

Henry shuffled nervously. "We know we have to be out by the fifteenth. We will be gone the first week of January."

"Whose truck is that over there?"

Jesse looked at the green truck Elijah had given him. "That's mine."

Sam looked surprised. "How could you afford a truck like that?"

"I work for a farmer named Baines when I'm not working here. I make deliveries for him."

"Oh yes, I know the Baineses. So, it isn't really your truck, then?"

"No, it's my truck. Their nephew, Elijah, gave it to me when he went away to college so I could make deliveries for his aunt and uncle."

"Do you have a registration?"

Jesse nodded and walked over to the truck. He opened the passenger door, reached up, and took a piece of paper from the sun visor. "Here's the registration."

Jesse handed the registration to Sam, who looked at it, then nodded and gave it back to Jesse.

Henry interjected, "Did Mrs. McKinley tell you about the heifers?"

Sam frowned. "We bought all livestock and materials. Mrs. McKinley said that there are four heifers Mr. McKinley gave to you, but that doesn't matter because we bought all the livestock, so unless you have a bill of sale, the heifers are staying here."

"He didn't give us a bill of sale. He bought them and gave them to us. So, you are just going to take them?"

"No, I'm not taking them. They already belong to the farm."

Jesse looked frustrated. "Sir, that ain't right. Mr. McKinley gave us those heifers to help get us started."

Sam shrugged. "When we bought the farm, we bought all the livestock."

Jesse stepped forward, prepared to challenge Sam. Henry reached out and took his arm. "Let it go, Jesse," he whispered.

Jesse looked at his father with frustration, then pulled away. He was troubled by the unfairness of Sam's comments, but he knew there was nothing he could do. Sam was going to steal the heifers, and that was the end of it. Then Jesse realized the reason Sam had inquired about the truck. If he could, he would take that too and there would be nothing Jesse could do about it.

On Monday, January 3, 1916, Jesse drove the truck slowly down the dirt road from Waco to Robinson. Next to him was Cassie. Billy and Jenny were in the back of the truck with the furniture they were moving. Jesse drove slowly so the two horse-drawn wagons could follow. In the Model T truck and two wagons was everything the Washington family owned. Occasionally, Jesse would notice that the wagons were falling behind, and he would slow so they could catch up. The drivers of the wagons did not know the way to the Fryer farm. Jesse had been to the farm earlier when he and his father interviewed with Lucy Fryer about the sharecropping position, so he led the way.

Finally, they arrived at their destination. The Fryer farm consisted of four hundred acres with the main house and several outbuildings, including a barn and a bungalow for the sharecroppers. Jesse maneuvered the truck along the side of the bungalow where the Washington family would live. Lucy Fryer, a fifty-three-year-old, sightly heavyset woman, came out of the house and began talking loudly. "Pull the wagons up to the front door of your house. You can unload the truck from the side of the house."

The firmness in Lucy's voice, combined with her British accent, made Jesse a little uncomfortable. She didn't seem kind, like Mrs. McKinley. She seemed firm and harsh, with little sense of humor. "The well's over there behind the cabin." She pointed in the direction of the sharecropper house. "It's got a hand pump on it. After you get everything unloaded, I'll bring you some food."

Lucy turned abruptly and walked to her house. She looked back toward Jesse. "Jesse, park your truck over behind the barn when you get it unloaded."

Jesse knew when Mr. McKinley died, things would never be the same. Reality confirmed his foreknowledge. As they unloaded the truck and wagons, no one said anything. Somehow, it felt as if darkness had befallen them all. *What is this strange feeling?* Jesse asked himself. *What does this constant question mean?*

After the unloading was complete, Lucy brought a plateful of sandwiches and set it on a table in the yard. Jesse walked to the table to help. Lucy said, "This is just for you and your family, Jesse. We don't have enough to feed an entire village."

Lucy's words seemed odd to Jesse. The Fryers owned cattle, and Jesse knew they had just butchered a steer two weeks ago because Mrs. Fryer had mentioned it during their interview. *How could there not be enough beef to make sandwiches for everyone?*

Jesse walked over to his friends, who were standing by the wagon. "Sorry, Mrs. Fryer didn't make enough food for all of us. Here are a few dollars. Why don't you guys get some barbecue from Lou's Place?"

"Thanks, Jesse." The men climbed into the wagon. Cassie, who had ridden with Jesse in the truck, asked, "Should I go back with them?"

"No," Jesse replied. "I'll take you back in the truck later tonight."

As the men drove their wagons back to the road, Cassie said, "Jesse, I don't know what it is, but everything here feels strange . . . really bad. It's like something bad is going to happen or is already happening. I can't get rid of this feeling. Do you feel it too?"

Jesse nodded. "I do. I feel it. I know it ain't just because Mr. McKinley died, 'cause I felt it before he died. I feel like it will be very bad, but something important will come out of this evil. I don't understand it neither."

"Do you think it's just us, or all colored people, or all people? What is it?"

"I don't know. I just hope everything will be OK. For you and me it means gettin' our feet on the ground so we can get our own place."

Cassie laughed. "Jesse, did you just propose to me?"

"No, I was just thinkin' out loud." He laughed.

Jesse and Cassie walked to the table to get something to eat. Billy and Jenny came to the table to join them. Billy said, "Hey. I guess this is our new place. It ain't as nice as the bungalow at McKinley's, but it ain't bad neither. What do you think of Lucy Fryer?"

Cassie remained silent. Jesse shook his head. "I don't know. We'll see. She ain't as nice as Mrs. McKinley. Maybe she's having a bad day."

Perhaps Lucy Fryer was having a bad day. The next time Jesse saw her was two days later. She seemed much more pleasant. The Washingtons were relaxing on the front porch of their bungalow in the early evening. Lucy walked over to them and said, in proper British English, "I feel that I owe all of you an apology for my rudeness when I last saw you . . . I wasn't feeling well. Mr. Fryer says that sometimes I am like two different people. I don't feel it. I know that somedays I don't feel right, but I don't feel like I'm significantly different. I just wanted to say, I'm sorry."

"Not at all," said Henry. "We thought you was just fine, ma'am."

Lucy smiled. "We're having a big barbecue on the Saturday night after next with several local churches. It will be in the pasture down by the creek. There are tables and a firepit there. You can't miss it. You folks are welcome to join us. It would give us a chance to introduce you to the community. It starts at four o'clock."

"Will they allow colored folks at the barbecue?" asked Jesse.

"The churches invite the colored churches to attend their picnics and barbecues, but colored folks usually don't come unless they're working for one of the White families that's attending. But we'd like you to attend. It will be a good time to introduce you to the community, and you will have some great food."

"We would like that very much," said Henry. "We'll be there." He nodded to his wife for support.

She nodded and smiled. "Yes, we'll be there."

Jesse listened to the conversation. He noticed the stark difference in the current demeanor of Lucy Fryer. She seemed like a completely different person today in comparison to the other times he had seen her. When she interviewed Jesse and his father, she seemed sharp, aloof, and unfeeling, and when they moved their belongings to the farm, she seemed the same. But today she seemed very pleasant and friendly. Jesse didn't trust her but decided to give her the benefit of the doubt.

During the first week on the Fryer farm there wasn't much to do. They moved their furniture and clothing into the sharecropper cabin, which only took Monday afternoon. The rest of the week Jesse and Billy looked around the farm during the day;

then, on Wednesday evening, Jesse went to the McKinley farm to visit Cassie. The weather in Waco was cool in January, with an average high temperature in the low sixties. The evenings typically delivered a brisk chill. That Wednesday evening was no different. Jesse and Cassie sat on the bale of hay next to the barn where they always sat when Jesse lived on the McKinley farm. They were both wearing winter jackets and covered themselves with the wool horse blanket they always used when they were sitting on the bale in cold weather. Jesse had started a fire in front of them to help keep them warm. They talked softly in case anyone was listening.

Cassie leaned her head against Jesse's shoulder. "Was your pa upset about the heifers?"

Jesse threw his head back. "Oh yeah. He was really mad." Jesse lowered his voice to a whisper. "Pa says Sam stole them, the same as if he had used a gun. What did your pa say?"

"He was upset, but I think he was more sad than mad. He was really excited about havin' those heifers. He said it was a good beginnin' for us. Pa was hopin' Sam would be nice, like Mr. McKinley. But now, he said he wants to leave sometime soon. He don't want to work for a man who would do that. How is it on the Fryer farm? Lucy Fryer didn't seem very friendly when we were there."

Jesse leaned back against the barn. "She was strange that first day, but the next time we saw her she seemed really nice. I think she was havin' a bad day when you met her. She invited us to a barbecue on the Saturday after next. I thought you could come."

"Who's gonna be there?"

"It's gonna be people from the White church in Robinson."

"She invited you to a White people's barbecue?"

"Yeah, and I want you to come."

Cassie took ahold of Jesse's hand. "I think I would be nervous at a White people's barbecue. We'll probably be the only Black people there."

"I don't think it would be any different from the volleyball games at the university."

Cassie laughed. "That time at the volleyball game at the university. What a night that was."

The air was silent for a moment as they thought about the evening they played volleyball at Baylor. Then Cassie continued. "We even met the president of Baylor that night."

"Yeah, that was a great night."

As the clock approached midnight, Jesse decided it was time to drive back home. He had enjoyed Cassie's company. They said good night, and he drove back to the Fryer farm.

On Friday morning George Fryer met Jesse coming out of the barn. "Jesse, I was wondering if you would like to make the trip into the general store in Robinson to pick up supplies. This is just the small items. I always have the big deliveries brought out to the farm, but someone needs to pick up groceries, and sometimes a bag of seed or other supplies about once a week."

Jesse nodded. "I could do that."

"Good. I made a list. I'm thinking you could go in at about four o'clock, before it gets busy on Friday afternoon." George gave Jesse the list. "They allow coloreds in the store, so you shouldn't have any problems."

"All right, sir. I'll go in to fetch the supplies."

Jesse worked on the farm until early afternoon. Finally, at three thirty, he climbed into the truck and traveled into Robinson. As he drove down the main street, he saw the general store on the right side of the road. He pulled up in front of the establishment and went inside. He looked around, surprised at the size. Although it wasn't obvious from the road, the store was like a small barn. An attractive, young White girl walked up to Jesse. "Welcome to the general store. Are you looking for anything in particular?"

"Yes, ma'am. I have a list, but I can't read it. Mr. Fryer said you would find the items if I gave you the list."

The young woman smiled. "Oh, you work for the Fryers. Sure.

My name is Rachel Blakely. My father owns this store. I work here on weekdays. I'm happy to help the Fryers. May I see the list?"

Jesse gave Rachel the list. "I'm Jesse Washington. I'll be pickin' up supplies every Friday afternoon from now on." Jesse noticed a teenage girl sitting at the soda fountain, listening to their conversation.

Rachel laughed. "Washington, like the president?"

"Yes, ma'am."

"OK. If you follow me, I'll point out the supplies for you. There's a pull wagon over there you can use to haul everything. You have several big bags on this list."

Jesse saw a wooden wagon next to the wall by the door. He took ahold of the wagon handle and followed Rachel through the store as she identified various items on the list. She pointed at a fifty-pound bag of rice. The bag was made of burlap and had rope handles on either end. Rachel's eyes widened when she saw Jesse pick up the bag with one hand and throw it on the cart. She looked at his large biceps.

"That's amazing," she said. "I have never seen anyone toss a fifty-pound bag of rice like that. You must be incredibly strong."

Jesse laughed. "I don't know, ma'am."

"Jesse, you don't need to call me 'ma'am.' You may call me Rachel."

"OK, ma'am. I mean, Rachel."

Rachel and Jesse both laughed.

Rachel and Jesse talked as they collected the items for purchase. After twenty minutes of collecting supplies in the store, Jesse loaded the supplies into the back of his truck and asked Rachel to put it on Mr. Fryer's tab. Rachel helped him load the lighter items, then watched him toss the heavy bags like they were filled with cotton. "I still can't believe how strong you are, Jesse. I have never seen someone toss heavy bags like you."

Jesse stood by the truck and talked to Rachel for about fifteen minutes. She asked about his family, where he was from, and how long he had lived in Robinson. Then she told him about her family. Her father owned a big ranch near Robinson where Rachel was born and raised.

Jesse thought it unusual that a White woman would spend this much time talking to him. But Rachel seemed very friendly. She didn't seem to see him as a Black man; she just saw him as a man. She mentioned that she did not have a boyfriend, and Jesse sensed that she was interested in him. But Jesse would never consider a relationship with her because of the laws prohibiting interracial marriage. It was too dangerous. Besides, he already had Cassie. *Why complicate that?*

"Thank you for your help, Miss Rachel."

"Just Rachel is fine. You don't need to call me miss either."

Rachel followed Jesse up to the front of his truck, where he used the crank to start the engine. "Are these hard to start with that crank?"

"No, ma'am . . . I mean Rachel."

Unbeknownst to Jesse, two members of the KKK were watching him from the other side of the street. One of them spat on the ground. "Where do you suppose that N_____ got that truck? I bet he stole it."

The other man replied, "I don't think he stole it. He wouldn't be drivin' it into town if it was stolen."

"Well, that's a pretty nice truck for a sharecropper. There must be some kinda story behind this. I think it's Morrison's truck. In fact, I saw Morrison driving it before."

Rachel waved goodbye as Jesse pulled away from the curb.

Jesse thought about Rachel several times throughout the week. *She is a really nice girl,* he thought to himself, *and pretty too.*

The next Friday Jesse drove into Robinson and parked in front of the general store. As he walked inside, he thought he overheard someone say, "That's him. That's the stud." He noticed the same teenage girl who was sitting there last week, looking at him, only now there were six other girls with her. "Oh yes," replied one of the other girls. "Now that's a prize stallion, right there." The girls laughed.

Jesse handed the list to Rachel as he had the previous week. "Would you help me again, Rachel?"

Rachel took the list. "Sure, I don't mind, but I showed you where everything was the last time you were here."

"Yes, I remember where everything is."

"But you asked me to help you again. Do you just like my company?" Rachel laughed.

Jesse smiled. "No, ma'am, that isn't it. I mean, I enjoy your company, but that isn't why I asked."

"Oh? What is it, then?"

Jesse whispered so no one could overhear his words. "You see, Miss Rachel, I can't read."

"Oh, I see. Well, that's alright, Jesse. I think you told me that last time, but I didn't know what you meant. I don't mind helping you when you come in. By the way, ignore those girls over there. Julie, the one on the end, she was in here when you came in last week, and she told her friends about you."

"I don't understand. Why are they all looking at me?"

Rachel laughed. "Because you are a very handsome fellow, Jesse. After you left last week, Julie talked about you for a half hour. She wanted to know where you live. I didn't tell her you live at the Fryers' place. I figure the last thing you need are a bunch of White girls coming around to watch you work."

"No, ma'am. I don't think that would be good."

As Jesse walked past the row of girls at the fountain, he heard a few comments. One girl said, "Now that's a stud."

Another said, "Hey, Jesse, why don't you come and play in the barn with us?"

All the girls laughed. Jesse pretended not to hear them.

After Jesse paid, he turned to walk out the door and saw one of the same men who had been across the street the week before. The man wore an angry expression on his face but didn't say anything as Jesse pulled the wagon out to his truck. Rachel came out to talk to him while he loaded the supplies. The man turned around and walked away abruptly.

Jesse said goodbye to Rachel, then started the truck and headed back to the Fryer farm. As he drove, he felt uncomfortable with the way the girls had spoken to him. He wondered if the man across the street had heard it. He remembered Steve Dixon's warning about catching him with White girls, and he remembered Richard, the man they dragged and murdered on the road in Waco because of a White woman. This concerned Jesse. *Why can't they just leave us alone?*

On Saturday morning Jesse went to the McKinley farm to pick up Cassie. He was a little nervous about bringing her with him due to his unfamiliarity with the people who would be attending the barbecue that evening. *What if they are rude? They are a group of people from local churches. Maybe they would not be as kind as the students on the volleyball teams.* Jesse had promised George that he would return by 9:00 a.m. to help put a side of beef on the skewer. This would allow it to slow cook all day.

Jesse arrived at the Williamses' bungalow and Cassie came out the front door. She was wearing a new light-green dress. Her beauty overwhelmed him as he opened the passenger door of the truck.

Cassie embraced Jesse, then kissed him gently on the lips. "I have missed you so much. This was the longest week of my life."

Jesse laughed. "I know what you mean. It seems like forever since I last saw you." He helped Cassie into the truck, closed the door, then walked around to the driver's side and climbed in. He had left the engine running so he would not have to restart the truck.

Cassie bounced a bit on the seat to achieve comfort. "How do you like it on the Fryer farm, Jesse? How's Lucy Fryer been?"

"She's been pretty nice. She was really nice when she stopped by to invite us to the barbecue. I think maybe she just wasn't feeling good when we saw her before. She said that is why she wasn't friendly."

Cassie nodded. "Maybe she's a really nice person. I am a little scared about going to the barbecue. I hope they are like the White people at Baylor."

"Me too," replied Jesse.

When they arrived at the Fryer farm, Jesse parked the truck next to the Washington bungalow. Cassie went inside to visit with Jesse's parents while Jesse went with Billy and George Fryer to the barn where they had slaughtered a cow the evening before. They had cured it with salt, then put it in the walk-in ice cooler. The cooler was insulated with thick boards and straw, and there were large blocks of ice on the floor. It generally took three or four men to toss a two-hundred-and fifty-pound side of beef onto a wagon. Without pausing for thought, Jesse walked over, picked up the side of beef as if it was a heavy bag of grain, and tossed it on the wagon. Billy had seen Jesse's strength in the past, so he wasn't surprised. George, however, was astounded. "I have never seen any man exhibit so much strength. That side weighs at least two hundred fifty or three hundred pounds. How did you do that?"

Jesse suddenly realized the subject of George's comment and laughed. He shook his head, then shrugged. "I don't know."

George glanced at Billy. "Did you see that?"

Billy chuckled and nodded. "Yeah."

"Doesn't that surprise you?"

Billy didn't respond. He looked at George, then Jesse, uncertain of the subject of the conversation.

George laughed. "You've seen him do that before." He turned to Jesse, "You must be the strongest man I have ever seen. I think I will call you Samson."

Jesse had been exercising every day since he was a child. He took for granted his own strength until George drew his attention to it. He laughed. "I don't know about that. I just always exercise."

"You mean like in the army? Push-ups and things like that?"

Jesse nodded. "Yeah, that's it. My pa and grandpa always exercised. They taught me. They said it makes a man better for workin' and for breedin' if he exercises and is strong."

George stroked his chin. "That's interesting. I suppose that's true."

Jesse walked over toward the other side of beef. George stepped forward. "Wait up. We'll all do it. I don't want you tossing your back out."

"Yes, sir," said Jesse.

They loaded the second side of beef into the wagon. Then they loaded a bucket of barbecue sauce, some utensils, and a bundle of kindling for starting the fire. As they climbed on the wagon, George said, "We'll bring everything else tonight. For now, we're just going to start the fire and get the beef cooking. Billy, can you stay there and turn the beef on the skewers? That way Jesse can spend a little time with Cassie."

"All right, sir," replied Billy.

As they pulled the wagon up to the pit and the picnic site, Jesse appreciated the atmosphere. There was a large barbecue pit and a dozen tables made of oak logs and two-by-six planks. The tables were painted brown and blended in nicely with the terrain. They were laid out around a stage constructed of stones. Next to the stage was the creek and a small waterfall where the land dropped abruptly from a hill. The men took a steel rod of about ten feet in length that was sharpened on one end and skewered one side of beef, weaving the rod in between the ribs. They then hoisted it onto two tripods, each made of three steel poles, on each end of the rod. Once the beef was roasting, they hoisted the second side of beef on a different skewer. There were six hundred pounds of beef to feed two hundred people at most. George always overcooked so the guests could take several pounds home with a jar of barbecue sauce. Many folks would come back to buy the sauce after George hosted one of these barbecues, which he did about twice per year.

In the fall it was generally combined with a small rodeo on the premises, which would usually double the number of people in attendance. They called the fall event a hoedown. George generally cooked two whole steers at the hoedown, and there was always plenty for the guests to take some home.

After the beef was roasting Jesse and George climbed back on the wagon while Billy stayed at the pit so he could turn the beef every twenty minutes or so. The end of each skewer had a crank handle, resting on ball bearing wheels, which was helpful in turning two hundred and fifty pounds of beef. As they rode back to the barn, Jesse reflected on his new surroundings. *I think I will like this place,* he thought to himself. *The Fryers are good people.*

George pulled the horses to a halt next to the barn. He smiled at Jesse. "Take your time visiting with Cassie. I can get the rest of the supplies. The kids will help me. Now, you ask that girl to marry you if that is what you really want. She is a good catch for sure."

Jesse laughed as he jumped down from the wagon. "Thanks, George. We will be over there at four o'clock."

When the evening arrived, Jesse noticed several horse-drawn wagons and automobiles making their way to the pasture down by the creek. They slowly parked in rows, wagons in one row and cars in another. The visitors disembarked their vehicles and looked for a picnic table where they could eat.

Jesse took a bath and put on clean clothes. He then climbed into the truck with Cassie in the front seat and his parents in the bed of the truck sitting on bales of hay. Jesse drove to the picnic site and parked the truck along with a row of other vehicles. Many people turned to see who was driving the flashy green truck and were quite surprised to see a Black family in the vehicle.

They climbed out of the truck and quickly noticed they were the only Black family at the picnic. They nervously walked around the outer edge of the picnic area as they made their way to a table far away from the stage. Lucy Fryer spotted them from a distance and smiled. She waved for them to come over. They complied.

Lucy put her hand on Martha's shoulder. "Ladies, I want to introduce you to Martha Washington. The Washingtons just moved into the bungalow. They will be living here now. This is her husband, Henry." She gestured toward Jesse and Cassie. "This is Jesse and his girl. I'm sorry, I have forgotten your name."

Cassie laughed and nodded. "I'm Cassie, ma'am."

"Yes, Cassie. Everyone, please make them welcome."

Several of those standing nearby stepped forward and introduced themselves. An elderly couple came over to Jesse and Cassie. "Hello, young ones. I'm Margaret, and this is my husband, Larry. Welcome to our barbecue."

Jesse smiled. "Thank you, ma'am."

"So where did you folks come from?"

Cassie replied, "They used to live on the McKinley farm. Mr. McKinley passed on just before Christmas. Jesse and his family had to move over here."

Larry shook his head. "We heard about McKinley. That was tragic. We didn't know him very well, but they would come to some church functions. I guess he had a nice spread over there toward Waco."

Jesse nodded. "Yes, sir. It was 'bout a thousand acres."

"That's a big farm. Too bad he didn't get to enjoy it longer before he passed."

Jesse looked awkwardly at the ground, not knowing where the conversation should go next. "Mr. McKinley was good to all the people who worked for him."

Margaret stepped forward. "Do you kids have anyone to sit with? Our table is right over here."

Jesse noticed that his parents had been seated at a table with another couple Lucy had introduced them to. Jesse and Cassie joined Margaret and Larry at their table. Another elderly couple joined them. Finally, Lucy's twenty-one-year-old daughter, Ruby, and her sixteen-year-old son, George Fryer Jr., came to the table and sat down.

"I'm Ruby, and this is my brother, George Jr. George and Lucy are our parents. We just got back from a trip to Dallas where we were traveling with a family from church."

Margaret replied, "When did you get back? Were you with the Steubings?"

"Yes. We got back today. We were attending a family camp with them. Mom and Dad couldn't go because they have too much going on here right now, so the Steubings invited George Jr. and me to go with them."

Soon Jesse had forgotten the differences in color and social skills. He noticed that Cassie blended in well, and the group was asking her questions about many topics, from history to medicine. Jesse liked this feeling of acceptance. These were good people.

Jesse and Cassie stayed and talked until nearly nine o'clock that night. As people began to leave, Jesse took water and doused the fires to make sure each one was out. George gave each family a jar of barbecue sauce and several pieces of leftover beef wrapped in butcher cloth. They loaded the rest of the leftover beef, sauces, and utensils on the wagon and took them to the main house. Billy drove and Jesse, Cassie, and Jesse's parents followed in the truck. They arrived at the house and placed the food into the ice cooler wrapped in the waxed cloth. When they were finished cleaning up, Jesse drove Cassie back to the McKinley farm in the truck.

Jesse stayed at the McKinley farm, talking to Cassie and her family until midnight. It was nice to be with Cassie again. Life wasn't bad on the Fryer farm, but it wasn't as pleasant as living at McKinley's. The McKinleys seemed to genuinely care about the sharecropper families. They treated them almost as extended family. It was different on the Fryer farm. The social structure was clear. It was obvious that the Fryers were the owners and the sharecroppers were employees. Perhaps that wasn't so much the result of the actions of the Fryers, but rather the way others in the community behaved when the Fryers were around. Treated with almost celebrity status, the Fryers were known to nearly everyone in the community. Lucy Fryer was considered pleasant and attractive. Well liked in the community, the Fryers were the kind of people others enjoyed socially.

Jesse and Cassie decided they would visit each other every Tuesday and Thursday, as well as on weekends. Usually, Jesse would drive to the McKinley farm after work, have dinner with the Williams family, then stay up with Cassie until after midnight, just talking. It seemed they were never at a loss for words or topics to discuss.

As was often the case, on a Thursday evening in March, the conversation turned to their romantic connection. Without explanation, Jesse leaned over and kissed Cassie on the lips. She giggled. "What are you doing, stud?"

Jesse laughed. "What'd you call me?"

"I called you stud. That is what the White girls call you over in Robinson, isn't it?"

"Where'd you hear that?"

"My friend's mother is the housekeeper for the Blakely family. Rachel Blakely works at the general store. She's their daughter. She's our age."

Jesse laughed. "Yeah, I know her."

"I think she wishes she knew you better. Did you ever notice that there are lots of White girls when you go into the store?"

"I did, but I didn't know why. Why are they there?"

"They come to see you. They call you the stud. She said you come in every Friday afternoon at about four to pick up supplies. They are always there to see you."

Jesse laughed. "That's really bad."

"They all like you, Jesse."

He shook his head. "I wouldn't go near one of those girls. They lynch colored guys for less than that. How'd ya find out about this?"

"My friend's mom said the girls stay at the house on weekends and have what they call slumber parties. They come to the store every Friday so they can see you, then they stay over at the Blakely house and talk about guys. She said you are the guy they talk about the most. They call you 'the forbidden stud.'"

Jesse frowned. "I don't think I like that. That could be bad with the White men. But it don't matter 'cause you're my girl."

"Am I your girl, Jesse?"

Jesse hugged her. "Yeah, ya are. Don't ya wanna be my girl?"

"I do, but I can't compete with all those girls."

"Yeah, ya can. I don't love them, I love you."

Cassie laughed and hugged Jesse.

Jesse pulled Cassie closer to him. "Maybe it's time to think about gettin' married and startin' a family."

"Are you serious, Jesse?"

"Yeah, I am."

"Well, you have to ask. A girl ain't gonna just fall into your lap."

Jesse laughed. "What do you mean, fall into my lap?"

"I mean you have to tell a girl you want her to be your wife and you have to act like you really want her."

"If I asked you to marry me, what would you say?"

Cassie laughed and punched Jesse in the shoulder. "Why do you always ask that? I told you, it doesn't work like that. You can't ask 'what if.' You just have to ask."

Jesse shrugged and held his arms in the air. "Who made all these rules? Why can't you say what you would do?"

"I don't know who made the rules. But somebody did. Since you are so afraid of asking me without knowing what I would say, I will help you. Obviously, I would say yes. If I didn't love you, I wouldn't be spending all this time with you. I'm investing in our future. But if you break my heart, I will hunt you down and spank you with a wire horse brush. I will make your cute little butt sore, Jesse Washington."

Cassie and Jesse both laughed again.

"So, you are saying that if I ask you to marry me, you will say yes?"

"Yes, Jesse. Yes, yes, yes. How many times do I have to say it before you ask me?"

"Then let's get married."

"When?"

"How about September 30, 1917?"

"Do you even know what day of the week that is?"

"No. But I do want to do this."

"OK, September 30, 1917, we will be married. Now you have just proposed to me. It's official. I am your fiancée, right?"

Jesse smiled. "Yep, that's right. We'll do this."

Jesse and Cassie had joked about this often in the past. This time it was official. They decided they would announce their engagement to everyone. Only as they talked, they decided there was no reason to wait for 1917. They would get married in September of 1916. They checked the calendar and realized that September 30 was a Saturday, so the day Jesse chose was perfect. They would be married on Saturday, September 30, 1916.

Jesse and Cassie decided they would tell Cassie's family on Saturday, when he came to pick her up, and then they would go to the Fryer farm on Sunday and tell Jesse's family. They both wanted to be there. But Jesse decided he needed to ask permission of Cassie's father before announcing it. So, they decided that Jesse would talk to John on Saturday morning, then announce it to the family if John said yes.

On Saturday morning, March 25, 1916, at 8:00 a.m., Jesse got up, warmed some water, and took a bath. He put on his best clothes, went outside, and walked over to the truck. As he drove down the dirt road toward the McKinley farm, he rehearsed in his mind what he would say to Cassie's father. Cassie was going to tell her father that Jesse wanted to talk to him, but that she didn't know why. He would ask permission then, if John said OK, he would talk to Cassie, so it would look like he asked her after he had permission.

Jesse pulled into the driveway of the McKinley farm and drove over to the Williamses' bungalow. John came out of the front door as Jesse turned off the engine.

"Hey, Jesse. How's it going?"

Jesse jumped out of the truck and closed the door. "Good, sir. How are you doing?"

"Doing OK. Cassie said you wanted to talk to me. I hope it ain't bad news."

"No, sir. I think it's good news."

"OK. Come on in and let's get a cup of coffee."

Jesse and John walked into the house and into the kitchen. John motioned for Jesse to sit at the table. Cynthia, Jenny, and Cassie walked out of the room and through the living room to the front door. "We're going to work in the garden this morning," said Cynthia as they walked out and closed the door behind them.

John poured two cups of coffee, one for Jesse and one for himself. They sat at the table.

"So, ya wanna marry my daughter," said John.

Jesse was flustered for a moment. "Uh, well. I wanted to ask you."

John laughed. "I'm just messin' with ya. Cassie didn't say anything about it. She just said you wanted to talk to me. I figured that must be the reason. How's everything on the Fryer farm?"

"It's good. I liked it better when we were all here, but it ain't bad."

"What'd ya like better?"

Jesse took a drink of his coffee. "I just liked it better when we were all together."

John nodded. "Of course you can marry my daughter. I just wondered what took you so long to ask." John roared with laughter and slapped Jesse on the shoulder. "That is what you wanted to talk about, right?"

Jesse smiled. "Yeah, that was it. This was a lot easier than I expected."

They both laughed.

"So, what are your plans now, Jesse?"

"Well, I was plannin' to save money so I can buy a farm and grow cotton. But I promised Cassie I would learn to read. She says I might want to be a colored doctor."

Jesse and John roared with laughter. John repeated, "A colored . . . a colored doctor." John had to pause to get over his laughter. "I know why she says that. We took her to see Dr. Connor one time when she was about ten. She was sick, and he gave her some medicine that made her better. He was nice to her, and he was a good-looking man. Since then, she always talked about colored doctors."

"If I like readin', I don't know what I will do, but she says I can choose. I thought maybe I would be a farmer *and* a colored doctor. There are lots of months we don't have to work on the farm. Maybe I can do doctoring then. But right now, I just want to save for a farm."

"I don't know why a guy couldn't do both if he wants to. It'd be a lot of work, though."

"Cassie thinks if I could read, I could choose. I don't know."

John leaned back in his chair. "Makes sense to me. When were you thinking you would jump the broom?"

"We were thinkin' on September 30. I thought we'd tell people in July. If we tell people too soon, I think they might forget."

John nodded. He stood up and walked to the front door. He opened it and Cynthia, Jenny, and Cassie were standing on the porch. John smiled and motioned them in. "We got some good news."

Astounded, Cassie looked at her father. "What?"

John grinned. "Cassie's getting married to Jesse on September 30, 1916."

Cynthia laughed and hugged Cassie. "We wondered what was takin' you kids so long. Praise the Lord. You're going to give us lots of little babies, I hope."

Cassie stepped back and spoke emphatically. "Mom? That's

not proper. Dad, it ain't supposed to happen like this. We were supposed to announce it to you, not you to us."

Everyone laughed. John said, "Oh, it's just us. We don't have to have rules. So, you are gonna announce it to everyone in July, right?"

Cassie nodded. "That's what we were thinkin'."

Cynthia asked, "Did you tell Jesse's family yet?"

Cassie shook her head. "No, we thought we would tell them tomorrow. I have something special to ask."

"OK," replied John.

"Now that Jesse and I are getting married, would it be OK if Jesse stayed here tonight? He could sleep out here in the living room. We got that spare straw mattress in the attic."

Cynthia looked at John. "I think it would be OK. John?"

John nodded. "I think it would be fun to have another man around."

"Hey," said Cassie, "he will still stay up talkin' to me, not you."

John laughed. "This is a good day."

That night Cassie and Jesse didn't sit alone in the barn as usual. Instead, they stayed up late with Cassie's family in the living room of the bungalow. It was a cool evening in March, and they had a fire in the woodburning stove. They played checkers for several hours and talked about everything imaginable. But mostly, John and Jesse talked about having a farm. Cassie only mentioned colored doctors one time when they were talking about Jesse's options.

Eventually, John, Cynthia, and Jenny went to bed. Jesse and Cassie sat on the couch. After a time, Jesse lay down and Cassie lay down next to him. Jesse placed his arm under Cassie's neck, and she cuddled close to him.

The following morning Jesse and Cassie got up and went to church with Cassie's family, then drove to the Fryer farm, where they told Jesse's parents of their decision to marry. Sunday afternoon was a celebratory time. It was now official. Cassie and Jesse were engaged.

CHAPTER
TWELVE

THE FOLLOWING MONDAY morning, George Fryer walked across the barnyard with Jesse and Billy. His British accent sounded dignified to the southern Texas community. Well educated, he would often speak at public events and sometimes spoke in church. "Have you fellows used a donkey to plow before? It's not as common as using a horse or oxen."

"No, sir," said Billy.

Jesse shook his head. "We haven't worked with donkeys before."

George smiled. "A lot of people don't like them. They can be very stubborn. But they are loyal and strong. I find that if you treat a donkey well, he will be obedient, but if you beat him . . ." George laughed and shook his head, "It's like he doesn't forget. Then, when you want him to do something, he ignores you."

"Then why do people use them?" asked Jesse.

George opened the barn door and they entered. "Because they're loyal, they work hard when they want to, and they don't require much maintenance." George opened a gate and led Billy and Jesse into a stall occupied by a mule. "I don't use donkeys on the farm, but we use mules."

"I thought a donkey and a mule were the same thing," said Billy.

George patted the mule on the back. "Yes, that's a common misconception. A donkey is a breed of its own. A mule is the offspring of a male donkey and a female horse. This one's called Betsy. Mules are much gentler than horses and they are much smarter than donkeys. For farming, I prefer a mule over anything but oxen. Mules and oxen have a similar personality."

George took ahold of Betsy by the bridle and led her out of the barn and into the barnyard. "One thing you don't want to do is let Lucy see you whip the mule. She loves Betsy like a house dog. I don't suppose I need to tell you guys about Lucy's depression. Most of the time Lucy is the nicest person ever. But every few weeks she has severe depression."

Billy asked, "What's depression?"

"Do you know how sometimes you catch a cold, and you don't feel well for a time? Well, the human mind can do that as well. It can become tired, or even sick. Every so often you will see that Lucy seems very sad. It's best just to stay away and give her plenty of room. It only lasts a day or two. Then she's back to normal. But don't let her see you whip Betsy. One time she saw me whip Betsy and I thought she was going to shoot me." George laughed; Billy and Jesse joined in.

George showed Jesse and Billy how to hitch Betsy to the plow. "Plowing season for cotton starts in early April. You have to be careful with cotton seeds. If the temperature drops below forty degrees within the first three days of planting, and the seeds have moisture, it can kill them. For that reason, many cotton farmers wait until mid-May to plow and plant the seeds. I usually plow the first and second week of May. I think that's the best time. It's better if the seeds absorb moisture from the soil during planting season because then they need less moisture later during the dry months. So you balance the benefit of planting early and getting a lot of moisture but risking the cold versus planting later and maybe not getting enough early moisture. I play it safe by plowing during the first two weeks of May. I like to have everything plowed and planted by May 15."

As George spoke, Jesse realized he was doing what Mr. McKinley had been doing. He was teaching Jesse and Billy about operating a cotton farm. It occurred to Jesse that George and Lucy Fryer were nice people, just like the McKinleys, only they were different. They had different personalities than Mr. and Mrs. McKinley, but in their own way, they were just as nice.

In the early spring, before planting time, there was plenty of work to do. In exchange for farming for the Fryers, Jesse's family was given the opportunity to plant their own crop. The Washington family had rented twenty acres in exchange for their labor, on which they could plant whatever crop they believed would perform the best. They decided to stay with the plan of the farm and produce cotton while maintaining a one-acre garden for their own fruit and vegetable consumption. Since Mr. Fryer liked to put his crop out later, Jesse had an opportunity to put out his own family's crop before planting for the Fryers.

The Washington family planted a crop of corn, beans, potatoes, tomatoes, and squash. Because the climate was mild in the Robinson area, the vegetable crops could be planted in late March, after the last frost. This gave the Washington family several weeks to plant their crops before planting the Fryers' cotton. Jesse also planted several acres of vegetables for the Fryers in April and still had plenty of time to get the Washington crops planted before planting the cotton for the Fryers.

As the Washington family blended into the community, Jesse found friendship in several young men from Robinson. Two of them, Mike and Jason, were White, and one of them, Andrew, was Black. Jesse had first met Mike through Elijah, when they traveled to Dallas to hear the band at the Phrygian Club. They began spending time together, which attracted attention in the

Robinson community. Within three weeks of Jesse's arrival in town, he began to "hang out" with these young men. The quartet began visiting a popular local bar in the town of Rosenthal, not far from Robinson. Soon they acquired the nickname Checkerboard because they comprised two White men and two Black men. Most in the community found them amiable and amusing. Although Black people did not ordinarily socialize with White persons, there were exceptions. Notwithstanding the warm reception the young men typically received, there were some who found their association offensive and distasteful. Some of them were members of the Ku Klux Klan.

Perhaps it was the novelty of seeing Black and White persons interacting socially that was of interest in the community. A novelty of such interest that those in the bar would sometimes sit near the young men to overhear their conversations and sometimes join in the laughter. Soon Jesse's sense of humor had become an attraction in the bar. He would tell jokes he had learned over the years. He possessed an uncanny ability to tell them in a particularly amusing way, which those in the bar found quite entertaining.

On weeknights after work, Jesse and Cassie would get together, usually on Tuesdays and Thursdays. They would also see each other on Saturdays and Sundays. Jesse usually went to the McKinley farm to see Cassie, and they would stay up late and talk, as they did when Jesse still lived there. Now that Jesse and Cassie were engaged, Jesse would sometimes spend the night at the Williams house, and Cassie would sometimes stay overnight at the Washington house. Although Jesse missed Cassie on the days he didn't see her, he enjoyed spending evenings with his male friends.

One Wednesday evening in April, Jesse, Andrew, Mike, and Jason decided to drive into the popular bar in Rosenthal. Jesse never knew if it had a name because there was no sign above the door. Most people called it the Watering Hole. They entered the establishment and made their way to their favorite table on the left side of the bar. As they took their seats, a pretty young waitress came to the table. She looked at Jesse and Andrew inquisitively. She had just moved to Rosenthal from Waco and was surprised to see the young men break the segregation laws. "Howdy, gents. What can I do ya fir?"

Mike laughed. "Do you mean what can you do for us?"

The waitress laughed and said, "Yeah, that too."

"We'd like a pitcher of beer," said Mike. "You got any of that Anheuser-Busch beer from Saint Louis?"

"You mean Budweiser? Yeah, we have it. Is that what you want?"

"Yes, a pitcher of that," replied Mike.

"How old are you guys? You look young. I'm Anna, by the way. You know, Texas has a drinking age minimum of twenty-one. You guys don't look twenty-one to me. And also, do they allow uh . . . coloreds in White places here in Rosenthal?" Anna looked at Jesse, then Andrew. She held the palm of her hand toward them as if to say, *wait a minute*. "It doesn't bother me. I just know in Waco you would get in trouble for coming into a White bar."

Jason leaned back in his chair. "It's OK, Anna. Larry lets us come in and buy beer."

Anna's brow formed a slight frown. She pointed toward the kitchen behind her with her thumb. "Larry, the owner?"

Mike nodded. "Yeah. We come in here all the time, and he serves us."

Anna nodded. "I'll have to check with him. This is my first day here and I can't afford to lose my job."

Anna took the notepad from the pocket in her flowing skirt. "Do you guys want any food?"

Andrew looked up at Anna. "We usually get hamburgers and beer."

"Y'all want hamburgers and a pitcher of beer? I will have to check with Larry on the beer. If he says it is OK, then I'll bring a pitcher out."

Anna turned around and walked to the kitchen. Mike looked

at Jesse and laughed. "Now that is a pretty girl. Not as pretty as Cassie, but she's pretty."

Jesse laughed. "Cassie is the prettiest there is. Not that I'm partial or anything." The others joined in the laughter.

Jason leaned forward on his elbow and lowered his voice. The others leaned in to hear him better. "Jesse, have you ever thought about what it would be like to be married to a White woman?"

Jesse looked startled. "Oh, no. Not me. I got Cassie. She is all I need."

Jason looked at Andrew. "How about you? Have you ever wondered what it would be like to be married to a White woman?"

Andrew shook his head emphatically. "No, sir. I never think about that. When I see a White woman, I look the other way. I don't want any White woman to think I am being forward. That's dangerous for a Black man."

Jason nodded. "That's probably a good idea. When these White guys get the notion that a White woman likes a Black guy, it can be dangerous for the Black guy."

As they talked, the kitchen doors swung open and Larry walked over to the table with a pitcher of beer in one hand and a plate with four hamburgers in the other. "Good afternoon, boys. What do you think of my new waitress, Anna? Ain't she a sweetheart?"

Jesse and Andrew both avoided the conversation about Anna. Mike laughed. "Yeah, she's nice."

Larry set the pitcher of beer on the table, then set the tray of hamburgers on the table next to the beer. "She didn't mean to be pushy. She didn't know I allow you to have beer in here."

Jesse spoke up. "No, she was fine. She was just doing her job to make sure it was OK to serve us."

Larry stood up and put his hands on his waist. "You guys are gonna like that hamburger. I butchered that one myself."

Jesse took one of the burgers from the tray in the middle of the table. "Thanks, Larry."

"It's no problem. From now on, Anna will bring your beers. She just didn't know I allow it."

Jason asked, "What would happen if the law found out you gave us beer? We don't want you to get shut down."

Larry shook his head. "We don't really have any law officers here. The ones in Waco never come down here. If they did, they would be more likely to do something about violating the segregation laws than about serving beer to minors."

The boys became cautiously quiet. They were unsure what Sam meant about segregation laws. *I wonder if he really wants us here,* thought Jesse.

After eating the hamburgers and drinking two pitchers of Budweiser, the young men leaned back in their chairs and watched Anna wait on tables. Now and then, Anna would glance over, though her attention seemed focused primarily on Jesse.

Jason set his beer mug on the table. "Hey, I got an idea. Let's go night fishin' on the Brazos. There's largemouth bass and catfish that feed now. The largemouth come up into the shallows at night. I like to fish from the shore with a lantern. They're attracted to the light. It's good fishin'."

Jesse nodded. "Oh yeah, I have done that a lot. The largemouth hunt food with their eyes. They like the light at night. I got four poles in the back of the truck. I took Billy, Cassie, and Jenny fishing yesterday. I also have some huge night crawlers."

Jason asked, "Do you think the crawlers are still alive in the back of the truck?"

Jesse nodded. "Oh yeah. They are in a big tub filled with dirt. It has been cool, so they should be fine."

Andrew grinned and stood up. "Let's do this."

The men paid, then left the bar and climbed into the truck except for Jesse, who went to the front to start the engine. The well-tuned engine started on the first turn as usual. Jesse walked around to the driver's door, jumped into the seat, released the brake, made a U-turn, then headed north toward a bend in the river near Waco. They were traveling to Jesse's favorite night fishing spot.

After driving for about fifteen minutes Jesse pulled off onto a dirt trail that wound down to the river. The truck bounced along on a horse trail that was filled with dips and mounds. Finally, after driving slowly for a half mile, Jesse parked the truck on the bank of the river. He turned off the engine and everyone climbed out.

Jesse reached in the back of the truck and pulled out the four cane fishing poles. He lit the lantern and sat it on the corner of the tailgate. He then took two tin cans, reached into the tub, and pulled out a handful of night crawlers. He put them in one can, then reached in the tub a second time and placed a handful of night crawlers in the other can. He took the lantern from its position and the four men walked to the edge of the river. They all sat on the bank and Jesse gave each of them a pole. He put one can of worms between Jason and Andrew and the other can of worms between Mike and himself.

Mike took a large night crawler from the tin can and put it on his hook. "Do you come here often, Jesse?"

Jesse nodded. "It's my favorite place for fishing at night. I've caught a lot of fish here. Ya have to watch for rattlers, though. There's lots around here. I seen a den on the other side of the river one day that was filled with rattlers. There were hundreds of 'em."

Andrew overheard the conversation. "They can't cross the river, can they?"

Jesse laughed. "Oh yeah, rattlesnakes are great swimmers. We'll probably see a few cross the river tonight since we have a full moon."

Andrew laughed. "Well, if I see one coming at me, I'm gonna be back in that pickup truck before it gets near me."

All four young men laughed. This was a good time for the men. A time of conversation and fishing. Jesse caught the first fish, though it was a catfish. "Looks like the cats are out tonight. They ain't bass, but they're good eatin.' That thing is huge." Jesse held the catfish up so everyone could see it.

Andrew said, "Nice catch, Jesse. That fish is twenty-four inches at least. That's one of the biggest catfish I ever seen."

Jesse grinned. "That's lunch tomorrow."

The men sat quietly on the bank fishing. Suddenly, Jesse said, "Look there is a rattler crossin' the river right now. Look toward the moonlight. We can only see the one in the moonlight, but there'd probably be a lot in the river right now where we can't see 'em because of the dark. Sometimes at night I will see one swimming toward me and the lantern. I usually yell and smack the water. The snake turns and swims the other way. They don't like going where people are."

Mike said, "Jesse, didn't you say you got bit by a rattler once?"

"I did. I was in the hospital for a couple of days."

"How did it happen?"

"One day I was running along the creek early in the morning and it bit me."

"Wow," said Andrew. "Did you see it before it bit?"

"Only for a second. But I didn't have time to do anything."

Jason stood up and walked down by the water. "Hey, Jesse, I have been meaning to ask you something. Do you do anything to make the White girls like you?"

"No, I do just the opposite. I try not to give them any attention."

"Do you know that some of them like you? They like to be at the general store on Friday afternoons so they can see you."

Jesse nodded. "I heard that. I don't like it, though. I think it's dangerous for me that they do that."

Jason dropped his line in the water. "I was thinking the same thing. Those girls shouldn't do that and they shouldn't talk about it. Somebody might think you are doing something to cause them to like you."

"Yeah. There ain't really anything I can do about it, though. I don't even talk to those girls except when I am talking to Rachel about the supplies."

Jason paused for a moment reflectively. "I wonder if it would be better if someone else picked up the supplies. It's known throughout town that these White women are enthralled with you. That could be dangerous for you, Jesse."

Jason's words rang loudly to Jesse. He knew Jason was right. It might be better if someone else picked up the supplies on Fridays. But who? He couldn't send Billy. The girls might turn their attention to him. Then *he* would be in trouble.

The young men caught over a dozen fish, mostly bass. As they drove back to Robinson, Jesse continued to reflect on the conversation and the warning about the White women. Jason was riding in the cab with Jesse. After a time, Jesse asked, "Jason, how'd you hear about the girls at the general store?"

"Quite a few people in town have been talking about it. It has some of the men angry. I heard that last Friday there were about ten girls in there waiting to see you. That's bad, Jesse. These White guys get mad. Maybe Mike and I could pick up the supplies for you for a few weeks. Just 'til things quiet down."

Jesse shook his head. "I couldn't let you do that. That's too much to ask."

"I'm really worried, Jesse. These men can get pretty mean. Just let us do it for the next two weeks. Maybe by then the girls will settle down."

"Well, at least let me pay you for it."

"No, Jesse. It's fine. If they ask where you are, we'll tell 'em you have business at the farm and won't be coming in anymore."

Jesse nodded. "Thanks, Jason. This is a good thing you're doin' for me. But please let Rachel know what is going on. I don't want her to worry."

"OK. I just don't want anything bad to happen."

The following Friday afternoon, Mike and Jason drove Jesse's truck into Robinson to pick up the supplies. It was a warm afternoon. As they pulled up to the front of the general store, they noticed a dozen girls sitting on the front porch of the store watching Jesse's truck approach. As Mike and Jason got out, one of the girls asked, "Where's Jesse? Why are you driving his truck?"

Jason answered, "Jesse had business out on the farm he couldn't get away from, so he hired us to pick up the supplies."

The same young woman asked, "Are you working for him?"

"I guess so."

As they entered the store, Jason and Mike could hear the girls giggling. One of them said, "I told you that Jesse is a stud. He's got White guys working for him."

Another said, "I would give anything to see Jesse loading seed bags without his shirt today." The young women laughed.

The following week, when Jason and Mike arrived at the general store to pick up the supplies, there were no women in sight. Mike laughed. "Well, I guess they think Jesse is better-looking than the two of us combined."

Jason smiled. "I guess it worked. That's the important thing."

The following week Jesse decided to return to the store. When he arrived, he saw three women at the store. This did not cause much concern for him. As he paid for the supplies, Rachel said, "We haven't seen you lately, Jesse. Have you been busy?"

"Yes, ma'am, I have. Didn't Mike and Jason tell you I wouldn't be in for a while?"

"Yes, but they didn't say why. How's your family?"

Jesse smiled. "We are all OK. We're all busy on the farm."

Rachel walked over to the door and held it open for Jesse as he carried a bag of seed. "Will we see you next week?"

Jesse passed through the door and loaded the seed into the bed of his truck. "It depends what's happening on the farm."

"OK. You know all the girls really like it when you come in."

Jesse paused, "I know. I don't think they should do that."

"Do what?"

"I think it isn't good that they try to see me when I come in."

"They don't mean any harm. They're just having fun."

"I know, ma'am, but that isn't good for a colored man. People won't like it."

Rachel paused and leaned against the truck. "You think people will get mad because the White girls come in to see you?"

"Yes, ma'am. White folks don't like that kind of thing."

"Oh, I see what you mean. Is that why you didn't come in the last two weeks?"

"Yes, ma'am. I don't want no trouble."

"I never thought of that, Jesse. Maybe it would be better if I tell them you weren't here this week."

"Yes, ma'am. I would be obliged if you did."

Rachel cast her gaze downward. "I think it's partly my fault. I told them you come in every Friday around four o'clock, and I told them how handsome you are. I didn't think they would come around to see you like they did. They just come in and buy soda, but I know they didn't think it would cause harm."

"I thought Julie told people. Anyhow, it's OK. I know you didn't mean any harm."

"Julie told them first, then after that I figured everybody already knew, so it didn't hurt to tell them when you come in."

"It's OK. I wish they didn't know I come here, though."

"Could you come on a different day? Like on a Thursday? Maybe if you come on different days, they won't know when to come around to see you."

Jesse nodded. "I'll do that. I'll come in on different days. That way they won't know when I am coming, and they won't be here to find me."

Jesse walked around to the front of the truck to crank the engine. "Thank you, Rachel. I will see you next time, on Thursday."

Rachel waved. "OK, Jesse. I'll see you next time."

Jesse climbed into his truck, put it in gear, and drove away.

CHAPTER
THIRTEEN

APRIL WAS PLEASANT in the Waco area. Jesse always liked the spring season. Although Central Texas did not suffer severe cold in the winter, spring and summer were Jesse's favorite seasons. He enjoyed the heat. It was dry heat, so the hot weather was not uncomfortable except during the occasional extreme temperatures.

George, Billy, and Jesse would meet by the barn every morning before they started working, to share a pot of coffee. George would tell them the latest news, usually about the war in Europe. England had entered the war in 1914, which was of great interest to him, considering his roots in Britain.

George puffed on his pipe as he leaned against the barn. "That war in Europe is causing tremendous devastation and loss of life. I received a letter from my aunt. One of my friends from childhood died on the battlefield in Belgium. She said he was hit by a sniper while crossing a field. He is the third person I knew who died in this horrible war."

Jesse rubbed the side of his neck with his hand. "How long you think this war's gonna last?"

George shook his head. "I don't know. It's bad. Tens of millions of people have died already."

"What are they fightin' about?" asked Billy. "Why would they kill so many people?"

"There were disputes and minor conflicts throughout Europe in the early part of this century. But it was the assassination of Archduke Franz Ferdinand in 1914 that caused the war to escalate. It still amazes me that people can fight each other that way."

Jesse interjected, "Sometimes I think about signin' up."

George frowned. "Why would you say that? Are you really thinking about joining?"

"I been thinkin' about it, but not much. Hearing you talk about it got me thinkin' that maybe I should join."

"Many Black men join the army. It's a way of getting room and board as a benefit, and a small wage for spending money. Plus, they get medical benefits. But it's dangerous and very difficult. Many men go in but never come out."

Jesse listened intently. "When did England get into the war?"

"On August 4, 1914. It has been the worst war in history. It is the place where there is no God."

Billy replied, "That sounds bad. Why do men join up?"

"Most places conscript them."

Billy's expression grew puzzled. "What is conscript?"

George paused a moment. "You probably call it the draft."

"You mean they have to join. They don't get to choose?"

"Yes, that's common in Europe. That was done here during the Civil War."

The thought of the Civil War attracted Jesse's attention. He thought of the stories he had heard from the older men who had been slaves. "Do ya think the war might come here?"

George took a sip of his coffee. "I sure hope not. I think it won't because that part of the world is so far away. It would be too hard to bring military equipment to the United States."

George stood upright and poured the last of the coffee in his cup onto the ground. "I suppose we better get to work. That field won't plow itself."

Jesse thought about Cassie, as he usually did when working in the field. On Thursday afternoon he climbed into his truck and drove to the general store in Robinson. He got out of the truck and walked into the store. Rachel was the only person there.

"Hi, Jesse. How are you doing?"

"I'm fine, ma'am."

Rachel smiled. "Well, this might work. As you can see, there's no one here."

She took the list and began pointing at the items on it. Jesse threw them on the cart.

"This is like the first day I came in. There was no one here except you and Julie."

By changing the days he came into the general store, Jesse was able to avoid drawing attention to himself. It seemed a safer way to proceed. For him, it was a necessary plan to avoid confrontation with the White men.

Jesse was very busy during the plowing season. He would awaken before dawn, get dressed, then prepare his equipment by the light of a lantern. He would generally be plowing at first light and would have several hours in before nine o'clock. He would try to finish his day early so that on some days he could visit Cassie at the McKinley farm. Although he was always tired after plowing the entire day, he would find time to visit Cassie at least twice during the week and on Saturday and Sunday.

Jesse operated a plow that had four blades, allowing him to plow four rows at one time. He had to stand on the plow to provide sufficient weight to hold it down as Betsy, the mule, pulled it forward. On a good day, with soft dirt, he could plow an acre in a little over an hour. By putting in seventy hours each week, he could plow fifty acres.

Henry and Billy also operated a plow, but they didn't usually start until around 8:00 a.m. They would still meet George in the morning, and Jesse would take a break from plowing to join them unless he was plowing on the opposite side of the farm. Henry and Billy usually plowed the smaller field, where they grew potatoes, strawberries, peppers, green beans, onions, and squash. A single-blade plow was adequate for plowing the vegetable garden. On occasion Jesse would use the single-blade plow and Henry would use the four-blade plow.

George would generally work around the farm during the day and occasionally operated a plow. He preferred working with the animals, though he spent quite a bit of time in the Concord grape vineyard. He also maintained the yard around the house. He would rotate the cattle in the yard every week to keep the lawn trimmed.

Lucy Fryer worked in the house most of the time. She would occasionally come outside with a pitcher of lemonade or iced tea for the men when they took a break. Jesse noticed that Mr. Simon, a neighbor, often stopped by the house to talk with Lucy. Jesse thought this odd and wondered if it bothered George. Although he never commented about it, George seemed to notice, especially since Mr. Simon never came around when George was working near the house.

Mr. Simon was a tall slender man with a full head of hair. Appearing to be in his late fifties with slightly graying sideburns, he had a nervous demeanor, almost as if he was concerned about an unseen risk. He seldom smiled except when he saw Lucy. He seemed to avoid George and when he was forced to greet him it was usually a simple *hey* or *hey, George.*

One morning in mid-April, shortly before lunch, Jesse was standing on the four-blade plow being pulled by Betsy. The dirt was soft, so the plowing was easy. Jesse leaned forward onto the handle of the plow to assure himself that he was pressing as firmly as possible, though such gestures had no real impact. The soft, well-used soil turned easily under the blades. Jesse thought of the need to have this field lie fallow in the rotation on the farm. He knew that fields were to be left fallow every five years for a period of two years. That prevented overuse of the soil and allowed it to gather nutrients that were stolen by the cotton plants. His biceps bulged as he thrust downward onto the plow in his dialogue with nature.

Jesse was plowing the edge of a field next to one of tall winter grass immediately to his right. As he moved forward, something caught his eye about two hundred yards ahead in the grass. It was a quick movement that he barely saw and wasn't even sure he had seen. Unconcerned, in part because of the distance between his location and that of the movement, and in part because of his uncertainty that it had occurred at all, Jesse continued to focus his attention on the plow. He looked closely at the dirt below his feet as the blade fashioned it into a dry but soft wave. Its movement fascinated him.

Suddenly, another motion to his right distracted him. It was a fleeting movement as before, only this time it was closer. Perhaps one hundred yards ahead. Once again, Jesse's attention was heightened, and again he was uncertain whether he actually saw anything move at all. Nonetheless, he focused his eyes ahead across the horizon for any sight of movement. Suddenly, he saw it again, though even closer than before. Now he was more certain than ever that movement had occurred.

Jesse pulled Betsy to a halt as he stepped off the plow. He walked forward to the place where he thought he saw the movement. He looked around at the rows of tall grass but did not see anything unusual. He walked around in the field, looking for an animal, though he did not know what animal he should be trying to find. After walking through the grass for about five minutes, Jesse finally concluded that he may have imagined the movement. It seemed odd that he could be mistaken three times, but he saw no sign of an animal.

Looking across the field, he thought how good it would be to have his own land. He thought of how wonderful it would be if

Cassie were his wife and they had a farm together. A small one at first, and a larger one later.

Suddenly, Jesse heard a loud snarl as a cougar flew through the air in front of him and landed on Betsy's haunches. Betsy bucked and kicked. Jesse looked at the ground for a rock to throw but didn't see any. He didn't have a staff with him, so he ran forward and hit the cougar several times in the back between the front legs with his fist. The animal snarled but continued to tear into the flesh of the mule with its claws and teeth. Jesse then grabbed the cougar by the tail and jerked as hard as he could, pulling it off Betsy. Before the cat hit the ground, it attacked Jesse. Jesse began swinging at the cat with all his might, landing two solid blows to the head. The cougar retreated, then looked back at Jesse, growling. Jesse bolted directly toward the lion while roaring like a bear and waving his arms in the air. He was prepared to fight this animal to the death if need be. The cougar turned and retreated into the field.

Jesse felt a sharp pain on his left side and arm. Looking down, he saw blood. He knew he had sustained significant injuries from the attack. He unhooked Betsy from the plow and walked her to the barn. As he was securing the mule in a stall, George walked in. "What happened to you? I saw you walking across the yard with Betsy . . . all bloody."

"Cougar. That's why we came up to the stable. He attacked Betsy while we were plowing. I jerked it off by the tail, so it turned on me. Got me pretty good."

George took hold of Jesse's arm. "You better come over to the house. We need to clean those wounds and bandage you up."

Jesse and George walked over to the well next to the main house. George retrieved a towel from the house and came back out. Lucy followed him.

George moistened the towel using the pump, then gave it to Jesse. Jesse wiped his wounds to stop the bleeding. Lucy went back into the house to fetch some hot water.

George gave Jesse a dry towel. "We might have to shoot it if it comes around here again. It will kill our livestock."

Jesse nodded. "I was thinking the same thing, sir."

"It probably lives in one of the ravines. The mountain lion, which most people call a cougar, has a hundred-mile hunting range. They have been known to travel more than a hundred miles in a day."

"How do they know that?" asked Jesse.

"There was a cougar in the San Antonio Zoo that escaped wearing a collar. Later that same day the cougar was found hiding in a barn on a farm near Waco. That cat had traveled two hundred miles in a few hours."

"I wonder what it was looking for."

"The zoologists said it was from the Waco area and just wanted to come back home when it escaped. There are ravines here where they live. There is no way to know where this one came from, but we can't let it destroy people's livestock."

Lucy came back out with a pan of hot water and set it on a picnic table near the well. She went back into the house and came out a few minutes later with a bottle of wine and a bottle of laudanum. Lucy took a cup from the pocket of her apron and gave it to Jesse with the bottle of laudanum. "Drink half a cup of this, Jesse. It will make the pain stop."

Jesse did as instructed. George poured the bottle of wine into the pan of hot water.

"What's that for?" asked Jesse.

George stirred the hot water with a wooden spoon Lucy had brought out. "We need to sterilize the wound. Those are deep gashes. We might have to stitch you up."

Lucy took a dry towel and put it in the pan of hot water. "Jesse, lay down on the ground."

Lucy took the towel soaked in hot water and wine and applied the solution liberally to the wound site.

Henry, Billy, and Martha came out of the bungalow to investigate. "What happened to you?" asked Henry.

Jesse winced as Lucy applied the hot water and wine to his wound. Lucy explained. "Jesse was attacked by a mountain lion. The lion got Betsy too. We're going to take care of Betsy as soon as we are finished with Jesse. George, I think you should go into Waco and fetch Dr. Connor. I think Jesse's going to need stitches."

George nodded and walked over to his Model T truck. He cranked the engine, then drove to Waco.

Lucy finished cleaning Jesse's wound. "Just stay on the ground until George gets back with Dr. Connor. If you move around, it might start bleeding again."

Lucy and Henry went into the stable to care for Betsy. Martha stayed by the well. "Jesse, you sure have a lot of fights with animals. Last year it was a rattlesnake and now it's a lion."

Jesse laughed. "Ouch. Don't make me laugh, it hurts."

Martha laughed. "OK."

Henry and Lucy came back from the stable. Henry walked over to Jesse. "How are you doin', Jesse?"

"I'm OK. That laudanum really works, but it makes me sleepy too."

After about an hour George drove into the yard. He climbed out of the truck and walked over to Jesse. "Dr. Connor wasn't in. I went to four doctors' offices. None of them would come out. I went back over to Dr. Connor's office and left a message for him to come out."

"Why wouldn't the other doctors come out?" asked Lucy.

George shook his head. "They only treat White people. If Dr. Connor doesn't come, we can take Jesse to the hospital at Baylor."

Jesse remembered Elijah telling him that there was no real difference between Black people and White people except for skin color. He wondered why the White doctors wouldn't treat him if that was true.

Eventually, they helped Jesse up and took him to the

Washington bungalow. He lay down on his bed and waited for Dr. Connor to come. About an hour later a shiny black surrey pulled up in front of the Fryer house. "Over here," shouted Henry from the front porch.

Dr. Connor entered the bungalow and was led into the bedroom where Jesse was lying on the bed. He examined the wound. "You will need a few stitches on your arm. The wounds on your chest won't need stitches, but you'll need to keep them clean. You shouldn't do any farmwork for at least two weeks."

Jesse protested, "I can't stop working for two weeks. This is plowing season. If we don't get the cotton planted now, it will be too late."

Dr. Connor did not respond. He poured some laudanum into a cup and gave it to Jesse. "Here, drink this. It'll help. Close your eyes and try to relax."

Dr. Connor took a needle and thread from his medical bag and threaded the needle. Jesse watched inquisitively. "What's that for?"

"You have open wounds on your arm. I need to suture them so the hypodermis isn't exposed. It looks like you blocked the swipe of the mountain lion with your arm. That might have saved your life. If you hadn't blocked it, the claws might have penetrated a vital organ. Looking at the claw marks on your arm, it appears the mountain lion partially retracted its claws while striking."

"What does that mean?"

"This mountain lion wasn't trying to kill you. You were interfering with its food source, namely the mule, but the lion didn't see you as an enemy. It saw you as a competitor."

"What? You mean the cougar saw me as another cougar?"

Dr. Connor nodded. "Maybe, or as another animal, but not an enemy. I studied veterinary medicine before I went to medical school. There's a lot we don't know about the animal kingdom, but we learn by looking at small details. I would say this lion was challenging you, not trying to kill you. Maybe he had been watching you for weeks and saw you as friendly. It's hard to say. Animals don't think like humans. They lack the ability to ask why something is happening. They can only think about what is happening or what happened."

Martha laughed. "So, you mean if an animal sees something strange, it doesn't ask why it is strange? It can only ask what is happening?"

Dr. Connor laughed. "That's what I believe. To ask why something is happening requires three-dimensional thought. Animals have two-dimensional thoughts. That's why nothing usually surprises them. They just accept it as reality and respond."

Jesse coughed and held his chest. "But I remember hearing of a pack of wolves hidin' and surroundin' their prey. Wouldn't that be thinking more like people?"

"Don't get me wrong. Animals are very intelligent, but they don't have the ability to see things abstractly the way people can. They don't have the ability to reflect on their own consciousness. They don't have the ability to think about what they are thinking or doing."

Jesse found Dr. Connor's words fascinating. The more he reflected on this concept, the more fascinating it became. He thought about the cougar hiding in the grass before the attack. Was it trying to give Jesse a glimpse of it before attacking? If so, would the cougar be reflecting on itself? In fact, just knowing to hide would require the animal to reflect on itself and what it was doing. "Dr. Connor, before the cougar attacked, it stalked us and tried to hide. Wouldn't trying to hide mean it was thinkin' about itself and where it was and what its victim saw?"

Dr. Connor laughed. "You're thinking deep, Jesse. Something fascinating about animals is that most of them have one or two talents that humans don't. Those talents are unique to that species. One of the most amazing, which far exceeds anything humans can do, is the ability of cats, dogs, and birds to navigate. They can find a location hundreds of miles away, even if they have never seen the route. But that doesn't mean those animals are smarter than people. It's more like an instinct. We don't know exactly how they do it."

Dr. Connor finished the suture placement and laid his instruments in a metal basin. "There is one thing you need to know. When a predator like a cougar injures its prey but can't complete the kill, it will continue to hunt it. It's almost like an obsession. You should expect that the lion will come back and try to kill the mule unless it gets distracted by one of the other animals on the farm."

"How soon will it come back?" asked Henry.

"Probably tonight. Now that it is aware of human inhabitants, it would likely try to come under cover of night."

Jesse looked at Henry. "We need to put all the animals in the barn and make sure all the doors and windows in the barn are locked tonight." Henry nodded.

"Try to rest as much as you can. Try not to do any work for two weeks. If you can't go that long, under no circumstances work before five days have passed."

"I'll try."

Everyone left the room so Jesse could sleep. He looked out the window and saw the sun was high overhead. He assumed it was about three o'clock. He laid his head back on the pillow.

The next thing Jesse knew, he was awakening to sounds in the barn. The animals seemed restless. It was dark outside. He got out of bed and walked into the sitting room. Henry was coming out of his bedroom. Billy was sleeping on the couch in the sitting room. Jesse lit a lantern. Billy sat up and rubbed his eyes. "What's going on?"

Henry replied, "There is a ruckus in the barn. We need to check it out."

The three men put on their jackets and walked over to the gun rack. Henry took down two Winchester 1912, pump-action, 12-gauge shotguns and handed one to Jesse; the other he gave to Billy. He took a third 12-gauge down from the rack and laid a box of shotgun shells on the table. Each took six shells and loaded the guns. Jesse picked up the flashlight from the table. Henry and William ran out the front door and went out to the barn. Jesse hobbled a distance behind. They opened the barn door and entered. Jesse shone the light around the barn and into the stalls. "All the doors are locked. I wonder what riled the animals."

Henry checked the back door of the barn. "Whatever it was, it isn't here now. Why don't we go back to . . ."Suddenly, Henry stopped talking. He was looking up at the top of the haystack. "What is that up there? It looks like a big animal."

Jesse shone the flashlight to the top of the haystack in the loft. Lying on a bale of hay, at the peak of the haystack, was the cougar, looking down at the men.

"Don't shoot inside the barn unless he attacks," said Henry. "The buckshot will blow a hole in the wall."

Jesse shone the light on the walls at the top of the ceiling. "How did he get in here? All the doors were locked." At the top of the barn, by the peak of the roof, Jesse could see an open window. "That must be how he got in. But how did he get that far up? That must be forty feet up."

Suddenly the cougar jumped and ran straight up the wall to a large beam adjacent to the open window at the top of the barn. The cougar rested on the beam and looked back at the men on the ground.

Henry pointed his shotgun at the large cat. "Is that the cougar that attacked you and Betsy?"

"Yeah, I think so."

The cougar jumped onto the ledge of the window, then jumped through the window onto a roof that covers an extended portion of the building below. The men ran outside the barn and around to the side where the window was located. The cougar was nowhere to be seen.

Jesse turned and began walking back to the front of the barn. "I better go up and close that window so the cougar can't get inside again."

Henry followed him. "You better not, Jesse. You were attacked by that cougar today. You might tear your stitches. I'll go up and close it."

"Be careful. You don't want to fall, and that lion might lunge at you if he is still by the window."

Henry climbed the ladder up to the hayloft. He then pulled up the ladder and leaned it against the wall next to the open window. Jesse was shining the flashlight so he could see. Henry climbed the ladder and closed and locked the window. After he climbed down the men stood in the door of the barn. Jesse remained puzzled by the actions of the cougar. "Why didn't the cougar attack Betsy? And why did he stare at me all the time it was sitting in the loft? Was it because I had the flashlight?"

Billy put his shotgun on safety. "Dr. Connor said that when a cougar attacks its prey but can't complete the kill, it will continue to hunt it. So, Betsy was the prey, right?"

Henry also put his shotgun on safety. "Yeah, that's right."

Billy seemed puzzled. "So, why did the cougar not attack Betsy when it was in the barn, before we got there?"

For a few moments, everyone remained silent. Finally, Henry said, "Maybe because Betsy isn't the one he is hunting after all."

Jesse frowned. "What do you mean?"

Henry continued, "Maybe Betsy isn't the one the cougar is hunting."

"Then who is he hunting?"

Henry closed the barn door and locked it. "Betsy wasn't the only one attacked."

Jesse started walking toward the bungalow. "Are you sayin' the cougar is huntin' me?"

"It looks like it. The cougar ain't interested in Betsy. But it stared at you all the time it was in the barn. I think it's you the cougar's huntin'."

His father's words troubled Jesse. "But what about what Dr.

Connor said? Remember, he said he didn't think it wanted to kill me."

Henry shook his head. "No one knows for sure. He was just telling you about one possibility."

"If he is huntin' me, I have no choice. I have to kill him."

The men entered the bungalow and leaned their shotguns against the wall by the front door. Jesse sat down at the table. "So, if that's right, how do we get the cougar to come around so we can kill it?"

"I don't think we have to worry about it. I think the cougar is going to come to us. I don't think we'll see it again tonight, though. Jesse, you better get back in bed. You need to get well."

The men went back to bed. The night was bright from the moon's reflection. Jesse lay on the bed looking out the window until he finally fell asleep. Several hours later he awakened with a strange feeling that something was wrong. He looked out the window, and there was the cougar, staring at him from outside. Jesse held perfectly still as he tried to focus to make sure he was seeing clearly. He noticed a little bit of light coming from under the window; then he remembered he had left it open an inch. Concerned the lion might break the window to get to him, he slowly crept out of bed to get a shotgun from the living room. He took one of the shotguns and went back into the bedroom then looked out the window. The cougar was gone.

Jesse lay back in bed. He put the gun on safety and went to sleep with the barrel pointing toward the window and resting across his abdomen. A few hours later Jesse awakened to the sound of a shotgun blast. It was light outside, and Jesse estimated it was about 7:00 a.m. He walked into the other room, where Henry and Billy were grabbing their shotguns and running out the door.

Jesse followed them and saw George in the middle of the yard with a shotgun, looking toward the cotton field.

"What happened?" asked Henry.

George began walking toward the field. "I woke up this

morning, looked out the window, and saw that mountain lion lying on the ground there under Jesse's bedroom window. I picked up my shotgun and went out the door as quietly as I could. It must have heard me anyway because all of a sudden it took off running toward that field. I fired a shot, but I don't think I hit him square. I would have if I had my rifle, but a shotgun just isn't that accurate at a distance. I think he got a few pieces of buckshot, though, because he jumped as he ran."

Henry began walking with George. "We better track it. It was in the barn last night. It got in by the window, way up at the peak of the barn."

"How did it get way up there?"

"That cat can run straight up the side of the wall. That is how it got out. Then it jumped down on the lower roof. By the time we got back outside, it was gone. That's the last we saw it."

Jesse, who was following the men with Billy, said, "Not really the last time. I woke up later, about three o'clock, I suppose, and the lion was staring in at me through the window."

George replied, "That is a scary story, but it makes sense. It was sleeping right below your window, partly under the house, when I saw it this morning. Have you fellows ever tracked before?"

"No, but I've heard about it," replied Henry.

George motioned for Jesse and Billy to catch up. "OK, tracking is meant to find the animal you are hunting. I noticed blood on the ground, so the lion is bleeding. I must have hit it better than I thought I did. Right now, the tracks are right in front of me. We should go in a straight line about twenty feet apart. I will follow the tracks, so if you stay with me, we will all be following the same tracks."

The men paused and looked across the ground at the grass that had been depressed. "Ordinarily we would walk about forty feet apart, but this grass is tall. Don't fall behind and keep your guns pointed to the ground with the safety on. The only track we will see here is the compacted grass. So, watch for any unusual formation in the grass."

They began walking forward with their guns pointed toward the ground. "We don't want this cougar to double back on us. Remember, we are tracking a very dangerous animal. If a one-hundred-twenty-pound cougar hits you at forty miles per hour with its claws extended the impact alone could be fatal."

They walked along in silence about twenty feet apart, as George had instructed. Jesse thought about his experience with the mountain lion. He thought it strange that it just looked through the window at him but didn't try to break the glass to get in. He thought it even stranger that the cougar had slept under his bedroom window. He remembered Dr. Connor's comment that the cougar might see Jesse as friendly, and that the cougar wasn't trying to kill him when they fought. Jesse thought how interesting it would be to give the cat food and water and see if, over time, it could become a pet. He knew it wasn't possible because the cougar was too dangerous, but he thought that if he lived alone in the wilderness, he might try to do that to see what would happen.

The men tracked the cougar for over an hour. They couldn't move too quickly or they might not see it and it could attack more easily. Suddenly, Henry held up his hand for everyone to stop. He pointed at something ahead in the grass. He moved forward slowly to investigate. As he got closer, he crouched down a little and turned his gun's safety off. The men all closed in and saw the cougar lying on the ground, not moving. They all pointed their shotguns at it. Finally, George kicked it with his boot. The cougar was lying on its side and looked like it was sleeping. They all stood and looked at the cat. Jesse thought it looked magnificent, even in death. He felt a bond with the cougar. It was a bond he couldn't understand. It was as if he and the dead cougar had something in common.

"Have you men ever eaten cougar?" asked George.

Everyone replied. "No."

"I haven't, but I have eaten African lion meat. It tastes like pork. I heard cougar is about the same. We'll have a barbecue with this one."

Jesse reached down to pick up the lion so he could carry it. Henry said, "No, Jesse. You will tear your stitches. I'll carry it."

Henry bent down and grabbed the cougar by the legs. George took hold of the cougar from the other side and helped Henry hoist it onto his shoulder. Jesse picked up Henry's shotgun and carried his and Henry's back to the bungalow.

Jesse didn't work for two days. He mostly stayed in bed and slept. The injury had drained his strength and he needed time to recover. When he was awake, he thought often about the lion. He couldn't stop thinking about Dr. Connor's comment that maybe the cougar saw Jesse as friendly. *Maybe it wasn't trying to kill me at all. Maybe it was acting like we were friends.* It saddened him a little to think that he would never know the cougar's true intentions.

On the second day of recovery, Jesse decided he was well enough to visit Cassie. He was a little concerned about trying to crank the Model T with his injury. Billy helped him by cranking it for him. Jesse arrived at Cassie's house at around seven thirty. He told her everything that had happened and that on Saturday they were going to have a barbecue with the cougar's meat. He invited Cassie's family. Cassie and Jenny said they would join them, but Cassie's parents thought they would be uncomfortable and chose not to come. It was the second weekend in April, and it was a happy time for Jesse and Cassie.

CHAPTER
FOURTEEN

ON THE FIRST Saturday in May, Jesse had a big day planned. He picked up Cassie at the usual time of 9:00 a.m. and drove to a part of the Brazos River in the countryside, away from people. They were attempting to avoid another confrontation with Steve and the other hoodlums by staying away from the areas where they had previously encountered them.

Jesse pulled the pickup truck off the road onto a grassy area next to the water. Cassie took a picnic basket she had brought and climbed out of the truck. Jesse laid out a clean horse blanket on the ground under a shade tree. They sat down together on the blanket and placed the picnic basket behind them. The air was fresh, and the sound of the flowing water was pleasant.

For some reason, Jesse felt sentimental. He appreciated every breeze, the wonderful smells, and the fresh air. But mostly, he appreciated Cassie's beauty. As they talked, he admired her. Her soft skin and light-green eyes. They were mesmerizing and seductive. He watched her speak. He noticed the way her lips pronounced certain words. Her upper lip moved in a symmetrical form that Jesse had noticed among some people of European descent. He was intrigued. "Cassie, do you know much about your family? I mean your ancestors."

"No, I don't. I know my great-great-grandfather was a French officer in the Revolutionary War. My great-great-grandmother was his maid. Before the War broke out, he was planning to resign his commission and move to Barbados, where he would live in peace and quiet on a plantation with my great-great grandmother. He made a will leaving his entire estate to her in case he died in the war. He died in the war, but because she was a colored woman, she could not own property, so his entire estate went to the commonwealth of Virginia. I think the politicians took it and divided it among themselves. I don't know if all that's true, but it is the story that was passed down through my family."

Jesse laughed. "It has to be true."

"How do you know that?"

Jesse moved forward and placed his finger under her chin. He moved close and kissed her. "How else can you explain an African girl with light-green eyes? You look naughty with those eyes. I mean, really, naughty."

Cassie laughed. "Jesse, you are so bad. I only look naughty because you think naughty. You are like the guy Becky talked about in Sunday youth classes. The guy with evil inclination."

Jesse smiled. "If evil inclination means wanting to cuddle with you, I am guilty for sure."

Cassie and Jesse enjoyed a nice lunch of thinly sliced beef on rye bread with an amazing sauce Cassie had made in the morning. They laughed and joked all afternoon and into the early evening. Finally, Jesse said, "I told the guys we would meet them at the bar in Rosenthal at eight o'clock. We need to run past the house to get cleaned up. We have been in the hot sun all day."

"Why don't we save time and get cleaned up here?" said Cassie. "I have clean clothes in the bag. You're wearing your new white shirt. We just need a bath to wash off the dust."

"Are you saying we should take a bath in the river with no clothes?"

Cassie smiled. "We're engaged to be married. We can do that now."

"You ain't ashamed for me to see you without clothes?"

"I didn't say you are going to see me without clothes. I said we can take a bath. You look the other way while I get undressed and get into the water. Then I will look the other way while you get undressed. But you have to promise you won't get too close to me in the water. We will have plenty of time for that after September 30."

Jesse nodded. "OK, I promise."

Jesse turned and faced the truck while Cassie undressed and walked into the river. When she was neck deep, she said, "OK, you can turn around now."

Jesse turned around and saw Cassie's head above the water. He saw her clothes lying in the grass on the bank of the river. "OK, now you turn around."

Cassie turned away until she heard Jesse dive into the river. Then she turned around. Jesse swam toward her. She said, "OK, that's it. Don't get any closer than three feet while we're disrobed."

"OK," said Jesse. As they swam around three feet from each other, Jesse extended his hand. "Is it OK if we hold hands?"

"Yes, that's OK," replied Cassie. "We just can't touch our bodies. That would not be appropriate."

Jesse was fascinated at how close Cassie was willing to be with him but trusted him to keep his distance in the water. He was tempted as he gazed into her pretty eyes, but he would honor her request and keep his distance.

They swam in the water for about twenty minutes. Finally, Cassie said, "We should be clean now." She held up her hands. "Look, my fingers are wrinkled from the water."

Jesse looked at his hands. "Mine are too."

They both laughed. Then Cassie said, "OK, I'm going to get out now. You know what to do."

Jesse turned away as she climbed out of the river and put on her clothes. Then she said, "OK, now it's your turn. You can come out now." She faced away from the water so Jesse could climb out. He walked up to the bank and was walking out of the river. Suddenly, Cassie turned and looked directly at him. Jesse covered his private parts. Cassie's eyes opened wide, and the pupils dilated as she giggled in astonishment.

Jesse shouted, "Hey! What are you doing? You aren't supposed to look. I didn't look when you climbed out."

Cassie laughed. "You had your chance. You should have taken it. Next time be more alert."

"See, you are bad. I knew those were naughty eyes."

Cassie laughed, then tossed Jesse a towel. She turned her back toward him and said, "It's OK. I promise I won't look again."

Jesse laughed. "Well, now I get to look."

"You will have plenty of looking after we are married. Until then, you will have to take a peek whenever you can." Cassie laughed and jumped in the truck.

Later that evening, Jesse and his companions were seated at a table toward the rear of the bar in Rosenthal where they liked to sit. The room was a large, open space with twenty tables and an area for playing pool. The aroma was pleasing to Jesse. The wood-paneled walls smelled like cedar and the tables and chairs were made of oak. The majority of the people present were White, though some were Black. No one seemed concerned about segregation laws.

Jesse noticed a man he recognized was staring at him from the bar. It was Steve Dixon. Jesse wondered what Steve was doing in Rosenthal. He knew he had a farm near Waco. Eventually, Jesse grew weary of Dixon staring at him, so he shouted across the room. "Is there something you want?"

The room grew silent for a moment. Dixon did not respond. He just kept staring at Jesse, who shook his head and ignored the man. Eventually, Jesse needed to use the restroom. He stood up from the table and walked directly toward the restrooms, which meant passing in front of Steve who continued staring at him. As Jesse passed, Steve suddenly extended his foot, causing Jesse to trip and fall to the floor.

Jesse heard the men at the bar laugh. He stood up slowly and turned toward the young man who had tripped him. Before Jesse could say anything, Steve struck Jesse in the nose with his fist, causing him to fall a second time. Jesse jumped up quickly and ran toward Steve and tackled him, knocking him off the barstool onto the wooden floor with a thud. Almost immediately Jesse was grabbed from behind and pulled up from the floor. His nose was bleeding profusely all over his clothes, destroying his new shirt and overalls.

Steve shouted, "If you get in my way again, I will blow your damned head off."

"What is the matter with you? Do you want trouble?" shouted Jesse.

Steve pulled himself up by hanging onto the bar. He turned toward Jesse, startled that a Black man had tackled him. It simply was not done, and if it was, the consequences could be quite severe, if not fatal.

Jesse lifted his arms abruptly, pushing away the men who were holding him from attacking Steve. "You didn't answer, punk. Do you want trouble? I will give it to you right here and now."

By this time, the entire bar had become silent as everyone looked to see what would happen next. Still astounded that Jesse had tackled him, Steve suddenly realized that Jesse could beat him in a real fight. Uncertain how to proceed, he turned toward the bar, embarrassed but afraid to risk being beaten by a Black man. One of the men with him asked loudly, "What are you doing, Steve? Are you just going to let him get away with that?"

Steve looked at him and said quietly, "Shut up, Joe."

Joe walked over to Steve, stood next to him and whispered,

"What are you doing? This looks bad. It looks like you are afraid of him."

"I told you to shut up. He is a big guy, and I don't want to get dirty. I'll find another way to take care of him."

Joe took a drink of his whiskey. "If you say so. But for you to turn away and not do anything makes you look afraid."

"I told you to shut up. I meant it. In a few days, everyone will know who's in charge."

"What?" Joe looked puzzled, then nodded. "OK."

Jesse went into the restroom and tried to wipe the blood off his shirt to no avail. He seethed with anger as he thought about Steve. He waited in the restroom, anticipating that Steve and his companions might come in and assault him. He welcomed the thought of beating Steve, though he knew it wouldn't be one on one. Still, it would be worth it.

The door opened, but it wasn't Steve; it was Jesse's Black friend, Andrew. "Jesse, we should go. You tackled a White man. They might gang up on us."

"Let 'em try," said Jesse gruffly. "I would love a chance to beat that pig within an inch of his life or even further."

Andrew opened the door to leave. "It's dangerous to talk like that, Jesse. They kill colored people for sayin' things like that."

"I don't care anymore. I am tired of caring, and I am tired of Black folks being afraid of White folks."

Andrew left the restroom and walked around one of the tables to avoid walking past Steve at close range. He looked at Steve, whose attention was focused on Jesse, who was walking out of the restroom and directly toward Steve. Steve and Jesse glared at each other as Jesse passed. Steve said, "This ain't over yet."

Jesse glared back at Steve. "You got that right. This is a long way from over." Jesse noticed that Cris Simon, the Fryers' neighbor, was sitting next to Steve on a barstool. *He will probably tell the Fryers I started a fight in a bar,* he thought.

Jesse and Andrew returned to the table and their friends.

Cassie said, "Jesse, are you OK? You got blood on your shirt and overalls."

"Yeah, I'm fine."

"You can't fight White people, Jesse. It's too dangerous."

Jesse spoke loudly. "I ain't afraid of those stupid KKK dunces. Those Kitty Kat Klub punks ain't nothin' to me."

Several people at nearby tables heard Jesse's comment and looked in his direction, surprised to hear a Black man speak so openly and so loudly about the KKK.

Andrew leaned forward. "Be careful, Jesse. Maybe you don't care if you die, but the rest of us do."

Cassie put her arms around Jesse. She whispered, "Please, baby, I don't want to lose you. Stop talking like that. It ain't safe."

After midnight Jesse and Cassie left the bar and headed for the McKinley farm to take her home. Waco was only fifteen minutes from Rosenthal, but during the drive Cassie reiterated her concern. "Jesse, I am worried you've gone too far. I have never heard of a Black man standing up to a White man like that. They kill Black folks for that. Don't you remember just two years ago, when Sheriff Buchanan shot ol' Will Bradley in the back? He didn't get into any trouble at all."

Jesse replied, "Yeah, but Bradley was breakin' into his house."

"That's what Buchanan said, but Will's family says he had gone to Buchanan's to deliver some eggs and collect past due money. And remember, that was the third colored man Buchanan killed."

"Well, Buchanan ain't sheriff no more. Fleming is."

"What makes you think Fleming will be any different? All those White government people treat us bad."

They arrived at the McKinley house shortly before 1:00 a.m. Jesse stopped beside Cassie's family's bungalow. She got out of the truck, but Jesse stayed inside.

Cassie turned back and looked at him. "You ain't comin' in, Jesse? Are you going back to Fryers' place?"

"Yeah. Since I was gone all day today, I have to do some chores early in the morning, but I will pick you up at eight for church."

Cassie came around the truck to the driver's door. Jesse got out. "Don't hug me. I got blood on my clothes."

"OK, Jesse, I'll see you in the morning." She leaned in and kissed him on the lips.

After dropping Cassie off Jesse had a few beers as he drove back toward Robinson. The longer he drove, the more anger swelled up inside him. He had learned that Steve lived on a farm between Robinson and Rosenthal. Perhaps it was the continuous harassment by Steve every time Jesse saw him that had pushed him over the edge, but he decided to pay Steve a visit. Shortly after 1:00 a.m. Jesse arrived at Steve's residence. He drove his truck into the front yard, shone the truck lights into the front windows of the house, and began blowing the horn. He saw the lights come on in the house, and several people looked through the window to see who was causing so much noise. Then he saw Steve looking through the front window.

Jesse climbed into the bed of his truck and shouted several times, "Now blow my head off." Eventually, the lights inside the house were turned off. Seeing that no one was going to come outside, Jesse climbed back into the truck and blew the horn several more times. He turned around in the front yard, then drove away blowing the horn. When he arrived back on the Fryer farm Jesse parked next to the bungalow and went inside. He fell on his bed and was soon fast asleep.

The following morning Jesse awakened early to shouting outside. Looking through the window, he saw Lucy Fryer chasing Betsy the mule down the lane toward the road. He quickly put on his trousers and shirt, then ran out the door. He stopped by the stable to grab Betsy's bridle and then chased after Lucy and Betsy. He quickly passed Lucy and chased Betsy to the end of the lane. He finally caught up with Betsy and, grabbing her by the mane, he began striking her with the harness as punishment for running.

Lucy caught up with Jesse and Betsy, as did Ruby and George Jr. Lucy shouted, "Jesse, I have told you before not to whip the mule. That is a rule of this farm. If you can't abide by the rule, you will have to leave."

"Yes, ma'am. I just wanted to teach her a lesson."

"That is fine, but don't do it with a whip."

Jesse walked Betsy back up to the stable and led her into her stall.

Jesse drove to the McKinley farm, picked up Cassie and they went to church. During Sunday youth classes, Jesse's mind wandered. He could not stop thinking about Steve Dixon and the altercation of the night before.

CHAPTER

FIFTEEN

FORMER LAW ENFORCEMENT officer and fire commissioner John Dollins was inaugurated as mayor of Waco on April 12, 1916. Dollins ran unopposed, which some ascribed to respect whereas others suspected it might be because it was dangerous to run against him.

The city seemed to be on edge in part due to stories about Black persons committing violent crimes in and around Waco. Newspapers terrified the White families with claims that Black persons were dangerous, violent, out-of-control criminals. They were described as creatures with no morals and no possibility of redemption. Politicians and law enforcement officers were motivated to prosecute Black persons for public gratification and to mete out harsh punishment as a deterrent to crime. They wanted to warn others and at the same time satisfy the townspeople's insatiable appetite for violence and retribution.

Waco had a long history of violence. It was a town with a history of gunslingers and cowboys. It is said that in the late 1800s, there were gunfights nearly every weekend. It was once a violent town where the fastest gun and the biggest wallet decided right from wrong.

It was at this time that Waco was so inflamed that even the most minor offense became a public spectacle. The anticipated release of the movie *The Birth of a Nation* by director D. W. Griffith brought racial tension to new heights. The climate was so intense that several ministers and leaders of church-affiliated academic institutions, including Samuel Palmer Brooks, the president of Baylor University, held a press conference to decry the mistreatment of Black people and the lynchings that had occurred throughout the community over the past decade. Hatred swelled. Black persons soon became undesirables in the eyes of many residents in Waco. Some wanted all Black people to be driven out of town. Others wanted to send a strong signal that any misbehavior by Black people would be dealt with harshly and even outside of the law if deemed necessary.

On Monday, May 8, 1916, at around noon, Jesse was planting cotton not far from the seed house. He saw Cris Simon walking around the house. He waved. Mr. Simon looked at him and nodded his head, then quickly turned away. Jesse went on about his business. About an hour later, he saw someone walking near the edge of a field on the Fryer property, down by Robinsonville Road. He couldn't see clearly who it was, but he didn't think it was George because Jesse knew he was plowing on the opposite side of the farm, and the person seemed too tall to be George Jr. *Perhaps it is Mr. Simon.*

Jesse spent the entire day plowing the field. The warm weather exacerbated fatigue as the temperature rose into the high eighties. It seemed unusually warm to Jesse, which caused him to wonder if the soil would be too dry to properly moisturize the seeds. He remembered what George had taught him about planting at the right time. He decided to act quickly to get the planting finished before it was too late. He worked all day, moving quickly and stopping only occasionally for a swallow of water. Late in the afternoon, George Jr. and Ruby returned from Robinson. They entered the house looking for their mother. Not finding her, George Jr. opened the door to go outside to look for her when he suddenly heard Ruby screaming hysterically. Returning into the house, he found Ruby looking through the window at something outside. He looked through the window and saw his mother lying in the doorway of the seed barn, covered with blood.

Jesse was walking in from the field and heading toward the seed barn to deposit the seed bags when he heard Ruby screaming. He ran up to investigate and saw Lucy lying in the door of the seed barn. Mr. Simon happened to be passing by when he heard the screaming and came to the seed barn as well. He looked at Lucy, lying in the doorway, covered in blood. She had been struck so hard in the head that a portion of her brain had escaped through the fracture in her skull. Her clothing was disheveled, but the investigating forensic physician later determined that she had not been raped. It appeared that someone wanted to create the image she had been. He also determined that she had been murdered around noon.

Simon went to find George. After bringing him to the seed barn, he drove into town to fetch Sheriff Fleming. Fleming was out, but his two deputies, Lee Jenkins and Barny Goldberg, returned to the Fryer farm with Simon. As soon as Fleming returned to the sheriff's office, he learned what had occurred and immediately went to the Fryer farm with Constable Leslie Stegall and Deputy Phil Hobbs.

By the time Fleming arrived, Jenkins had already identified a suspect: Jesse Washington. Simon had seen him near the house planting cotton in the morning. The evidence against him was compounded when it was learned there was a report of Jesse being involved in a fight with a White person in a bar on the Saturday evening before the murder, and that he had gone to the house of that person, driven his truck into the front yard and screamed at the house. Then it became known that on Sunday morning Jesse was chastised by Lucy Fryer for whipping a mule. This, in the eyes of Jenkins, was an open and shut case. To Jenkins, Jesse was exactly the dangerous Black person the newspapers had been warning people about.

Who was Jenkins? Although Fleming got the most credit for identifying the perpetrator, Jenkins was the one who made the call. Jenkins began his career in law enforcement in 1880 at the age of eighteen, when he joined the Texas Rangers. Three years later he was elected constable and later served as chief of police. He was regarded as one of the best forensic investigators in Texas history.

Lucy Fryer's body was found at approximately 6:00 p.m. At 9:00 p.m. Jesse was on the front porch of his family's bungalow whittling. His mother, father, and brother Billy were on the porch with him. They were waiting to see what would happen but did not anticipate it would involve them. Among themselves they had talked about the possibility that Cris Simon had done it. Simon was there around noon, when no one was around but Jesse and Simon just happened to be there when they found the body.

The five officers approached the Washington residence with their guns drawn. They were convinced that Jesse was a cold-blooded murderer. Jesse looked up and saw them approaching slowly in a wide *V* formation.

"Jesse Washington, Get down on the ground!" shouted Jenkins. "One move and you're dead."

Jesse lay down on the ground as instructed. Martha, Henry, and Billy also lay prostrate. Jenkins grabbed Jesse by the shirt collar and jerked him up off the ground. They arrested Jesse, his parents, Martha and Henry, and his brother Billy. They were all taken to Waco, to be detained in the McLennan County jail. Jesse consistently protested his innocence. He said he was as shocked as everyone else by the event but that he had nothing to do with it. On the way to Waco, Jesse curled up in the back seat of the 1916 Model T sedan police car and appeared to sleep. In reality, he knew what was coming and wanted to block everything out. Jesse was taken into a cell, where he was interrogated by Jenkins and McLennan County attorney John McNamara without the benefit of his own attorney being present.

Jesse was seated behind a table in the interrogation room of the county jail, wearing the bloody shirt and overalls he wore when he had the fight on Saturday night. He had tried to wash the blood out to no avail, so he decided to wear the clothes as work clothes, although the shirt was new. Fleming was seated directly across from Jesse and McNamara was at the end of the table to Jesse's left.

Fleming glared intensely at Jesse. "Look, Jesse, we know you did it. There's a lynch mob forming as we speak. If you continue to deny that you did it, they are eventually going to find you. You know what those lynch mobs do. They don't just lynch somebody. They cut off their fingers and toes and genitals, they set them on fire. Sometimes they torture them for hours or even days. If you confess, I can protect you from them. But I can't save you from thousands of people if you continue to say you are innocent. It is about more than you. If you don't confess and they go looking for the killer, your family is in danger. They often kill entire families if they can't find the guy who did it. Your family is the only colored family living on the Fryer farm. Your family is the number one group of suspects. If you didn't do it, one or all of them did."

Fleming took a puff of his cigar and blew the smoke toward Jesse. "Tell me again how you got the blood on your shirt."

"A guy hit me in the nose with his fist on Saturday night."

Fleming took another puff and blew it toward Jesse again. "And why did he hit you?"

Jesse shrugged. "I don't know."

McNamara stood up and walked next to Jesse. He kicked the chair, causing Jesse to fall hard on the concrete floor. "You're wasting our time. Stop lying and tell us what happened."

"He just hit me. I don't know why."

"What were you doing?"

"I was walking past him. He stuck his foot out to trip me. When I started to get up, he hit me in the face with his fist."

"Why did you drive to his house later that night and yell at him?"

Jesse glanced up toward Fleming. "Because I wanted him to leave me alone. I thought I could scare him."

Fleming leaned forward and glared directly at Jesse. "What were you doing in a Whites-only bar?"

Jesse did not respond.

"You know what it looks like to us, don't you? You're an angry hothead, and you got mad at Lucy Fryer because she yelled at you for whipping the mule. And we don't believe you got your shirt bloody in a fight. People in the bar say you started the fight, and you were yelling at the other guy, and they say you didn't get your shirt bloody there. You got your shirt covered with Lucy's blood when you killed her."

Jesse shook his head, "No, that isn't true. I saw Mr. Simon by the house while I was plowing. Maybe he did it."

McNamara jerked Jesse up from the floor, sat up the chair, and threw Jesse into it. "So, now you are going to blame a White man? It's because of Simon that we know you were up by the house around noon, when no one else was there. He is an upstanding citizen, a pillar in the community. If you think you are going to push the blame onto Simon, you are sorely mistaken."

Throughout the night they continued to question Jesse, but the questioning was little more than an accusation to which they sought admission. The details of the interrogation were never made public, but for Jesse it was an unimaginable horror. Jesse's only hope was that someone would find evidence that would prove his innocence. Meanwhile, law enforcement officers from throughout the county were scouring the Fryer farm, looking for the murder weapon and other evidence of the crime.

By this time, a vigilante posse had formed in Robinson and set out to help find Lucy's killer. Anticipating a lynch mob, Fleming arranged to transport Jesse to Hillsboro, a small town about thirty-five miles north of Waco. Henry, Martha, and Billy, were all released given that they appeared to have no knowledge of the murder.

Jesse was told he could sleep for a few hours when they got to Hillsboro, but that the questioning would resume in the morning.

Fleming and McNamara left the room and walked to the front of the jail. McNamara asked, "Do you think there is any chance he didn't do it?"

"Not a chance," replied Fleming. "All the evidence points to Jesse."

"There is one piece of the puzzle I don't understand," said McNamara. "If he did it, why would he stay around, working on the farm the rest of the day? Don't you think he would have run away? George Fryer and his kids all said Jesse seemed as surprised and upset as everyone else when he learned that Lucy was dead."

Fleming shook his head, "You know he's slow. I think he's so stupid, he thought no one would suspect him if he stayed around."

"If that's what he really thought, I would consider that smart, not stupid. It is causing me to question whether he did it."

Fleming said, "Look, we got our guy. We all know it. Let's get his confession and announce it as soon as possible to ease the tension in the county. He is our guy, and we need this to assure the public. I need this. I just took office. The public is expecting results. I can give them results fast. Are you with me? All we want is justice. We don't need to get hung up in a rodeo sideshow while a murderer goes free."

"I want justice too, obviously. I'm just not convinced he is our guy."

Early Tuesday morning at sunrise, Fleming was in the interrogation room in the jail in Hillsboro questioning Jesse. "According to George Fryer and his kids, there is a blacksmith's hammer missing from the seed house. Is that what you used to kill Lucy Fryer?"

Jesse did not respond.

"Where's that hammer now?"

Jesse still did not respond.

"Do you have any idea where it might be? We spent the entire night looking for the murder weapon. They have been plowing the field and looking for the hammer. Where is it, Jesse?"

"I don't know, sir."

"Where do you think it is?"

Jesse said softly, "I saw a man at the end of the field down by the hackberry tree. It was by Robinsonville Road."

"Who did you see there?"

"I don't know, but I thought it might be Mr. Simon."

"Cris Simon? So, we are back to that again? Is Cris Simon some kind of ghost who floats around from place to place?"

Jesse looked down but did not respond.

Fleming leaned forward. "So you threw it in the field by the hackberry tree down by Robinsonville Road? That's where we'll look."

Again, Jesse did not respond.

Fleming stood up and left the room. He motioned for deputies Lee Jenkins and Joe Robert. "There is a hackberry tree near the Robinsonville Road on the Fryer farm. That's where we'll find the murder weapon. It's a blacksmith's hammer."

"Is that what he said?"

"Yeah, that's what he said. Let's head out there. I'll finish up with Jesse and I'll meet you out there with McNamara. Wait for us when you get there. Let's all witness the evidence simultaneously, so we have four separate eyewitnesses to the same evidence when it is found."

The deputies nodded.

Fleming went back into the interrogation room. "This is what it has come down to, Jesse. There is a big mob forming in Robinson. They're looking for you. When these lynch mobs form, sometimes there are thousands. We have had them here before. But they don't just lynch somebody. They torture them to send a warning to other coloreds in the community. It's a very painful death that lasts for hours, sometimes even days. These mobs do some of the worst things you can imagine. I have seen them shove fishhooks up a man's rectum and hang him by his rear end from a tree. I have seen them set people on fire. This is what you are going to face if you don't confess. If you confess, I can protect you until the trial, and I can protect your family. Once you confess, everyone will calm down and you will be hanged, but it will be quick and painless, and your family will be safe. It's your choice."

"What do I have to do?"

"Just confess and say you killed Lucy Fryer. I will ask you one more time. Did you kill Lucy Fryer?"

Jesse looked at the table and mumbled, "I guess so."

"Either you did, or you didn't. It isn't a guess. Did you kill Lucy Fryer? I suggest you think long and hard about the answer you give. This is the last chance I'm going to give you."

Jesse tried not to show emotion, though tears were forming in his eyes. He was terrified of what they might do to his family. He had already decided there was no way for him to save himself, but the thought of his family going through this was more than he could bear. Fleming opened the door. "I'm going out to the farm to get the hammer. When I get back, we'll go through the story from start to finish. Try to get a little sleep so your mind is clear."

Fleming, McNamara, and the deputies went to the Fryer farm and found the blacksmith's hammer by the hackberry tree where Jesse said he saw a man walking. It was reported to the press that Jesse confessed at the jail in Hillsboro on Tuesday morning and that he told the police where the murder weapon was located. People began gathering at the jail in Hillsboro. Fleming arranged to move Jesse to the jail in Dallas, ninety-four miles north of Waco. In Dallas, Jesse confessed again in front of witnesses and signed his name with an *X* at the bottom of the written confession.

Sheriff Fleming returned to Hillsboro, where he encountered a crowd estimated to be at least five hundred in number. Many were newspaper reporters and government employees. He got out of his car and walked up to the crowd. "I know everyone is angry because of this terrible event. But within twenty-four hours I have already identified the criminal, made an arrest, and obtained a confession. There is nothing for you to do. We moved Washington to Dallas. You need to understand that I have to continue upholding the law. That includes making sure Jesse Washington is safe until his trial. By the way, he confessed that he acted alone, so there is no reason to pursue anyone else."

Someone in the crowd shouted, "We have a duty as citizens of the state of Texas to make sure that our womenfolk are protected. We need to make sure that nothing like this ever happens again, and the only way we can do that is by making an example of this one. It's our duty."

The self-righteousness exhibited by many people in Waco was encouraged by the local newspapers, which compared the vigilantes to Revolutionary War patriots fighting for their country to preserve their way of life.

Fleming stepped away from the vehicle to engender trust. "If you doubt that I am telling you the truth about the whereabouts of Washington, come with me to the jail in Waco and you can search it."

A tall man with a rifle, who seemed to have influence over the crowd, said, "That's exactly what we're gonna do. We'll be right behind you."

Fleming nodded and looked at the crowd. "Let's go."

The mob got into their vehicles. About half drove back home, but half drove to Waco to search the jail.

CHAPTER
SIXTEEN

IN DALLAS, JESSE sat in the jail cell curled up in the corner, trying to stay warm. It had been very hot in McLennan County, but Dallas County seemed to have a slight chill. After signing the confession with his *X* mark Jesse waited for the next event in this nightmare.

Meanwhile in Waco, several hundred vigilantes surrounded the jail. They searched every square inch, inside and out. After about an hour they concluded that Fleming was telling the truth and Jesse wasn't there. They gathered in the street and in the yards around the jail.

Fleming walked to the center of the street. He shouted, "Now you can see I was telling the truth." He paused for emphasis. "If anyone still does not believe me, I am happy to take you to the jail in Hillsboro and you can search there too."

The crowd mumbled for a moment. Finally, the tall man with the rifle said, "Naw, that's OK. We've done enough for tonight. We'll get that guy tomorrow."

The crowd slowly disbursed, and Fleming acquired a long-needed slumber.

On Tuesday afternoon the newspapers announced that the murderer had been apprehended, had confessed, and had said where the murder weapon was located. The newspapers did not say that the suspect was interrogated without an attorney, that he was threatened, and that the only reason he confessed was to protect his family and Cassie. They said he was a local hothead who often had altercations with White men, and that he had threatened to kill a White man one day before he was scolded by Lucy Fryer, and that one day after that he bludgeoned her to death with a blacksmith's hammer. And further, he was found with Lucy Fryer's blood on his clothes when he was apprehended. Absent from every account was the fact that Jesse had stayed and plowed the field all afternoon after allegedly killing Lucy Fryer.

Jesse Washington was held up as an example of the violent nature of dark-skinned people. They were described as animals with no morals, no conscience, and no ability to feel empathy, love, or emotional pain. They were seen as violent and brutal by nature, with no redeeming qualities. They were seen as a blight on society.

By Tuesday afternoon the newspapers were describing the event as rape and murder, even though there was no evidence on Lucy's body that she had been raped. Although Jesse could not read the confession he had signed with an X, it was published in the newspaper as factual. Anger swelled in the community, and the vigilante mob stayed up all night. By now the roving mob had grown to several thousand people.

Back at the Fryer farm, the Washington family remained in their bungalow with the doors locked and the curtains pulled shut. They were terrified that the mob might show up and kill them if they could not find Jesse.

Henry said, "We need to leave. It is too dangerous here."

Martha shook her head. "How can we leave? The law took Jesse's truck. If someone sees us going down the road in a wagon, they will say we are running because we did it. Everybody is crazy right now. We should just stay here and hope they don't come for us."

Billy said, "I don't know what to do. What are they doing with Jesse? He didn't do that thing. Why did they say he did?"

Martha said, "Mr. Simon was around all morning that day. I seen him talking to Mrs. Fryer after George and the kids left. Jesse was out in the field all morning."

Henry replied, "Yeah, you said that. Couldn't you hear anything they was sayin'?"

"No, they went in the house. He's been here before, so I didn't think much of it."

"He's been here before when George was gone?"

"Yeah, I seen it."

Billy nodded. "Me too."

Henry appeared puzzled. "I wonder if Lucy Fryer and Mr. Simon were doin' the naughty."

Martha shook her head. "I don't know. I would never have thought of that until now, but now I am wondering if maybe so. Should we go talk to Sheriff Fleming again?"

"They already talked to us. You already told them about seeing Mr. Simon and Lucy Fryer together. He didn't care. It won't matter."

"But if there is any chance it can save Jesse, we should try."

They sat about the table wondering what to do. There was a gentle knock on the door. Then two more, a little quicker. Billy opened the door. It was Ruby and George Jr. They came in. Ruby took ahold of Martha's arm. "How are you holding up?"

Martha fought back tears as she said, "We'll make it. How's your father?"

Ruby looked at the floor. "He isn't well. I wanted to invite you to come to the viewing if you feel up to it. The house is open until nine tonight and tomorrow night. There will be a small service. I know it might make you uncomfortable, but if you want to attend the service, you're welcome."

"Thank you so much," replied Martha.

Ruby looked around the room. "I know you feel trapped in here. Is there anything you need?"

Henry stepped forward, "Well, there is, ma'am. But we don't know how we could do it. We want to go to Waco to talk to Sheriff Fleming, but we is worried that it might not be good for Black people there right now. Sometimes these things boil over into the whole town. We're worried that might be happening here."

Ruby said, "They don't think this one will boil over because when Jesse confessed, he said no one else was involved."

Martha burst into tears. "Jesse confessed? Oh no."

Ruby said, "I'm sorry, Martha. I assumed you knew."

Everyone was silent for a time while Martha cried.

She said, "I don't understand. It doesn't make sense. Jesse would never go to his maker with a lie on his lips. He was taught that since he was a baby. Yet, he would never do the things they said he done to your mama. Does your father think Jesse done it?"

Ruby shook her head. "I don't know. He's really confused. He's greeting the guests, but he doesn't say much."

George Jr. stepped forward and looked at Martha. "Pa told me he didn't think Jesse did those things the paper said. But he said he doesn't know, and that we need to let him have a fair trial."

Martha looked at Henry. "Do you think he can have a fair trial?"

Henry knew that Black men did not get fair trials when it came to cases of rape and murder of a White woman, but he couldn't bring himself to say it. So, he said, "Let's pray that he does."

Ruby said, "It's only a few minutes to the Waco jail if we take the car. Would you like for me to drive you there?"

Martha said, "Oh Miss Ruby. If you could, that would be so good for us."

"OK, I'll go tell Daddy and I will be back with the car in twenty minutes. Georgie, you should stay here."

George Jr. frowned, "But I want to come too."

"If Dad says it's OK."

Ruby left the bungalow and went to the main house. Ten minutes later she was back with the Model T sedan. George Jr. climbed in the front seat with Ruby. "Did Dad say it was OK for me to come?"

Ruby nodded. "He said go straight there and back. He said Fleming will want to know what they say. He said if we see any big crowds turn around and go a different way."

When everyone was in the car Ruby drove to the road and turned right, headed for the Waco jail.

On the McKinley farm, Cassie stayed locked alone in the room she shared with Jenny. She had learned of Jesse's arrest on Tuesday morning when everyone was talking about it, especially people on the McKinley farm where Jesse had been working just six months earlier. No one who knew him believed it was possible that he murdered anyone, especially not a woman. Jesse was very kind to everyone. It was true he had a temper but only when he believed that someone was unfair to him or to someone close to him. For Cassie, this was too much to bear. She knew that when a Black person is accused of the rape or murder of a White woman it meant not only death, but often a painful and brutal death. From the moment she heard what happened she believed in her heart there was no hope for Jesse. She also believed Jesse was innocent. Her only hope was that someone would come forward and confess or say that they had seen someone else murder Lucy Fryer. Then she learned that Jesse had confessed and even signed a written confession an embellished version of which had been published in a local newspaper. She requested her father to obtain a copy of the paper.

Cassie heard a tap on the bedroom door. Then she heard her father's voice. "Cassie, I have the newspaper, but I don't think you should read it. I know it isn't a true confession. There is no way Jesse would do the things this article says. He signed it with an

X because he can't read or write. I don't think it was even read to him."

Between sobs, Cassie opened the door and reached for the paper. "I have to read it, Papa. I have to know what it says." She took the paper from her father's hand and gently closed the door. She put it on the bed and saw the confession on the front page. She immediately noticed that the newspaper had misspelled the name Fryer.

"On yesterday May 8th, 1916, I was planting cotton for Mr. Fryar [sic] near Robinsonville close to Waco, Texas, and about 3:30 o'clock P.M. I went up to Mr. Fryar's barn to get some more cotton seed. I called Mrs. Fryar from the house to get some cotton seed, and she came to the barn and unfastened the door and scooped up the cotton seed. I was holding the sack while she was putting the seed in the sack, and after she had finished, she was fussing with me about whipping the mules, and while she was standing inside of the door of the barn, and still talking to me, I hit her on the side of the head with a hammer that I had in my hand. I had taken this hammer from Mr. Fryar's home to the field that morning, and brought it back and put it in the barn at dinner. I had picked up this hammer and had it in my hand when I called Mrs. Fryar from the house, and had the hammer in my right hand all the time I was holding the sack.

"When I hit Mrs. Fryar on the side of the head with the hammer she fell over, and then I assaulted her [pulled up her clothes and crawled on her and screwed her]. By screwing her I mean that I stuck my male organ into her female organ, and while I was doing this she was trying to push me off. When I got through screwing her I got off of her and I then picked up the hammer from where I had laid it down, and hit her twice more with the hammer on top of her head. I saw the blood coming through her bonnet.

"I then picked up the sack of cotton seed and carried it and the hammer to the field, where I had left the team. I left the sack of cotton seed near the planter and went about forty steps south of the planter and the mules, and put the hammer that I killed Mrs. Fryar with in some woods tinder some hackberry brush.

"I knew when I went to the barn for the cotton seed that there wasn't anybody at the house except Mrs. Fryar, and when I called her from the house to the barn, I had already made up my mind to knock her in the head with the hammer and then assault her.

"I had been working for Mr. Fryar about five months, and first made up my mind to assault Mrs. Fryar yesterday morning and took the hammer from the buggy shed to the field with me, and brought it back and put it in the barn at dinnertime, so that I could use it to knock Mrs. Fryar in the head when I came back for seed during the afternoon. I planted cotton the rest of the afternoon, then put up the team and went home to my daddy's house where I was arrested. There wasn't anybody else who had anything to do with the killing or assaulting of Mrs. Fryar except myself."

Signed Jesse Washington *X*, his mark.

Cassie could not read the entire confession. She read only through the second paragraph as she cried uncontrollably. She walked into the kitchen, where Jenny was sitting with her parents around the table holding the newspaper in her hand. She sat at the table and wiped the tears from her eyes. "Jesse couldn't have done this thing it says. Jesse didn't know how to rape a woman. Jesse had never seen a woman without clothes before. He wouldn't even know what to do. I know because we talked about it. I want to talk to the sheriff. I will tell him the truth."

Her father shook his head. "You can't go there, Cassie. These people don't care if he did it or not. If you go to talk to them, they might say you planned it with Jesse."

"Why would they do that?"

"Because that's what they do to us."

"But I have to try," cried Cassie.

Cassie's mother said, "Child you are still young and there's lots of things you don't know. Some White people don't need a reason to do what they do to us. They don't care about a reason. They just hate us."

"But why? Why do they hate us so much? What did we do to them?"

Cassie's father looked out the window. "We didn't do nothin' to them. It's just the way they are."

Still determined not to give up, Cassie said, "We have to get word to Elijah at Yale. He will know what to do."

Cassie's father replied, "How can we do that? And even if we could, what could he do? They are going to give Jesse a trial. But they always say the colored man is guilty. The judge is White, and the jury is White. There is nothing we can do now, Cassie."

"Papa, will you take me to see Sheriff Fleming? Please, Papa?"

Cassie's father took a deep breath. "It would be better if we went with a White person like Mr. McKinley, but he is gone now. I don't know who else we could ask. They might attack us just for being in town."

He looked at his daughter as a tear flowed gently down her right cheek. "OK, baby. I will take you, but you need to cover your head with a scarf, and I will wear a big hat. It will be better if no one knows who we are."

Cassie's mother reached for her arm. She looked at Cassie and John. "This is too dangerous. Don't do this."

Cassie took her mother's arm. "We have to try Mama."

Her mother closed her eyes and took a deep breath, then said, "OK, then I'm coming too."

"And me," said Jenny.

"Let's go then," said John.

They climbed into the wagon and headed toward Waco to see Sheriff Fleming.

On Tuesday afternoon, at the jail in Dallas, Jesse sat on a wooden bench in a small concrete cell. No one had come in or out for hours. The cell was equipped with a toilet and a wooden bench intended to serve as a bed. Food and water were passed through a small door at the bottom of the metal cell door. Jesse tried to understand everything that had happened, but it was all happening so fast. He tried to get some sleep to pass the time, but sleep would not come. Jesse heard the cell door clang as it was unlocked. He looked up to see the guard opening the door. "You've got some visitors. It's a couple of your lawyers."

Jesse stood up. "My lawyers? I ain't got no lawyers."

"The judge appointed them for you. Let's go."

Jesse, with his hands and feet shackled, walked to the attorney meeting room. For a moment Jesse felt a flicker of hope. He sat at the table and waited. The attorneys came in. Jesse noticed that they weren't much older than him. "You're my lawyers?"

They sat down at the table. "I'm Joe Taylor from Waco. This is Percy Wilie. Judge Munroe appointed us to defend you. There are four more."

"Why do I have so many lawyers?"

"That's how many the judge appointed. I don't know why."

Jesse looked at both of them with a feeling of hope. "With that many lawyers will you be able to get me off?"

"Get you off? You confessed to the rape and murder of a White woman. No one can get you off."

Jesse looked perplexed. "Then why do I have lawyers?"

"Because the law says you can have lawyers. The judge said this would be a good case for us to learn on. You have already confessed to the murder, so if we don't get you off no one will be surprised. That is what's expected."

"But I didn't do it."

"If you didn't do it why did you confess?"

"Because Sheriff Fleming told me that he would not be able to protect me from the lynch mob if I didn't confess, and he said that it would be dangerous for my family if I didn't confess." Jesse looked at Taylor, who looked familiar. "Don't I know you? I seen you somewhere before."

Taylor nodded. "Yeah, you've seen me. I was in the bar in Rosenthal Saturday night when you got into a spat with Steve Dixon."

Suddenly, Jesse remembered. "You are the one who told him to fight me. You said he would look afraid if he didn't fight me. He told you to shut up."

"That's right. It was me."

"You're my attorney?"

Taylor laughed. "Yeah, it looks like I am."

"But you can't help me?"

"The best thing we can do is to make sure the trial is done in an orderly manner. If we can do that the mob might not lynch you."

Jesse shook his head. "I don't understand. Sheriff Fleming said that he would protect me from the lynch mob if I confessed."

Taylor nodded. "I'm sure he'll try, but he won't be able to do much against a mob of several thousand people. Jesse, you confessed to murdering a White woman. Nothing can save you from hanging. Our job is to try to keep you safe until you are hanged. That is also Fleming's job."

Jesse looked at them in disbelief. "There really is no one who can save me?"

Wilie and Taylor shook their heads. "Not really," said Taylor.

Wilie leaned back in his chair. "I do have one question. It's the elephant in the room."

Jesse leaned forward on the table. "What? There was an elephant there when Lucy was killed?"

Wilie and Taylor laughed. Wilie continued. "No, that's just an expression. It means it's something that's obvious, but no one is talking about it. There's an elephant in the room in your case."

Jesse smiled slightly.

Taylor said, "Look at that. You smiled. Not many people would smile in your situation. I like you, Jesse. I liked you the night you tackled Steve. I knew it was a mistake, but I really admired your spunk. I kind of wanted you to kick Steve's ass. He deserved it.

Between you and me, that is why I egged him on to fight you. I wanted you to kick his ass."

Jesse laughed out loud. "Look, I know I'm innocent, but I know how it is. If they can find a colored man to pin it on that's what they do. I ain't afraid to die. I'm sad for my parents, and my brother, and my girl, Cassie, but I ain't afraid to die. That's why I went to Steve's house and told him to shoot me. I wasn't afraid to die."

Taylor stood up and walked around the table and put his hand on Jesse's shoulder and gave it a slight squeeze.

Jesse continued, "I just don't want them to cut me up and burn me and do all the bad things they do to coloreds before they kill them."

The room was silent for a moment, then Taylor said, "Damn, I hate to see this happen to you. But it's because you aren't afraid to die that people think you are so dangerous. You will stand right up to a White guy. That just doesn't ever happen. That's really scary to most White folks. And you're big and strong and athletic. You are scary to these White people. And the White guys really don't like you because the White girls call you the stud."

Jesse frowned. "The stud?"

Taylor replied, "Like I said, I actually like you, Jesse. I really wish there was something we could do, but this is how things are in Waco. It's just how it is. There are forces at work that are much bigger than you and me. The more we try to fight your conviction the angrier the mob will get and the more dangerous it will be for you and even for us. Yeah, it turns out that White girls in Waco used to call you the stud because they think you are a great-looking guy."

Jesse laughed. "I ain't never heard that." In reality, he remembered Cassie telling him that she had heard that the White girls call him stud but he didn't want these men to know for fear they might think he liked it.

Wilie cleared his throat almost nervously. "Let me bring it back to the elephant in the room. This is a question everyone is asking, and no one understands. Why did you stay around plowing the field after you killed Lucy Fryer? Why didn't you run? No one would ever do that. That is why I think you might be innocent."

Jesse stood up and said loudly, "Because I didn't do it. I didn't know she was dead until I came in from the field."

Taylor leaned forward on his elbows. "It doesn't matter now because you confessed."

"But can't I take back the confession? I only said that because Sheriff Fleming said he would protect my family and me from the mob."

Taylor shook his head. "I wish I had been your lawyer then. I would have told you not to confess. You can't retract a confession once you have given it. It's now a matter of the official record, in writing, with your signature mark. I mean, you could retract it, but that would only make things worse. The mob might storm the jail and get to you. But even if you did retract the confession, no one would believe you because you already confessed."

"It's because I'm Black, isn't it?"

Neither Taylor nor Wilie answered the question. They both cast their gaze downward, almost as if in shame.

CHAPTER
SEVENTEEN

RUBY DROVE THE Model T sedan into Waco toward the jail. George Jr. was in the front seat, and Henry, Martha, and Billy were in the rear seat. As they drove through the streets, the city seemed unusually quiet, given the news about Jesse. Not only were White people walking about at leisure, but Black people seemed to be going about their business as well.

Upon approaching the jail, they noticed a crowd standing by the front entrance. In the accruing darkness, many in the crowd had lanterns. Ruby parked along the right side of the street in one of the few parking places available. Gazing at the large crowd, Martha asked, "Do you think it's safe to go to the door past that crowd? What if someone recognizes us?"

Henry inhaled deeply, collecting his thoughts. "We came this far. We might as well go in."

They climbed out of the vehicle and walked toward the jail. pushing their way past bystanders. Upon reaching a clear spot in front of the jail, they noticed two sheriff's deputies standing in front of the door with rifles in their hands.

Henry walked toward them. One of them said, "No one is allowed in the jail now. Jesse isn't here."

Henry moved closer. "We came to talk to Sheriff Fleming about Lucy Fryer and Jesse Washington."

The deputy turned slightly to see Henry better. "What do you want to see him for?"

"We have information about Lucy's death. We were living on the . . ."

"Oh, I recognize you. You're Jesse's father."

"Yes, sir."

The deputy lowered his rifle slightly. Henry and Billy recognized him as Deputy Goldberg, who had questioned them the night before. "Jesse is in Dallas. Fleming isn't here either. Just between us, I believe Jesse is innocent. There are many people who believe that Jesse would win if there was time to prepare a good defense, but these guys are pushing it forward. Jesse didn't even waive his thirty days, but they took it from him like he waived it. The judge is in on it."

"What thirty days?"

"Every defendant is entitled to thirty days to prepare his defense. They took that away from him. They are doing his trial in eight days from the crime. This is terrible. It's a lynching. I can't do anything about it. Those in charge are too powerful. Some derelict named D. W. Griffith is calling the shots. I think the guy is a traitor and should be in prison, but if anyone heard me talk like this I would be arrested. I would like to take him out."

Henry frowned. "Take him out to where?"

Deputy Goldberg tried to hide his chuckle. "It's an expression. It means get rid of him."

As they talked, someone began singing "Amazing Grace." Billy turned around and saw that the people standing there were from Baylor University—from the church volleyball teams. They looked at Billy and waved and smiled as they continued to sing. Then Billy heard the familiar harmony parts he used to sing with Jenny,

Cassie, and Jesse. He distinctly recognized the voices of Cassie and Jenny. He walked past several people and saw them with their parents and several students from Baylor. They did not see him, so he began singing his harmony part. Jenny and Cassie recognized his voice and they turned to see him. Billy walked up to them, and they all embraced and cried.

When the singing finished Billy asked, "What's going on? When did you get here?"

Cassie replied, "We just got here, and they were all here. Most of these people are from the church volleyball teams. They came down here to tell Sheriff Fleming that they believe Jesse is innocent . . . that they know he would never do such a thing."

Henry, Martha, George Jr., and Ruby came over. Cassie had seen them around the farm and recognized them. The crowd began to sing another song and asked Billy, Cassie, and Jenny to sing their harmony parts. The trio complied. Although the harmonies were beautiful, noticeably absent was Jesse's voice singing his harmony part. Many in the crowd were wiping tears from their eyes.

As they continued to sing, a man walked to the front of the crowd. Cassie recognized him as Samuel Palmer Brooks, the president of Baylor University. Dr. Brooks began to speak, and the crowd grew silent. "Thank you all for coming out tonight. We need to be here to show our sympathy for the loss of the Fryer family, and also to show our support for Jesse . . . to make sure he gets a fair trial. That is what we came here to tell Sheriff Fleming, but he isn't here. I had a chance to speak with Officer Jenkins earlier today and I told him that those of us who know Jesse believe he is innocent. Of course, he said that is something that will have to be decided by the jury. We made our presence known and that is the important thing. Why don't we adjourn and meet in a half hour at the volleyball courts on the Baylor campus? There we will have an outdoor prayer service for Jesse and for the Fryer family. All we can ask is that he receive a fair trial and that this does not turn into the kind of horrible scene some other towns have experienced."

Dr. Brooks held up a piece of paper. "Before you leave be sure to sign the petition demanding a fair trial for Jesse. There are several people standing around with clipboards. They have the petition for you to sign. We have several thousand signatures already, but we need a lot more."

After signing the petition, the crowd began to disperse, heading for their cars and wagons to go back to the Baylor campus. As they left, Cassie's mother said, "Martha, why don't you folks come and stay with us tonight? I don't know how safe it is out there on the Fryer farm."

Cassie joined in the supplication. "Please come and stay with us tonight."

Jenny nodded. "Yes."

Martha looked at Ruby. "What do you think, Miss Ruby?"

Ruby nodded. "It is up to you, Martha. I think you are safe on our farm because everyone knows we are having a viewing of my mother. But it might be even safer at the McKinley place."

Henry said, "If it is OK, it might be a good idea. But we don't want to impose."

Cynthia said, "It will be fine."

The Washingtons and the Williamses climbed into the wagon and headed toward the Baylor campus, while Ruby and George Jr. drove back to the Fryer ranch for their mother's evening viewing.

That evening on the Baylor campus the volleyball players from church teams all over Waco came out for a prayer vigil for the Fryer family, for the Washington family, and, most of all, for Jesse. They sang songs and prayed together until midnight. Then they all quietly went home.

On Thursday morning, May 11, 1916, a grand jury returned an indictment after only thirty minutes. The court summoned fifty prospective jurors for the trial, which was scheduled to take place on Monday, May 15, precisely one week from the death of Lucy

Fryer. The county officials, including Mayor Dollins and Sheriff Fleming, promised swift justice.

Jesse remained in the Dallas jail until late Sunday night. He was driven back to Waco in the sheriff's Model T Ford. Upon arrival, he was driven to the rear of the jail. They entered by a back door so the public would not be aware that he had been brought back to Waco.

Jesse was taken into an interrogation room, where he was seated at the table. A few minutes later six young men came into the room. They were Jesse's attorneys. Jesse immediately recognized Joe Taylor and Percy Wilie, the attorneys he had met in the Dallas County jail. Jesse immediately felt a small sense of comfort, until he recognized a third person. Suddenly, his heart sank. One of the attorneys walked in, sat directly across from Jesse, and began looking at him with a sinister smile. He was Westwood Bowden Hays Jr. Although Jesse did not know his name, he clearly recognized him. He was one of the people who was with Steve Dixon at the river the day Elijah had come to his aid, punching Steve in the eye. He was in the pickup truck the day Steve Dixon and his comrades dragged the Black man, then poured tar and feathers all over him. He was at the bar with Steve Dixon and Joe Taylor the night of the altercation, but most terrifying perhaps, was that Jesse recognized him from the group of men in white robes when Jesse and his friends stumbled upon the KKK rally at Kay Mountain.

The rest of the attorneys took a place around the large table except the youngest one, who stood by the door, almost as if he was unsure if he should even be there. Taylor said, "Jesse, we're your legal team. We are your lawyers. You already met Percy and me in Dallas. The person directly across from you is Westwood Bowden Hays Jr. The man at the end of the table to your right is Frank Fitzpatrick, at the left end of the table is Kyle Vick. This gentleman standing by the door is Chester Machen. Chester is fresh out of law school, but the rest of us have been practicing around here for a while."

Jesse nodded but continued looking at Hays. "Why are you here? I know you. You is in the Kitty Kat Klub."

Hays tilted his head and smiled. "The what?"

"The Kitty Kat Klub."

Hays shook his head. "What's the Kitty Kat Klub?"

"You call it the KKK."

Hays leaned back in his chair. "What makes you think I am in the KKK? How would you know that? Have you been attending their rallies?" Everyone laughed except Jesse.

"Yeah, I have been to a KKK rally. I saw you there at Kay Mountain last summer."

Hays shook his head. "When were . . . ?" Suddenly Hays remembered the time they were seen by someone at the rally who ran up into the woods. "Was that you we chased with the dog?"

Jesse nodded.

"Who else was with you?"

Jesse didn't reply.

Taylor said, "Jesse, we're here to try to find any form of proof that you are innocent. Retracting your confession is not going to save you. But if there is anything you can remember, any piece of evidence that will prove that you did not kill Lucy Fryer, now is the time to tell us."

Jesse turned his gaze downward at the table. He knew there was nothing he could say that would save him.

Taylor continued, "Why don't you tell us the whole story again from start to finish? Tell us everything you remember about last Monday."

Jesse recounted the day the best he could remember. When he spoke about seeing Cris Simon at the farm on the morning of the murder of Lucy Fryer, he noticed that Hays seemed to be a little more attentive.

"Did you see anyone else with Cris Simon on the morning of the murder?" asked Hays.

"Naw. I was plowing the field not far from the Fryer house. I seen Mr. Simon there. I waved, but he didn't wave back. He turned away real quick. Then, about an hour later, I seen someone throw something into a hackberry bush down by Robinsonville Road. That person was too far away for me to see who he was. I don't see people down there very often. That's why I remember it."

Taylor said, "Jesse, if you were to give your best guess of who killed Lucy Fryer, who would it be?"

Jesse looked at Taylor. "I wouldn't really want to say, sir. I didn't see who done it, so I can't say for sure."

"It's OK, Jesse. This information will never leave this room. That is called the attorney-client privilege. We can't tell anyone what you tell us."

Jesse turned his gaze back to the table. "If I had to say who I think done it, I would have to say Mr. Simon 'cause he's the only one I seen around the house that morning."

"Had you ever seen him around the house before?" asked Taylor.

"Yeah, he used to come around a lot. Just about every day, it seems like."

"What did he come for?"

"I guess he came to see Lucy. She was usually the only one around when I saw him."

The room grew quiet for a moment. Then Taylor asked, "Are you saying that Simon would come around to see Lucy?"

"I guess so, because she was usually the only one there."

"Did you see him in the seed barn on the morning of the murder?"

"No, sir, but he was close to it when I seen him and waved, but I didn't see him go inside."

"Damn," said Wilie.

Hays looked over at Wilie. "Don't even go there. Simon is an upstanding citizen. There is no way we're going to pin this on Simon unless someone actually saw him do it. Someone other than a N_____."

Jesse looked perplexed. "He saw me there. I seen him there. Why am I the one being accused and not him?"

The room was silent again for a few minutes. Then Jesse asked, "It's because I'm Black, ain't it?"

No one responded. Finally, Taylor said, "Listen, Jesse. The evidence points to you, and you have already confessed. Just about the only possible way we can turn this around now is if we can find a witness who says they saw who did it. Are you absolutely positive you can't think of anyone who might have been there? One person."

"No. George Jr. and Ruby were not at the farm. Mom, Dad, and Billy had all gone into town for supplies. George Sr. was way over on the other side of the field. I didn't see anyone except Mr. Simon."

The interrogation continued until midnight. Despite all their questions, the young defense team could not find anything to prove that Jesse didn't kill Lucy Fryer, which meant they could not find proof that anyone else did it. In the absence of that proof, Jesse had no chance. He was a Black man seen near the scene of the crime at about the time of its occurrence.

Finally, Taylor said, "We can't get you off with this information, Jesse. We need more. We wanted to give you an opportunity to think of anything we might use, any witness we could find, who would support your version of the facts."

"But why am I the one who they go after and not Mr. Simon? We were both there. It could have been him. Why are they saying it was me and not him?" Jesse asked again, "It's because I'm Black, ain't it?"

No one responded. They all turned their gazes away from Jesse except for Hays, who glared at him with a sinister smirk.

CHAPTER
EIGHTEEN

BY SATURDAY PEOPLE had begun to arrive in Waco, in Model T Fords and horse-drawn wagons. They came from all over Texas to see the trial and execution of Jesse Washington. Samuel Palmer Brooks had launched a campaign to ensure a fair trial for Jesse. The news of Lucy Fryer's murder had spread throughout Texas and soon became a national news story. In Waco, Jesse's guilt was a foregone conclusion.

On Monday, Jesse was escorted through the halls of the courthouse by Deputies Goldberg and Jenkins. They opened the door from the back hallway and Jesse peered into the courtroom. He could not believe his eyes. The courtroom was packed with people. Most of the spectators were White but there were some Black persons present as well.

When Jesse finally entered, the crowd grew silent. He looked around the courtroom. Even the balconies were filled to standing room only. Deputy Barney Goldberg leaned over and whispered, "Jesse, there's thousands outside who couldn't get in. You're famous. Your name is known all over America. Lots of people believe you're innocent, including me. But we can't do anything about it.

Whatever they do, don't show any pain or worry. Don't let them have that satisfaction."

Jesse made eye contact with Goldberg and nodded. The deputy escorted Jesse across the courtroom to the defense table. The crowd began to shout at Jesse. They called him all sorts of names, some vulgar. Jesse thought about Deputy Goldberg's words. He told himself that no matter what they did, he would not show weakness. He would not give them the satisfaction of seeing him suffer.

Goldberg seated Jesse at the table and sat in a chair directly behind him. The deputy whispered, "I'm not supposed to talk to you, so listen to what I say." Jesse listened, and though he could not understand it all, the words gave him a sense of comfort.

"This might be bad, Jesse. If there was anything I could do to stop it, I would. I can only say, your pain and suffering won't be in vain. But whatever you do, don't let them believe they have hurt you. If you rise above the pain, your spirit will live forever in the hearts and minds of the good people of America. The good people of America are not in Waco today. There is evil in Waco worse than anything I have ever seen or heard of. I know a friend of yours, Becky Baines, who is on the mission field. I took classes at Baylor too."

"You know Becky Baines?"

"Yes. She doesn't know what's happening here today. But before she left for the mission field, she told me about you and your friends. She really liked you kids. Be strong for Becky and your girl. Her name is Cassie, isn't it?"

Jesse was so overcome that tears swelled up in his eyes and he felt a lump in his throat. "How do you know that?"

"Your parents, your brother, Cassie, her sister, and her parents all came down to the jail last week and told us you are innocent. Hundreds of people from Baylor University came to support you too. They all say they know you are innocent. They have been having prayer services for you over at the campus . . . the volleyball teams."

"They all came down for me?"

Goldberg nodded. "They have been at the Baylor campus every night for the past week. They say you would never hurt a woman. Why did you confess?"

"Sheriff Fleming told me if I confessed, he would protect my family and me from the crowd. After I confessed, he said there was nothin' he can do."

Goldberg shook his head. "He lied. He told us if the crowd tried to take you, we aren't to stop them. We're supposed to leave the courtroom immediately after the jury announces the guilty verdict if the crowd swarms us. I'm not going anywhere. I will fight as long as I can."

Those words amused Jesse, who smiled at the deputy. "I couldn't care less if I die. I'd rather not die, but if I'm gonna die, that's OK. Last week I drove to Steve Dixon's house and told him to shoot my head off. Fleming and Jenkins thought I was threatening him. I wasn't. I was saying go ahead and do it, because I would rather be dead than to live as a coward being pushed around by the likes of him."

Jesse paused for contemplation. "I like to not have a lot of pain when I die. But if that is what is gonna happen, I can take my licks. I heard what you said, and that's what I was thinking. I won't do anything that lets them know they caused me pain. That's how I will win. And maybe it will not be until this story is told in a hundred years that people will understand. But someday, they will understand."

As he listened, the deputy's eyes began to tear up too. He looked up at Judge Munroe as he entered the courtroom. "All I can say is, Jesse, you're a hero. You're everything that makes humanity good. These guys are wolves, but you are a lion. Lots of people think you're innocent, but the wolves are pushing this through."

"It's because I'm Black, ain't it?" Jesse expected that Goldberg would refuse to respond the way others had.

He was surprised to hear Goldberg say, "Yes, Jesse. It's because you're Black. A lot of these people hate me too because I'm a Jew."

That comment puzzled Jesse. "But you're White."

"Yes, but I am also Jewish. These monsters don't like Blacks and they don't like Jews."

The bailiff shouted "Order. Order in the court."

The room quieted as Judge Richard Munroe took the bench. Jesse looked around the courtroom and up at the balcony, almost as if to say, *You are what you do here today. This will be how Waco will be remembered forever.* As he looked in the crowd for someone he might know, he saw Cassie and her family sitting behind a row of deputies. He looked for his own parents but didn't see them. Unbeknownst to Jesse, his parents had been picked up again and were being detained away from McLennan County for their own safety. Cassie, Jenny, and their parents were all crying. Cassie made eye contact with Jesse. As the tears slowly flowed down her cheeks she mouthed the words, *"I love you, Jesse."* He said, "I love you." Inside Jesse cried, but he would not let the public see his tears. As he saw how pretty Cassie was, he realized he would never have her. He would never share his bed with her. He wished that he could have, but now he never will. He should have married her when he could have. At least then he would have known what it would be like to be with her.

Cassie's presence gave Jesse indescribable strength. Suddenly, he felt as if he had the strength of a hundred men. He would make Cassie proud. And he would make his new friend, Deputy Goldberg, proud. He would not let anyone see him cry. He would not cry out.

Outside, the crowd could not be quieted. Within the courtroom, the crowd moved dangerously close to one another. Sheriff Fleming shouted, "Try to be quiet."

Judge Munroe pounded the bench with his gavel and shouted,

"You will be quiet or there will be no court." He slammed the gavel on the bench again, this time with two loud cracks that reverberated throughout the courtroom.

The court grew deathly silent, and the trial began at ten o'clock. Judge Munroe said gruffly, *"State of Texas v. Jesse Washington."*

Judge Munroe conducted a brief voir dire (questioning of the jury members) that lasted only a few seconds and was more like an admonition. "Counsel for the state, do you have any questions for the jury?"

"No, Your Honor," said McNamara.

"Defense?"

"No, Your Honor," said Joe Taylor.

"Do you accept the jury as empaneled?"

"Yes, Your Honor," replied Taylor and McNamara almost simultaneously.

Prosecuting attorney Guy McNamara paced the floor in front of the jury. "The facts are simple. Jesse Washington murdered Lucy Fryer. He was seen within two hundred and fifty yards of the seed barn around the time of the murder, he fought with a White man the Saturday before the murder, he went to the White man's house and threatened him. This shows he has a temper and is reckless and dangerous and hates White people. He argued with Lucy Fryer over a mule the day before her murder and he confessed to the murder and told Sheriff Fleming where the murder weapon would be found. Blood was found on his clothes the day of the murder after Lucy's body was found. Ladies and gentlemen, there is no doubt this man is the murderer."

Judge Munroe said, "Mr. Taylor, are you going to give an opening statement?"

"No, Your Honor."

"Call your first witness, Mr. McNamara."

"Thank you, Your Honor. The state calls Dr. J. H. Maynard."

Dr. Maynard walked to the witness stand, was sworn in, and took his seat.

"Dr. Maynard, what's your profession?"

"I am a medical doctor and a forensic investigator for the state of Texas."

"And did you investigate the death of one Lucy Fryer who died on May 8, 1916?"

"Yes, I did."

"Please tell us what you know about this incident."

"I knew Mrs. Fryer. I was called to the Fryer home last Monday, May 8. I found Mrs. Fryer dead when I reached her home. I found several wounds on the head, two large wounds involving the bony structure. Two large wounds going or entering into the brain. A quantity of brain had escaped from the cranial vault. And there were four or five, possibly a half-dozen flesh wounds on the forehead going down to the skull. Over the right ear was the largest wound, which I would suppose to be two and one-half inches in circumference, possibly three inches in circumference.

"Mrs. Fryer's death was caused by the wounds she received. The wounds appeared to have been made with some blunt instrument . . . a heavy instrument. I should say that Mrs. Fryer received a half dozen round on her head. There were two wounds involving the skull, fracturing the skull, one in the back part, and either one of those wounds would have killed her. Mrs. Fryer was a married woman. She died in this county and in this state."

The judge looked at Taylor. "Do you have any questions for this witness, Mr. Taylor."

"No, Your Honor."

The judge looked at McNamara. "Call your next witness."

"Yes, Your Honor. The state would like to call Mike I. Lively."

Lively took the witness stand and was duly sworn.

McNamara said, "Mr. Lively, please tell us what you know about this incident."

"My name is Mike I. Lively. I am an attorney for Dallas County. I saw the defendant, Jesse Washington, in my office one day last week."

McNamara gave the witness a document . . . the confession marked by Jesse with an *X*.

Mr. Lively continued. "I took this instrument. It was made in my presence. The statutory warning about a defendant's right to make a statement was carefully given to this defendant. He was instructed that he did not have to make any statement and that any statement he made might be used against him and could not be used for him. This statement was given to me after that warning was given. The statement was then read over twice to the defendant very carefully and he then affixed his mark thereto in the presence of Joe Davie and M. G. Turney whom I called in to have present there and to witness his signature. The instrument related to the murder of a Mrs. Fryer who lived in this County near the town of Robinsonville. That murder was committed last Monday the eighth. Sheriff Long, of Hill County, brought the defendant into my office. This statement was made in my office in Dallas, Texas."

Jesse heard the words, not fully understanding their meaning. But he knew it was bad for him. The prosecution presented two more law enforcement officers who witnessed Jesse sign his confession.

Sheriff Fleming was then called to the witness stand and was duly sworn.

McNamara said, "Mr. Fleming, would you tell us what you know of this matter involving the murder of Lucy Fryer?"

"I am sheriff of McLennan County, Texas. I had a conference with the defendant in the Hill County jail last Tuesday. In that conference he told me that he had killed Mrs. Fryer with 'a piece of iron.' He finally told me that he killed her with a hammer. He told me what he had done with the hammer, stating that we would find the hammer next to the road at the end of the ground where he was plowing, just a little west, below these hackberry trees, along the main Robinsonville Road. I afterward went to the place where he told me that he had placed the hammer and found it. It is a medium-size blacksmith's hand hammer. It is not the largest nor the smallest. It was a sixteen medium-size hammer. The handle next to the hammer for about two-and-one-half or three inches was covered with blood and the hammer was covered with blood all over. At the time there was also some lint of cotton seed on the hammer. Mrs. Fryer was killed in a seed house in which there was a lot of cotton seed."

Judge Munroe asked, "Cross-examination, Mr. Taylor?"

Mr. Taylor stood and walked to the podium. "Was anyone with you when you found the hammer, Mr. Fleming?"

"Yes, Lee Jenkins, Mr. McNamara, and Joe Robert were present when I found the hammer."

"Thank you, Mr. Fleming."

Mr. Fleming took his seat near the defense table. McNamara walked to the podium. "The state calls Lee Jenkins."

Jenkins took the witness stand and was duly sworn.

McNamara said, "Mr. Jenkins, please tell us what you know about the murder of Lucy Fryer."

"My name is Lee Jenkins. I am deputy sheriff of McLennan County. I visited the home of Mr. Fryer on last Monday night. I arrested the defendant in this case on that night. I found blood upon his clothing at that time, some being on his shirt . . . on each side of his shirt. I am referring to his undershirt and some on his pants here in front."

Jenkins stood and pointed toward his own pant legs.

"I was present the next day when Mr. Fleming returned from Hillsboro and the hammer was found. The hammer was found right at the end of the rows where Jesse Washington was plowing . . . found it out in some brush there, out close, to a hackberry tree, on the inside of the field. There was quite a lot of brush and weeds . . . brush up about that high, and weeds all around.

"I was out there with Leslie Stegall that night. I had known the Fryers before this time. I suppose it was a couple of hundred yards from the Fryer home to the point where the defendant had been at work that afternoon. The little house in which Mrs. Fryer was killed is about forty or fifty yards from the residence . . . hardly so far; I suppose it is thirty-five or forty steps.

"You and Mr. Fleming and Mr. Robert, and myself saw the hammer before it was picked up, and there were several others passed . . . we stopped a man in a car and let him come over there and look at it. Mr. Reeter, I think it was, then we set up to the house and got Mr. McCullough."

McNamara paused for a moment while reviewing his notes. "Thank you, Mr. Jenkins. Nothing further, Your Honor."

Judge Munroe wrote something on a piece of paper. "Mr. Taylor?"

"Nothing, Your Honor."

The next witness was Cris Simon.

"Mr. Simon, please tell us what you know about this incident."

"I live at Robinsonville, about five or six hundred yards from Mr. Fryer. I was not working at all last Monday. My brother was not working at a point where you could see the Fryer field near the Fryer house. He was working on the other side of my house and was not anywhere close. I was not at home all day that day.

"I saw Jesse Washington last Monday morning at a distance. He was planting cotton about two hundred fifty yards from the Fryer home, something like that. I know where Jesse Washington lived. He lived on Mr. Fryer's farm. He had been living there, I suppose, about five months. I have seen Mrs. Fryer three or four times at a distance. I did not see her that day.

"I saw Jesse Washington in the afternoon about sundown. He was coming out from the field by the little house, going into a horse lot-mule lot. I know where Mrs. Fryer's body was found in the seed house. Her body was found about two minutes after the time I saw Jesse Washington . . . I was coming into the big gate at the road. The crying of the children attracted my attention."

McNamara said, "Thank you, Mr. Simon. No further questions, Your Honor."

Judge Munroe looked at Taylor. "Mr. Taylor?"

Taylor looked up at Judge Munroe. "No questions, Your Honor."

Judge Munroe said, "Mr. McNamara, your next witness."

"Thank you, Your Honor. The state calls Leslie Stegall."

Stegall took the witness stand and was sworn in.

McNamara continued. "Mr. Stegall, please tell us what you know about the murder of Lucy Fryer."

"I am constable of the precinct. I went out to the Fryer home last Monday evening. I saw Mrs. Fryer's body in the seed house as I passed by the window and looked through. I judge the cotton seed house to be about thirty steps from the dwelling house. It sits off to the right. I know where they were planting the cotton seed that day; it is about three or four hundred yards from the Fryer residence."

Stegall pointed at Jesse. "This is Jesse Washington. He was arrested that night."

After the witnesses had given their testimony, McNamara said, "At this time Your Honor I would like to read the confession of Jesse Washington into the record."

Judge Munroe nodded. "Go ahead."

McNamara took the confession and placed it on the podium in front of him.

"'The state of Texas dated May 9, 1916, County of Dallas. To whom it may concern:

"After I have been duly warned by M. I. Lively that I do not have to make any statement at all, and that any statement I make may be used in evidence against me on the trial for the offense concerning which this statement is herein made, I wish to make the following voluntary statement to the aforesaid person.

"My name is Jesse Washington. My address is on George Fryer's place near Waco, Texas, near Robinsonville. I was seventeen years old three months after last Christmas. On yesterday, May 8, 1916, I was planting cotton for Mr. Fryer near Robinsonville close to Waco, Texas, and about 3:30 o'clock p.m. I went up to Mr. Fryer's barn to get some more cotton seed.

"I called Mrs. Fryer from the house to get some cotton seed, and she came to the barn and unfastened the door and scooped up the cotton seed. I was holding the sack while she was putting the seed in the sack and after she had finished, she was fussing with me about whipping the mule and while she was standing inside of the door of the Barn and still talking to me I hit her on the side of the head with a hammer that I had in my hand. I had taken this hammer from Mr. Fryer's house to the field that morning and brought it back and put it in the barn at dinner. I had picked up this hammer and had it in my hand when I called Mrs. Fryer from the house and had the hammer in my right hand all the time I was holding the sack.

"When I hit Mrs. Fryer on the side of the head with the hammer she fell over. I then pulled up her clothes and crawled on her and screwed her, by screwing her I mean that I stuck my male organ into her female organ, and while I was doing this, she was trying to push me off. When I got through screwing her, I got off her and picked up the hammer from where I had laid it down and hit her twice more with the hammer on top of her head. I saw the blood coming through her bonnet.

"I then picked up the sack of cotton seed and carried it and the hammer to the field where I had left the team. I left the sack of cotton seed near the planter and the mules and put the hammer that I killed Mrs. Fryer within some weeds under the hackberry bush.

"I knew when I went to the barn for the cotton seed, that there wasn't anybody at the house except Mrs. Fryer and when I called her from the house to the barn, I bad already made up my mind to knock her in the head with the hammer and screw her.

"I had been working for Mrs. Fryer about five months. I first made up my mind to screw Mrs. Fryer yesterday morning and took the hammer from the buggy shed to the field with me and brought it back and put it in the barn at dinnertime so that I could use it to knock her in the head and I came back for seed during the afternoon.

"I planted cotton the rest of the afternoon, then put up the team and went home at my daddy's house where I was arrested. There wasn't anybody else who had anything to do with the killing or raping of Mrs. Fryer except myself."

After the reading of the confession the State rested its case, and it was time for Jesse's lawyers to open the defense's case. Joe Taylor stood and walked to the podium. "Jesse, do you want to tell this jury anything?"

Jesse was duly sworn.

"What would you like to tell the jury?"

"My name is Jesse Washington."

Taylor cleared his throat. "You are charged here with having murdered Mrs. Fryer and under this charge you have plead guilty. Have you anything you wish to say to the jury? You can tell them anything you went to tell them now?"

Jesse looked at the jury, then at Taylor. "I ain't going to tell them nothing more than what I said that what I done." Jesse mumbled something inaudible.

Judge Munroe asked, "Mr. Washington, do you have anything you would like to say to the court?"

Jesse said something inaudible.

Taylor said, "He says he is sorry for what he's done."

The judge asked, "Mr. Washington, is there anything else you would like to say?"

There was no audible response.

"That is all," said Taylor.

Judge Munroe looked at the prosecutor. "Mr. McNamara."

McNamara stood up. "This man has been given as fair a trial as there ever was. He has confessed. The only possible sentence in a case like this is death."

Judge Munroe motioned toward Joe Taylor. "Mr. Taylor. Your closing?"

Taylor stood. "Nothing further from the defense, Your Honor."

Judge Munroe turned toward the jury. "Ladies and gentlemen of the jury, you are now charged to render a verdict. The bailiff will escort you to the deliberation room. After you have reached a verdict, you will summon the bailiff, who will bring you back into the courtroom." He nodded toward the bailiff, who walked to the jury box and motioned for the jury to follow him.

The entire trial took only an hour. Jesse's attorneys offered no defense and asked only one question during the entire trial. Taylor asked who was present when the murder weapon was found. Sheriff Fleming testified that attorney John McNamara, deputy sheriffs Lee Jenkins, Joe Roberts, and himself were all present.

Jesse watched the jury walk single file from the courtroom. Knowing there was no chance he would be acquitted, he leaned over to Taylor and whispered, "What happens now?"

Taylor put his hand on Jesse's shoulder. "The jury will decide if you are guilty or not."

"How long does that take?"

Taylor shook his head. "Usually, about an hour or so. Sometimes it takes all day or even more than one day."

In four minutes, the jury returned to the courtroom.

Jesse leaned over and whispered to Taylor, "They're coming back in already. Is that good?"

Taylor shook his head. "No, Jesse. It isn't good."

The jury took their places in the jury box.

Judge Munroe looked at W. B. Brazelton, the jury foreman. "Have you reached a verdict?"

"Yes, Your Honor."

"How do you find?"

Brazelton stood to his feet. "We the jury find the defendant guilty of murder as charged in the indictment and assess his penalty at death."

Judge Munroe asked, "Is that your verdict, gentlemen?"

Unanimously, the jury replied in the affirmative.

Judge Munroe wrote in the Register of Actions, "Plea of guilty and verdict of guilty, and punishment assessed at death." He spoke the words as he wrote them.

For a moment, the courtroom was silent. The deputies rose to their feet to take Jesse into custody. Someone shouted, "Let's get that rotten N____. We have to protect our women folk." The crowd began to cheer and shout. Without warning, some of the men in the crowd rushed forward and pushed their way past the barrier. Jesse turned around upon hearing the commotion and saw several hundred White men moving directly toward him. *Oh, no. This can't be real.*

Almost immediately, Sheriff Fleming, his deputies, Judge Munroe, the court reporter, and the bailiff ran out the rear door of the courtroom, leaving Jesse alone with a surging crowd and his attorneys. The only deputy who remained was Deputy Goldberg. He drew his pistol and struck one man in the forehead, as he tried to grab Jesse, then another. He tried to stand between Jesse and the attackers and shouted, "Get back or I will shoot." Several men pushed Deputy Goldberg back on the table and one shouted, "Stop, or you will get the same thing as Jesse."

Goldberg continued to struggle as someone grabbed the gun from his hand. Finally, pinned to the table by half a dozen men, Deputy Goldberg could offer no further support to protect Jesse.

A tall man grabbed Jesse by the collar, and several men dragged him toward the rear door of the courtroom. Though his hands and feet were shackled, Jesse fought back to the best of his ability and caused several injuries in the process. He managed to lift one of the heavy chairs and slam it into the head of one of the attackers. Then he grabbed the table and, using it as a shield, ran forward, bulldozing a dozen men who fell on the floor. While being dragged down the backstairs, Jesse managed to use his feet to kick two of the men down the steps, then he dove on top of several more and body slammed a third on the stairs. Sublimating his love for Cassie, he fought with everything he had inside. Someone shouted, "That is one strong N_____." The mob dragged Jesse down the back stairs and out the back door into the street behind the courthouse.

As far as Jesse could see, there was a sea of people cheering and shouting for his demise. Some were laughing, others cursing. There were more people than Jesse had ever seen in one place. Fifteen thousand people, half the population of Waco, had gathered to watch Jesse be tortured. Jesse looked around for his family and Cassie but could not see them.

Two men with leather blacksmith gloves threw a heavy tow chain around Jesse's neck and locked it. The chain had been in the fire, and it immediately charred Jesse's skin, but he did not cry out. To save Jesse from unimaginable pain a man drew his gun to shoot him, but he was quickly overpowered by several other men. They used knives and began cutting off Jesse's clothes, stabbing him in the process, until he was completely naked. As they dragged Jesse into the street by the smoldering chain around his neck, some men grabbed his hands and, using sharpened knives, cut off his fingers, one by one, to sell as souvenirs. Another man reached between Jesse's legs and with a sharp carving knife, cut off his penis and testicles. He held them up and laughed. The crowd laughed and cheered.

As they dragged Jesse down the street, he fought with every bit of strength he had. He shouted and yelled at them, but he did not cry. At one point he was knocked to the ground. A man shoved his finger in Jesse's mouth to try to pull him back up. Jesse bit down on the man's finger so severely that it nearly severed the finger. As this man screamed in pain, another man stomped on Jesse's face repeatedly until he let go of the man's finger. Jesse hoped that his family and Cassie could not see this part of his tribulation. He would not want them to see how severely he suffered. At one point during the mayhem, Jesse shouted, "Do I not have even one friend who will help me?" Perhaps he didn't know Goldberg had been overtaken and was crying out for assistance.

Jesse believed they were taking him to the Washington Avenue bridge that spanned 430 feet across the Brazos River, where another Black victim, Sank Majors, had been lynched in 1905, nearly eleven years earlier. He continued to fight and resist the best he could, despite being clubbed and stabbed throughout the procession, with the crowd cheering like spectators at a sporting event. When the procession turned onto Second Street, Jesse realized he was not going to the bridge.

As they approached the town square Jesse could see a large pile of kindling and could smell oil. For the first time, it appeared to him that they might be planning to burn him in a fire. He began resisting the procession even more fervently than before, but still, he did not cry out.

When they finally reached the town square directly across from City Hall, where Mayor Dollins watched the entire event from a second-story window, the opposite end of the chain around Jesse's neck was tossed over the limb of a tree. By this juncture Jesse was lapsing in and out of consciousness due to loss of blood and shock from the pain. He was hoisted into the air by the chain around his neck.

Jesse was doused with oil, and the kindling at the base of the tree was ignited. The crowd cheered with pleasure as Jesse was turned upside down and lowered up and down into the fire for over two hours and slowly roasted alive. He attempted to pull himself out of the fire by grabbing the hot chain, but because his fingers had been severed, he was unable to grip it.

By the time Cassie had made her way down to the center of the courtroom, she found Deputy Goldberg lying on the floor with blood coming from a gash in his forehead. He was dazed but had begun to regain consciousness. "You shouldn't be down here. It is too dangerous," he said.

"I must be here for Jesse. I need to make sure he can see me."

Goldberg slowly stood with Cassie's assistance. "Jesse doesn't want you to see this. You should go on home."

Cassie replied, "No," as she made her way through the crowd to the back exit.

Cassie and Deputy Goldberg followed the crowd down the street. They finally caught up with Jesse as he was being hoisted up and down in the flames. She fell to her knees and screamed, "No, please stop!" as she fell forward with her face to the ground, crying uncontrollably.

Jesse could no longer see anything. His eyes were covered with sweat and blood. He felt only intense pain as they continued to hoist him up and down in the flames. Occasionally, someone would throw oil on him to keep him burning alive. The pain was indescribably horrid, with the only relief occurring when he would drift into a short-lived unconsciousness. Hearing Cassie's screams and knowing that he would soon be dead, Jesse wanted to see her one last time. Using both hands, he tried to wipe the blood and oil from his eyes. Finally, he could see a distant light, which he knew to be the light of day. He wiped his eyes some more and looked out at the crowd. The first object of his vision was Cassie, approximately forty feet away, on her knees, with tears streaming down her face, reaching both arms toward Jesse. Next to her, with his face covered in blood, was Deputy Goldberg, also on his knees, with his right arm around Cassie as he tried to comfort her.

As Jesse cleared his eyes and saw Cassie, he opened his mouth to speak. The crowd became silent, fully anticipating that Jesse was finally going to cry out in pain. Jesse did cry out, but not in pain. He cried "Cassie" as he tried to reach his arms toward her, then fell back into unconsciousness.

It was uncertain precisely when Jesse died, but eventually, he stopped moving. His body became charred, like a piece of burned wood. The crowd celebrated with cheers and laughter. Photographers took photos, which were later made into postcards. Children who had been let out of school for lunch came by and watched Jesse burn. Some of them stayed and took pieces of his body as souvenirs. Eventually, Jesse's charred body was tied behind a horse and dragged through the streets of Waco until the head fell off and was placed on the doorstep of a local prostitute. A group of local boys retrieved the head and sold the teeth for five dollars each.

CHAPTER
NINETEEN

THE EVENING AFTER Jesse's death, Cassie locked herself in her room and cried for hours. *How could such a wonderful young man come to such a horrible demise? Why did they refuse him a fair trial?* These questions were rehearsed in her mind over and again. Deep inside she knew there was an answer. One that she did not want to hear. It was the most obvious feature of this case. *Why was Jesse blamed for the murder, then horribly tortured without even the semblance of a fair trial?* Finally, she knew she was cornered. She tried to think of every possible reason Jesse might have been treated this way. There was only one answer and she had to face it. The answer was that it was because he was Black.

Finally, Cassie stopped crying and began asking herself questions. *Why are we so different from these White people? What is there about us that causes them to hate us so badly? First, they brought us to America and made us slaves, then they gave us our freedom, then they hate us for being in this country, even though they are the ones who brought us here under slavery. We have been under their thumb for centuries and now they hate us and want us to be gone. This is a people that is impossible to please. There is only one possible explanation. They hate us. They hate us because we look different from them and for no other reason.*

For Cassie, the thought of Waco saddened her. How could she live in a community where the man she loved was so brutalized? She remembered seeing how severely Jesse suffered because of some cruel, inhumane perception of people. Cassie decided that she needed to make sure Elijah knew what happened. She sent him a telegram:

> "Jesse is gone. Executed for murder. He was inno-
> cent. Deputy Barney Goldberg said it was because
> he was Black."

Given the urgency, Western Union delivered the telegram to Elijah's dorm room by courier. Sitting on his bed, Elijah felt an intense sadness. A depression of unfathomable depth. Could he have done anything to help Jesse if he had learned in time? He knew he could not, but somehow, searching his own soul obsessed his thoughts. But no matter how severely he tortured himself, his good friend Jesse was gone.

The Williams family decided that Waco was not the community where they wanted to live. They had saved some money working for the McKinleys, so they traveled to California and purchased a small avocado farm near San Diego.

Cassie never fully recovered from the loss of Jesse. She could have moved on, found a young man, and built a wonderful family, but she felt that no one would ever replace Jesse. She taught school until she retired, and she told her students about Jesse Washington but never told them she knew him personally.

Charred corpse of Jesse Washington after lynching,
Waco, Texas. Texas Waco, 1916. Photograph.
https://www.loc.gov/item/95517784/

Large crowd watching the lynching of Jesse Washington, 17 year-old African American, in Waco, Texas. Texas Waco, 1916. Photograph. https://www.loc.gov/item/95517067/

Spectators looking at charred corpse of Jesse
Washington hanging from tree after lynching,
Waco, Texas. Texas Waco, 1916. Photograph.
https://www.loc.gov/item/95518055/

Image of postcard of photo of charred corpse of Jesse Washington.
https://dailyhistory.org/images/8/8e/1200px-
*Postcard_of_the_lynched_Jesse_Washington%2C_*
front_and_back.jpg

Gildersleeve, Fred A., 1881?-1958, photographer.
Large crowd looking at the burned body of Jesse
Washington, 17 year-old African American, lynched
in Waco, Texas. Texas Waco, 1916. Photograph.
https://www.loc.gov/item/95517168/.

EPILOGUE

THE LYNCHING OF Jesse Washington was celebrated and justified by many residents of Waco to deter future crimes by Black persons but elsewhere across the nation, the event brought condemnation. Many Waco community leaders, including Samuel Palmer Brooks, the president of Baylor University, denounced the lynching of Jesse Washington as an inhumane and horrific sin. Despite the clear evidence and widespread knowledge of the event, no person was ever charged with a crime in the lynching of Jesse Washington. In time, the town forgot the occurrence and to this date, many lifelong residents of Waco are unaware that the lynching ever occurred. Many who are aware proclaim that it was justified as a deterrent to crime and was lawful at that time, which was clearly not the case. Lynchings were illegal in Texas and violated the Eighth Amendment to the US Constitution's prohibition on cruel and unusual punishment.

Mayor Dollins watched the event from a second-story window from city hall but took no action to stop the crowd or to save Jesse. No one attempted to save Jesse. None of the cowardly law enforcement officers, apart from Deputy Barney Goldberg, made any attempt to stop the crowd. The administration of justice in Waco over the event of Jesse's trial and execution is one of the worst examples of judicial and law enforcement incompetence and corruption ever seen in America. It raised many questions. Why was the trial not moved to another location further away from Waco? Why were the military and the Texas Rangers not brought in to control the crowd? Why did no one, except for members of the clergy and the universities, try to assist Jesse? The answer was that Mayor Dollins, Sheriff Fleming, and others wanted to please the crowd to secure their own re-election. They wanted to show that they could administer justice fairly and swiftly.

Because Deputy Goldberg had attempted to save Jesse after the trial, and because he was Jewish, many of the townspeople turned their anger toward him in the days following the lynching. Deputy Goldberg also held a part-time job at the local mercantile in Waco, so Sheriff Fleming told the public that Goldberg was working in the mercantile the day of the trial and that the deputy in the courtroom, who fought to save Jesse, was from out of town. This caused those who sought revenge to conclude that it must have been someone else who fought for Jesse, though some knew better.

In the years after the lynching of Jesse Washington, analysis ensued in large part because of the work of the NAACP and Suffragette, Elisabeth Freeman, and more recently the work of Patricia Bernstein, *The First Waco Horror*, Texas A&M University Press, 2005. The prosecution of Jesse Washington contained so many constitutional violations, it is difficult to know where to begin. First, the confession was coerced. Clearly, the public had no way of knowing what actual conversations took place between the investigators and Jesse because no defense counsel was present. Was he tortured? It is known he was threatened, which alone would have constituted coercion. He was told that the only way he could save himself and his family from a horrific death of torture and lynching was if he confessed and said he acted alone. So, at minimum the confession was obtained under duress, and he had initially denied that he was involved in the killing of Lucy Fryer.

The primary evidence against Jesse, blood on his clothes, according to some witnesses, was there from a few days earlier when he was struck in the altercation at the bar in Rosenthal. But that evidence was ignored, and the investigators only listened to the testimony of those who said Jesse didn't get bloody in the bar fight.

So, even this evidence is suspect. The location of the hammer could have been known in several ways. The interrogators could have told him where it was if they knew. This is a young man who would likely have said anything to avoid the horrors he and his family were facing. Alternatively, even if the interrogators were innocent of any wrongdoing, it is possible that Jesse saw someone place the hammer at that location. He was plowing the field, and the hammer was placed where Jesse said it was at the end of the field he was plowing. A witness reported that George Fryer had said he killed his wife. This information was ignored by the prosecution and the defense. In fact, a Black newspaper reporter was later arrested for publishing that the true murderer was George Fryer Sr.

The feature of the story that most likely suggests Jesse's innocence is that after Lucy Fryer was murdered, he continued plowing the field for the rest of the day. The prosecution explained this away by saying that Jesse was "mentally retarded" and didn't realize he would be caught if he stayed around the farm. The fact that he continued plowing after Lucy was murdered was not widely disseminated to the press and was not mentioned at all during the trial except in the prewritten confession that was submitted to the court by the prosecution. It was the elephant in the room no one wanted to talk about.

Another important inconsistency, which was not addressed in court, is that the handwritten confession Jesse signed with an X stated that Jesse raped Mrs. Fryer. However, the forensic physician who examined the body said it did not appear she had been raped, though it appeared her clothes had been disheveled to give the impression she had. This inconsistency between the confession and the forensic findings suggests that the confession itself was a fabrication.

Many of those who knew Jesse disputed that he was mentally impaired, but instead said he was just stubborn and did not want to learn to read and write. He wanted to be a cotton farmer and didn't feel a need. The lynching of Jesse Washington would have been a horrific case of cruel and unusual punishment even if he was guilty, but sadly we will never know if he was innocent or guilty because he was deprived of a fair trial and the greatest weight of the evidence suggests that he was innocent.

Waco was a college town with a population of thirty thousand. It was the home of Baylor University and two Black universities. Yet nearly half the population of the town came out to participate in the lynching. Over time this has become a horrible shame for Waco and one that many of the town's people wish had never occurred. Others simply dismiss it as a product of the time and place where Jesse lived, and many say it was justified and legal. Perhaps most amazing is the wide number of lifelong residents of Waco who, to this day, are unaware that this event ever occurred. The lynching of Jesse Washington is something we would have considered impossible to occur at that time and place. But perhaps most shocking is that to this day, not one person has ever been charged with a crime in the lynching of Jesse Washington.

Printed in the United States
by Baker & Taylor Publisher Services